D0046862

FUTURE TENSE FICTION

Stories of Tomorrow

**CHARLIE JANE ANDERS · MADELINE ASHBY
PAOLO BACIGALUPI · MEG ELISON · LEE KONSTANTINOU
CARMEN MARIA MACHADO · EMILY ST. JOHN MANDEL
MAUREEN MCHUGH · ANNALEE NEWITZ
NNEDI OKORAFOR · DEJI BRYCE OLUKOTUN
MARK OSHIRO · HANNU RAJANIEMI · MARK STASENKO**

EDITED BY:
KIRSTEN BERG, TORIE BOSCH, JOEY ESCHRICH,
ED FINN, ANDRÉS MARTINEZ, AND JULIET ULMAN

The Unnamed Press
Los Angeles, CA

Note

Future Tense is a partnership of *Slate*, New America, and Arizona State University that explores emerging technologies, public policy, and society. Beginning in 2016, Future Tense commissioned a series of stories from leading writers that imagined what life might be like in a variety of possible futures. *Future Tense Fiction: Stories of Tomorrow* is a selection of those pieces.

Table of Contents

FUTURE

TENSE

FICTION

Introduction:
The Future is Made of Choices

We seem inevitably drawn to two opposites when we tell stories about the future: will we finally reach a rationalist techno-utopia, or will we sow the seeds of our own destruction by innovating too aggressively? These extremes tempt us because they provide finality, and hence they scratch our itch for neatly packaged narratives where all the loose ends are carefully tied up. But they don't reflect how we encounter technologies in our everyday lives, or the history of actual technological change, which is always heterogeneous, ambivalent, growing out of and elaborating on our existing social structures and norms, cultures and values, and physical environments. There are no fresh beginnings or clean endings in real life. We don't get to terraform our planet and start over; the forces of evil probably won't wear highly visible insignia and matching uniforms. Instead, technologies as profound as personal computers, solar panels, and pacemakers and as mundane as toasters and headphones insinuate themselves gradually into our markets, our relationships, and even our sense of who we are.

Living with technology is profoundly weird. One year you have to drive to the next state or post a letter to talk to your sister or father, and the next you're able to summon them up instantly with the ring of a telephone. A few decades later, you're texting them the palm tree or mermaid emoji from the back seat of your rideshare as shorthand for "good morning" or "thinking of you." A few months after that, you find out that your own government might be monitoring these exchanges. Technologies deform existing social arrangements, not invalidating or erasing them but twisting them into unexpected shapes—and thereby provoking new feelings, allowing new thrills, eliciting new anxieties, opening up new vulnerabilities, creating new opportunities for self-expression, commerce, connection, and conflict. We get used to these changes quite quickly, and once we do, they become unremarkable, even invisible. A good science fiction story can help re-sensitize us by showing us people dangling over different techno-logical precipices, or realizing their potential in once-unimaginable ways.

It's the pursuit of this strangeness, this destabilizing feeling of cohabitating on our planet with multitudes of technologies seen and unseen, that inspires us at Future Tense Fiction. The project grew out of Future Tense, a collaboration among *Slate*, Arizona State University, and New America. Since 2010, we have been publishing nonfiction commentary and hosting events about emerging technologies and their transformative effects on public policy, culture, and society. We started experimenting with publishing fiction on *Slate*'s Future Tense channel in 2016, with Paolo Bacigalupi's disturbing, incisive robots-and-IP-law detective thriller "Mika Model," and then in early 2017, with Emily St. John Mandel's wistful, uncanny time-travel yarn "Mr. Thursday." In 2018, cheered by the enthusiastic reactions of our read-ers and keen to work with some of our favorite authors, we started publishing one story per month, accompanied by a response essay by someone with expertise in a related area (from theoretical physics to food systems) and original illustrations.

We view Future Tense Fiction as an urgent corollary to our nonfic-tion efforts. Fiction has the ability to transport us into a panoply of possible visions of the future, and to grasp at the weirdness of our pervasive interactions with science and technology through the eyes of people with identities and experiences entirely unlike our own. Stories evoke our empathy, allowing us to tunnel into someone's psychology, emotions, and worldview—and to viscerally experience the consequences, both desired and dreaded, expected and unfore-seen, of living in a technological world in perpetual flux.

The future isn't a fixed path, or a chute through which we're helplessly propelled. We make the future together through an agglomeration of choices small and large, minute and momentous:

whether and how to vote, which technologies to buy and adopt and which ones to skip entirely, how and where we live, how we get around, how we construct our families, where we work and what we work on. We're all constrained to various degrees by a dizzying array of social factors, but we do have decisions to make. And doing nothing in the face of scientific and technological change is a decision too. We hope that Future Tense Fiction stories help us imaginatively rehearse possible future scenarios, and help us get better at recognizing places where things could be different, even when they're hard to glimpse. Scientific and technological elites and leaders often present the future as a fait accompli. A good story can help us find a different point of view, to scout out the decision points so that we can muster our resources and act at the right moment.

This volume collects a full year of Future Tense Fiction, exploring quarterly themes like *home, memory, sport,* and *work*. It can be both tricky and rewarding, with such a range of topics, and such a stylistically diverse set of contributing authors, to tease out commonalities running through our first year of Future Tense Fiction. Instead of doing so ourselves here, we invite you to proceed on your own journey of discovery, to help us think constructively about our shared future.

In these stories, the future is a place where the concerns of short stories still matter: individual people living their lives not in black and white but the same stubborn blend of grays that we encounter today. Life in the future, in short, will not be so different from life today. The human choices we make will be inflected by technology, but ultimately we are the ones who will have to live with their consequences. We are also the ones who will have to make sense of them, telling stories and narrating ourselves into identities, communities, and societies that feel like they really matter. That is the essential role of fiction—to help us inhabit other worlds, and other minds, so that we can better understand our own.

—The Future Tense Editors
Kirsten Berg, Torie Bosch, Joey Eschrich,
Ed Finn, Andrés Martinez, and Juliet Ulman

MOTHER OF INVENTION
Nnedi Okorafor

"Error, fear, and suffering are the mothers of invention."
—**Ursula K. Le Guin,** *Changing Planes*

It was a beautiful sunny day, and yet Anwuli knew the weather was coming for her.

She paused on the lush grass in front of the house, purposely stepping on one of the grass' flowers. When she raised her foot, the sturdy thing sprung right back into place, letting out a puff of pollen like a small laugh. Anwuli gnashed her teeth, clutching the metal planks she carried and staring up the driveway.

Up the road, a man was huffing and puffing and sweating. He wore a clearly drenched jogging suit and white running shoes that probably wanted to melt in the Nigerian midday heat. Her neighbor, Festus Nnaemeka. The moment she and Festus made eye contact, he began walking faster.

Anwuli squeezed her face with irritation and loudly sucked her teeth, hoping he would hear. "Don't need help from any of you two-faced people, anyway," she muttered to herself, watching him go. "You keep walking and wheezing. Idiot." She heaved the metal planks up a bit, carried them to the doorstep and dumped them there. "Obi 3, come and get all this," she said. Breathing heavily, she wiped sweat from her brow, rubbing the Braxton Hicks pain in her lower belly. "Whoo!"

One of Obi 3's sleek blue metal drones zipped in and used its extending arms to scoop up the planks. The blown air from its propellers felt good on Anwuli's face, and she sighed.

"Thank you, Anwuli," Obi 3 said through the drone's speakers.

Anwuli nodded, watching the drone zoom off with the planks to the other side of Obi 3. Who knew what Obi 3 needed them for; it was always requesting something. Obi 3 was one of her now ex-fiancé's personally designed shape-shifting smart homes. He'd built one for himself, one for his company, and this third one was also his, but Anwuli lived in it. And this house, which he'd named Obi 3 (not because of the classic *Star Wars* film but because *obi* meant "home" in Igbo, and it was the third one), was his smallest, most complex design.

Built atop drained swamplands, Obi 3 rested on three mechanized cushioning beams that could lift the house up high when it wanted a nice view of the city or keep it close to the ground. The house could also rotate to follow the sun and transform its shape from an equilateral triangle into a square and split into four separate modules based on a mathematical formula. And because it was a smart home, it was always repairing and sometimes building on itself.

Over the past five months, Obi 3 had requested nails, vents, sheet metal, planks of wood, piping. Once it even requested large steel ball bearings. Paid for using her ex's credit card, most of the time she just had it delivered and dropped at the doorway, or she'd pick up the stuff and place it there, where she quickly forgot about it. By the time she came back outside, it was always gone, taken by the drones. None of this mattered to her, though, because she had real problems to worry about. Especially in the last eight months. Especially in the next hour.

"Shit," she whimpered, holding her very pregnant belly as she looked at the clear blue sky, again. There had been no storms in the damned forecast for the next two weeks, and she thought she *had* finally been blessed with some luck after so long. However, apparently the weather forecast was wrong. Very, very wrong. She felt the air pressure dropping like a cold shiver running up her spine. Mere hours ago, Dr. Iwuchukwu had informed her that this sensitivity to air pressure was part of the allergy.

Several honeybees buzzed around one of the flowerbeds beside her. The lilies and chrysanthemums were far more delicate than the government-enforced supergrass, but at least they were of her choosing. Just as it was her choice to stay in *her* house. She listened harder, straining to hear over the remote sound of cars passing on the main road a half-mile away. "Dammit," she whispered, when she heard the rumble of thunder in the distance. She turned and headed to the house.

The door opened, and she went inside and slammed it behind her before it could close itself. She stood there for a moment, her hands shaking, tears tumbling down her face. The house had drawn itself into its most compact and secure shape: a square, swinging the triangular sections of the kitchen and living room together. Outside, from down the road, the mosque announced the call to prayer.

"Fuck!" she screamed, smacking a fist to the wall. "*Tufiakwa*! No, no, no, this is *not* fair!" Then the Braxton Hicks in her belly clenched, and she gasped with pain. She went to her living room, threw her purse on the couch, and plopped down next to it, massaging her sides.

"Relax, oh, relax, Anwuli. Breathe," Obi 3 crooned in its rich voice. "You are fine; your baby is fine; everything is fiiiiiine."

Anwuli closed her eyes and listened to her house sing for a bit, and soon she calmed and felt better. "Music is all we've got," she sang back to Obi 3. And the sound of her own voice pushed away the fact that she and her baby would probably be dead by morning, and it would be all her fault. Pushed it away some.

Music and Obi 3. Those were all she and her unborn baby had had for nine months. Since she'd learned she was pregnant and stupidly told her fiancé, who a minute later blurted to her that he was married with two children and couldn't be a father to her child, too.

The city of New Delta was big, but her neighborhood had always been "small" in many ways. One of those ways was how people stamped the scarlet badge of "home-wrecking lady" on women who had children with married men. Her fake fiancé had deserted her, using the excuse of Anwuli playing the seductress he couldn't resist. Then her friends stopped talking to her. Even her sister and cousins who lived mere miles away blocked her on all social networks. When she went to the local supermarket, not one person would meet her eye.

Only her smart home spoke (and sometimes sang) to her. And then there was the baby. Boy, girl, she refused to find out. It was the only good thing she had to look forward to. But her baby was making her sick too, specifically allergic. Dr. Iwuchukwu had been telling her to leave New Delta for months, but Anwuli wasn't about to leave her house. The house was her respect; what else could she claim she'd earned from the relationship? She knew it was irrational and maybe even deadly, but she took her chances. So far, so good. Until today's diagnosis at her doctor's appointment. And right there in that anti-septic place, whose smell made her queasy, she'd decided for good: She wasn't going *anywhere*. Come what may. Now, as if the cruel gods were answering her, a storm was coming.

"Seriously," she muttered, sinking down on the couch, letting its massagers knead the tight muscles of her neck. "I have such bad luck."

"Bad luck is only a lack of information," Obi 3 said. "Dr. Iwuchukwu has sent you a message saying to go over it again."

"I understood it the first time," she said. "I just don't care. I'm not going anywhere. The idiot left me. He's not getting his house back, too."

Before Anwuli could launch into a full-blown rant, Obi 3 began playing the informative video the doctor suggested. She sighed with irritation as the image opened up before her. She didn't care to know more than the bits her doctor had told her, but she was tired, so she watched anyway.

The man walked with a cane and wore an Igbo white-and-red chief's cap like an elder from Anwuli's village in Arochukwu. The projection made it look as if he walked in from the bedroom door, and Anwuli rolled her eyes. This entrance was supposed to be more "personable," but she only found it obnoxious.

"Hello, Anwuli," the man said, graciously. "So, you live in New Delta, Nigeria, the greenest place in the world. Fun fact: 100 years ago, this used to be swamplands and riverways, and the greatest export was oil. Violent clashes between oil corporations and a number of the Niger Delta's minority ethnic groups who felt they were being exploited..."

"Skip," Anwuli said. The man froze for a moment and went from standing in the living room to standing in the middle of downtown New Delta. Anwuli was about to skip again, but instead she laughed and watched.

In the area between New Delta's low skyscrapers, buildings and homes were carpeted with its world-famous stunning green grass, and the roads were fringed with it, but in this scene the grass was covered with smiley-faced bopping periwinkle flowers. It looked ridiculous, like one of those ancient animations from the early 1900s or a psychedelic drug–induced hallucination. The man grinned as he grandiosely swept his arms out to indicate all the lush greenery around him.

"Grass!" he announced. "Whether we know it or not, grass is important to most of us. Grass is a monumental food source worldwide. Corn, millet, oats, sugar—all of them come from grass plants. Even rice was a grass plant. We use grass plants to make bread, liquor, plastic, and so much more! Livestock animals feed mostly on grasses, too. Sometimes we use grass plants like bamboo for construction. Grass helps curb erosion."

He walked closer and stood in the center of town square in the grassy roundabout, smart cars and electric scooters driving round him. At his back stood the statue of Nigeria's president standing beside a giant peri flower. "The post-oil city New Delta is now the greenest place in the world, thanks to the innovative air-scrubbing superplant known as periwinkle grass, a GMO grass created in Chinese labs by Nigerian scientist Nneka Mgbaramuko.

"Carpeting New Delta, Periwinkle's signature tough flowers are a thing of beauty and innovation. A genetic hybrid drawn from a variety of plants including sunflowers, zoysia grass, rice, and jasmine flowers, we can thank periwinkle grass for giving us the perfect replacement for rice just after its extinction. The grass produces periwinkle seed, more commonly just called 'peri,' which is delicious, easy to cook, quick to grow. And it can grow only here in New Delta, because of the special mineral makeup from its past as a swamp. What a resource!" He held up a hand, and the point of view zoomed in to the soft light-purple–blue flower in it. The man looked down at Anwuli as he grinned somewhat insanely. "One week a year, the harvester trucks come out to—"

"Ugh, skip," she said, waving a hand. "Just go to 'New Delta Allergies.' "

The man froze and then reappeared in what looked like someone's nasal cavity, the world around him red and smooth.

"Allergies," he said, looking right at Anwuli with a smirk. He winked mischievously. "Humans have had them since humans were humans, and maybe before that. One of the earliest recorded incidents was sometime between 3640 and 3300 BC when King Menses of Egypt died from a wasp sting.

"In New Delta, pollen allergies are commonplace. Milder symptoms include skin rash, hives, runny nose, itchy eyes, nausea, and stomach cramps. Severe symptoms are more extreme. Swelling caused by the allergic reaction can spread to the throat and lungs, causing allergenic asthma or a serious condition known as anaphylaxis.

"New Delta is a wonderful place of spotless greenery where one can walk about with no shoes on the soft grass, breathe air so clear it smells perfumed, and drive down Nigeria's cleanest streets."

At this Anwuli laughed.

"But in the last five years, due to an unexpected shift in the climate, pollination season has become quite an event. This means more copious harvests of peri. But because peri grass is a wind pollinator, it also means what scientists have called 'pollen tsunamis.' " The weather around the man grew dark as storm clouds moved in and the room vibrated with the sound of thunder. Anwuli glanced toward the side of the room that was all window. Outside was still sunny, but it wouldn't be for long.

"Skip to Izeuzere," she said.

The man froze and then was sitting behind a doctor's desk, wearing a lab coat. He still wore his Igbo chief cap. "...a few New Delta citizens were diagnosed with an allergy called Izeuzere. The name, which means 'sneeze' in Igbo, was given to the condition by a non-English-speaking Igbo virologist who liked to keep things simple. If someone with Izeuzere is caught in a pollen tsunami, there will first be severe runny eyes, sneezing fits, and then an escalation to convulsions, 'rapid rash,' and then suffocation. Most who have it experience a preliminary sneezing fit and then the full spectrum of symptoms the moment a pollen tsunami saturates the area. Deadly exposure to the pollen when a tsunami hits takes minutes, even when indoors, and is instant when outside. Treatment is to leave New Delta and go to an arid environment before the next pollen tsunami. Once there, one must be given a battery of anti-allergen injections for five months."

"What if I lose everything if I *leave*?" Anwuli asked the virtual man. "What if moving out of this house allows the father of my child to get rid of me without lifting a damn finger? Do you have answers for that in your database?" The man's eyebrows went up, but before the man could respond, she screamed, "Shut up!" She punched the couch cushion. "Off! Turn off!" The image disappeared, replaced by her favorite soothing scene of an American cottage covered in snow. The sound of the wind was muffled by the blanket of snow, and smoke was rising from the cottage's chimney. She knew what would happen if she couldn't leave the area. "Dammit," she hissed. "I refuse! I *refuse*!"

"Are you sure you don't want me to buy a ticket for you to Abuja?" Obi 3 asked. "There is a flight leaving in two hours. Your auntie will—"

"No!" Anwuli sat back and shut her eyes, feeling her frustrated tears roll down both sides of her face. "I'm not leaving. I don't care." She paused. "They probably all hope I'll die. Like I deserve it."

"What kind of dessert would you like? There is caramel crème and honeyed peri bread."

"*Deserve*," Anwuli snapped. "I said *deserve*, not *dessert*!"

"You deserve happiness, Anwuli."

Anwuli closed her eyes and sighed, muttering, "Left me alone here for nine months; their message is clear. Well, so is mine. I'm not going. This is his baby. He can't deny that forever." She paused. "Now this stupid storm rolls in out of nowhere when I could have this child at any moment. This is God's work. Maybe he wants all my trouble over with fast."

"Would you like some jollof peri and stew?" Obi 3 asked as Anwuli slowly got up. "You haven't eaten since before you went to your appointment."

"Why would I want to eat when I am about to die alone?" she shouted.

She got up. She stared around Obi 3. Not spotless, because Anwuli didn't like spotless, but tidy. *Her* space since *he* had left her to fully return to his marital home. One of Obi 3's interior drones zipped into the bedroom with a set of freshly washed and folded clothes.

"What do I do?" Anwuli whispered. And, as if to answer, the sound of thunder rumbled from outside, this time louder. "I don't want to die."

She'd always had allergies. Her father had even playfully nicknamed her *ogbanje* when she was little because she was always the one sniffling, sneezy, and sent to bed any time the peri flowers bloomed. Goodness knew that when her allergies flared, she did feel like a spirit who'd prefer to die and return to her spirit friends than keep living with the discomfort. But *never* did she imagine she'd eventually come down with the rare illness everyone had been talking about. And her doctor, also a local to her community, had been so cold about it.

"I don't know why you haven't left yet, but don't worry. You'll give birth any day now," he'd said at her earlier appointment, clearly avoiding her eyes by looking at his tablet. "Then you take your baby, fly to Abuja immediately and get treatment there. No storms are due in the next week, so you will be fine."

Anwuli had nodded agreement. What she didn't say in that room was that she had no intention of leaving. Obi 3 was her home as long as she lived in it. Bayo was an asshole, but he could never throw her out of the house, no matter how much he wanted the situation to go away. She was sure he still loved her, and above everything, this *was* his baby. However, his wife certainly would love for her and his "bastard" baby to simply leave the area. But none of it mattered now because here was the thunder.

Anwuli went to her room and curled up in her bed and for several minutes, minutes she knew would be her last, she cried and cried. For herself, for her situation, her choice, for everything. When she couldn't cry anymore, the thunder was closer. She got up. Her belly felt hard as a rock, and the pain drove even her fear of death away. At the same time, Obi 3 brightened the lights, which seemed to amplify the pain.

"Blood of Jesus!" she screamed, crumbling to the floor in front of the couch.

She was 29 years old and she'd watched all her friends settle into marriage and have child after child, yet this was her first. And there had been so much chaos around the fact of her pregnancy that although she went to regular checkups, she hadn't really thought much about the birth or what she'd do afterward. Shame, desperation, embarrassment, and abandonment burned hotter and shined brighter than her future. So Anwuli wasn't ready.

Now her pain had begun to speak, and it told vibrant stories of flesh-consuming fire that burned the body to hard, hot stone. It was as if her midsection was trying to squeeze itself bloody. She rolled on the floor, more tears tumbling from her eyes. And then...it passed. Her belly melted from hot stone back to flesh, her mind cleared, and a light patter of rain began tapping at the windows.

"Better?" Obi 3 asked.

"Yes," Anwuli said, grasping the side of the couch to pull herself up. Beside her hovered one of Obi 3's drones. "I'm OK. I can do it myself."

"That was a contraction," Obi 3 said. "The variations in electromagnetic noise my sensory lights are picking up tell me that you'll be entering labor soon."

Anwuli groaned, glancing at the window. *Of course*, she thought.

"Not yet but very soon," Obi 3 said. It beeped softly, and the lights flashed a gentle pink orange. "You have a phone call. Bayo."

Anwuli frowned. She shut her eyes and took a deep breath. "OK, answer."

There was another beep, and Bayo's face appeared before her. He looked sweaty, and his shaven brown head shined in the light of the room he was in. He squinted. "Anwuli, turn your visuals on," he said.

"No," she snapped, propping herself against the couch. "What do you want?"

He sighed. "Your doctor just called me."

"What did he say?" she asked, gnashing her teeth.

"That you're sick. That you have...Izeuzere. How can this be? Is it the pregnancy?"

"Is it legal for him to discuss confidential patient information with strangers?" she snapped. "Doubtful."

"I'm not a stranger."

"The last time you spoke to me was nine months ago."

His shifty eyes shifted. There was a shadow beside him; someone else was there. Probably his wife. Anwuli felt a wave of wooziness pass over her. "I...I think I'm in labor," she said.

He looked surprised but then shocked her by saying nothing.

"No ambulance will drive through this storm," she said. "Can you...?"

His wife's face suddenly filled the virtual screen. "No, he will *not*," she said. "He has a family and cannot afford to go driving into pollen storms. Clean up your own mess. And get out of *our* house!" Bayo's wife continued to block Bayo's face, and if Bayo said anything, Anwuli could not hear him.

"Whose house?" Anwuli shouted at her. "Did *you* design it? Build it? Pay for it? Does this house even know your name?"

"Go and *die*!" his wife roared. The image disappeared.

Anwuli flared her nostrils, but no effort could stop the tears and hurt from washing over her like its own contraction. She hadn't known a thing about that woman. Bayo had. Yet who did his family and the rest of the community embrace? Who still had his own body to himself? *Well*, Anwuli thought, *maybe I did know about her. Maybe. Let me not lie when I am so close to my death. I knew. I just chose not to see.*

"Call parents," she breathed.

Their phone rang and rang. No response. Not surprising. They'd stopped picking up her calls months ago. She sent a text explaining it all, then went to the kitchen.

❖❖❖❖❖

The strain of throwing up *and* having a contraction nearly caused her to pass out. One of Obi 3's drones pushed itself beside her to keep her from tumbling to the floor.

"The variations in electromagnetic noise my sensory lights pick up alert me that—"

"Shut up!" Anwuli screamed.

"—you are now in labor," Obi 3 finished.

Boom! the thunder outside responded. Sheets of rain began to pelt Obi 3. The lights flickered, and then Anwuli heard her backup solar generator kick in.

"What do I do?" she grunted, using a napkin to wipe her mouth. "What am I going to do?"

"Shuffling songs by MC Do Dat," Obi 3 cheerily said. Bass-heavy rap music shook the entire house, making Anwuli even more nauseous.

"Ladies do dat / Bitches do dat! / Get down low and / Do dat, do dat!" MC Do Dat rapped over the beats in his low raspy voice.

"Music off!" she screamed, tears squeezing from her eyes. She clenched her fists with rage. "No music! Ooh, I *hate* this song!"

The music stopped in time for the sound of thunder to shake the house. Anwuli slowly dragged herself up as the contraction subsided.

"I'll help you to the couch," Obi 3 said.

She nodded and leaned against the drone that floated to her side. As she did, reality descended on Anwuli. Obi 3 was only an extension of herself. She was only talking to herself, being helped by herself. She was alone. "The storm...pollen...I don't want to..." As she stumbled to the couch, the drone holding her under her armpit, she started to cry again. She cried more as she fell onto the couch and rolled onto her back, her clothes now drenched in sweat. She cried as she stared at the spotless sky-blue ceiling, which she had used Obi 3's drones to paint when Bayo left her. She cried as lightning flashed and the thunder roared outside, the unpredicted storm's winds blowing.

She'd been crying for nine months, and she cried for yet another 10 minutes, and then another contraction hit, and she forgot everything. As the minutes passed, and the contractions came faster and faster, she didn't remember where the pillow came from that propped her up or how her legs held themselves apart. What she did recall was the window across from her shattering as a palm tree fell through it. She remembered the wind and rain blowing into Obi 3, filling it with the heat and humidity from outside. Tree leaves, new and dry, slapped against the couch, onto the floor, but no peri flowers were blown in. Those were strong like men; they didn't even lose petals in the worst wind. *Built to survive and reproduce, not to keep from killing us*, she vaguely thought. She couldn't help but note the irony: Plant fertilizer was going to kill her as she was giving birth.

Her face grew damp with sweat and rain. As she gave the great push that thrust her first child into the world, the storm outside exhausted itself to a hard rain. The coming of her child felt like her body submitting after a battle. The sharp pain peaked and then retreated. And that is how the first to carry her squirming daughter was not a human being but a drone, using a plastic scooper as its long sharp knife cut the cord. When the drone placed the child in Anwuli's hands, she looked down at her daughter's squashed, agitated face. For several moments, she stared, unmoving.

"Don't you want to cry?" she asked the snuffling infant.

"Mmmyah," the baby said, turning her head this way and that. Anwuli found herself smiling. She poked her daughter's little cheek. The moment she felt the baby's softness, Anwuli began to weep. She touched the baby again, running a finger delicately across the baby's cheek to touch her lips. Immediately, her child began to suck on her finger.

"She's breathing strongly already," Obi 3 said. "Maybe she does not need to cry."

"Mmiri," Anwuli said, holding the child to her. "I'll name you Mmiri. What do you think, Obi 3?"

"Mmiri means 'water' in the Igbo language," Obi 3 said.

Anwuli laughed. "OK. But do *you* approve?"

"You do not need my approval to name your child."

"But I would like it, if you think to give it."

There was a pause. Then Obi 3 said, "How about giving her the middle name Storm? Storm was the American Kenyan superheroine from Marvel comics. She could control the weather and fly."

Anwuli's eyebrows rose. "Hmm, wow," she said. "Mmiri Storm Okwuokenye, then. I approve." The house glowed a soft lavender color that turned the ceiling a deeper sky blue as Anwuli stared up at it. "Mmiri Storm Okwuokenye," Anwuli breathed again, looking at her new daughter, who smelled like the earth. Bloody, coppery, yeasty. Hers. She held on to this beautiful thought and the sound of her daughter snuffling as the pains of expelling the afterbirth came. When this was over, she slumped on the couch, watching the drone take away the bloody mass.

She already felt much better. Then she sneezed, and her eyes grew itchy. "No," she whispered. Baby Mmiri decided it was time to start wailing. The rain had stopped, and the sun was already peeking through the retreating clouds. She sneezed again, and the house drone flew to her, a clean orange towel now draped over its scooper. Anwuli put her daughter into it and was wracked by a sneeze again. She sat up, surprised by how OK she felt. The second drone flew up beside her carrying a glass of water and her bottle of antihistamine tablets. "Hurry, take three," Obi 3 said. "Maybe—"

"There is nothing to be helped now," Anwuli blurted, looking at the shattered window. Already, what looked like smoke was wafting into the house. Soon visibility outside would be zero, and it would last for the next 24 hours. "I'm a dead woman."

No one had predicted weather patterns shifting. This is why scientists were calling the occasional spontaneous variation in weather patterns "climate chaos" instead of "climate change." That's what they'd recently been saying on the news, anyway. The pollinating grass was genetically staggered to release pollen at three separate times during the year, with one-third of the grass pollinating in each period. However, over the last 20 years, an unexpected shift in the length of the dry, cool Harmattan season had scrambled that timing, causing the pollination periods of all three groups to align.

The immense wealth made from peri production went directly to the Nigerian government and to the Chinese corporations who'd invested so deeply in Nigeria for decades, and next to nothing went to New Delta, much in the same way it had when the greatest resource had been oil. For this reason, the initially lovely city that was New Delta began to deteriorate, and the Chinese and Nigerian governments paid less attention to the pollination misalignment. News of pollen allergies had become nationally known only when Izeuzere set in during the last two years. But only because the way it killed was so spectacular. And this year, rainy season had been particularly wet.

"I'm dead," Anwuli muttered, using all the effort she could muster to get up. She threw her legs off the couch, planting them on the floor. Ignoring the blood soaking her bottom through the drenched towels, she pressed her fists to the cushions on both sides of her. Then she lifted herself up. The pain was far less than she expected, and she froze for a moment, glad to be on her feet.

"Standing," she whispered, her nose now completely stuffed and her eyes still watering. She sniffed wetly. Her insides felt as if they would plop out between her legs onto the blood-spattered carpet. But they didn't. She touched her deflated belly. Then she sneezed so hard that she sat back down. In the kitchen, her baby was crying as the drone put her in a tub of water to wash her off. Anwuli pushed herself up again and took a step toward the kitchen. But as she took another, her chest grew stiff. She wheezed.

She couldn't tell if the room was blurry because it was full of pollen or because of her watering eyes or the fact that she could barely take in enough oxygen. And then she was falling. As she lay on the floor, she heard Obi 3 talking to her, but she didn't understand. Her baby was crying, and if she could smile, she would have, because her baby was not sneezing. Then she closed her eyes, and it was as if the world around her was breaking.

◆◆◆◆◆◆

The floor shook, and Anwuli heard the walls cracking, shifting, crumbling. Her nose was too stuffed for her to smell anything, but she could feel pollen coating her tongue and blood seeping from between her legs. Things went black for a while. Mmiri's cries faded away and stopped. The noise of things breaking became a low hum. The shaking stopped. Anwuli must have slept.

She sneezed hard and wheezed, cracking her gummy eyes open. Everything was a blur until she blinked. She gasped. Then she realized that she *could* gasp. And the room was suddenly warm, like outside. She blinked several more times, wiped her eyes, and then just stared at where the broken window had been. Her daughter began weakly crying. The makeshift cradle the drone had began to gently rock, and Mmiri quieted a little.

Still staring but slowly sitting up, Anwuli said, "Bring her here." She took the baby into her arms as she stared at what looked like a smooth, shiny metal wall. So shiny that she could see the entire living room reflected in it. She remembered these metal sheets; Obi 3 had asked her to order them weeks ago. Something clanged, and the wooden wall beside the metal wall buckled in a bit. She turned and looked down the hall toward the front door, and there she saw another metal wall blocking the view of outside.

"What's...did you do something?" she asked. In her arms, baby Mmiri squirmed and nestled closer to her.

"I did," Obi 3 said. "Do you like it?"

Air was blowing near the ceiling, the Nigerian flag hanging from a bookshelf flapping, and for the first time, Anwuli noticed something. The vent grate was gone, and the air duct inside was a shiny aluminum, not the dull steel. She pointed, "What is that?"

"I built a duct to filter pollen from the air."

Anwuli glanced at the air duct again. And then she looked around the room. Then she looked back at the air duct. She sneezed, but doing so cleared the snot from her nose. She wiped her face with her sleeve and sat on the towel of blood, the coppery, yeasty smell of birth floating around her.

For months, Obi 3 had requested things. Had it been since before Bayo left? Anwuli couldn't remember. She hadn't been paying attention. The last nine months had been crying, shouting, back-turning, embarrassing. Swollen ankles. The day she was in the supermarket and all those women had pointed at her belly and laughed. Swelling body. Her parents ignoring her in church. Wild cravings. Running to her self-driven car after turning a corner and walking right into Bayo's wife. The heightened pollen allergies. And she couldn't stop crying. And all that time, her house had been asking her to buy things.

It would put the items on her phone's grocery list. Nails, sheets of metal, piping, plaster, tool parts and, yes, two air ducts. She'd hear banging on the sides of Obi 3, sawing, creaking, but who could care about repairs Obi 3 made to itself when her life had fallen into disrepair? Who could care about anything else?

"What have you done?"

After a long pause, Obi 3 said, "Please, can you walk?"

"Obi 3."

"Yes?"

"What have you done?" she demanded.

"Go to your room...please," Obi 3 said. "I will tell you, but please take baby Mmiri Storm to your bed. The pollen outside just increased. I can't...it's time for phase 2, or you *will* die."

Anwuli got up. This time, doing so was more painful. She bent forward. "Take her," she gasped. "I can't."

The drone swept up, and as gently as she could, shaking with pain that broiled from her uterus and radiated to every part of her body, she took a step. She felt blood trickling down her leg. "I...should... wash. Can—"

"Yes, but use the towel beside the bed to wipe it, for now, and just get into bed."

"Why?" Anwuli asked, stumbling to the back of the couch and then into the hallway to her room. She leaned against the wall as she stiffly walked.

"There's no time," Obi 3 said.

She took more steps. "Talk to me," she said. "It'll help distract... yeeee, oh my God, this hurts. Feels like my intestines are being pulled down by gravity." She stopped, leaning against the wall, panting. "Talk to me, Obi 3. Tell me a recipe, recite some poetry, *something*."

"You are 0.8 kilometers from the center of New Delta."

"T-t-tell me what you did to yourself...and why?" She shut her eyes for a moment and took a deep breath. *Just pushed out baby*, she told herself. *Pain is just from that. I'm OK. I'm OK.*

"I've listened to you," Obi 3 said. "One day, you said you wished someone would protect you like you protected the baby." Anwuli remembered that night. She'd been unable to sleep and thus had stayed up all night, thinking and thinking about all the weeks of being alone. Scared. She hadn't been talking to Obi 3. Nor the baby. She'd just talked to herself, to hear her own voice. Maybe she'd been praying.

"You were speaking and asking," Obi 3 continued. "I did my own research and then engineered my plans," it said. "I had answers. Every smart home watches the news, its central person, and its environment. Nearly one-third of all pregnant women will develop an allergy they have not previously suffered from, and the allergies they already have tend to get worse. You have always had bad allergies; you told me how they used to call you *ogbanje*. Also, remember the day your stupid, useless man left? You turned off my filter *because* he liked to have it on."

At this, Anwuli snorted a laugh, and she felt blood gush from her privates and a pang of pain strong enough to make her stumble. She'd been brash. *No one* turned off a home's filter. Not after all the incidents of smart homes being too nosy and intrusive.

"Ah, so you predicted I'd get Izeuzere?"

"Yes," Obi 3 said. "I used formal logic."

"Then you decided to find a way to protect me."

"Yes. I invented a way, then I built my invention."

"Necessity is the mother of invention," Anwuli said, with a weak smile. "Wow. Technology harbors a personal god; my Chi is a smart home." She laughed, and her body ached, but a good ache.

"I have decided to call it a 'protective egg,'" Obi 3 said. "Is this all right?"

Anwuli frowned for a moment. Then she shrugged. "It's kept me and baby alive."

"Watching you inspired me. Your body protects your baby. Steel-plated, impervious exterior, an air filter..." It paused, and Anwuli frowned.

"Tell me all of it," she demanded, entering her room. "Oh!" she said. Here, the window wall in front of her bed had mostly been fortified with metal except for about three by three feet of it. And outside, a blizzard of bright-orange fluff thick enough to mute the midday Nigerian sunshine. Never ever ever had the pollen been so thick. Towels had been placed on the bed and beside it. Anwuli grabbed one, wiped her legs, and then pressed it to herself. "No use hiding it from me now," she said. "We're in this together, no? We have been for months. Is this why you haven't tried so hard to get me to leave?"

"Yes."

Anwuli chuckled tiredly. "Interesting. So interesting."

As Anwuli laid herself on the bed, Obi 3 told her all about what it called "Project Protective Egg." And then, as she clutched Mmiri in her arms, watching her death swirl about outside, the entire house began to rise up. Obi 3 had rebuilt its own steel cushioning beams, used to support it above the delta swamp floor, into three powerful legs.

"I can take us beyond the tsunami before the filters are over-whelmed," Obi 3 said.

"If we can make it that far, there is no peri grass in Abuja."

As it walked, the room gently rocking, Obi 3 *hummed* the song Anwuli's mother always hummed when she cooked. Anwuli rested on the pillow the drone had pushed beneath her head, held Mmiri closer to her, and hugged herself. Yes, Obi 3 was like an extension of herself. *Like part of my immune system who has just saved my life*, she thought, staring at the window. *Or my Chi.* Anwuli hoped Obi 3 crushed the hell out of as much peri grass as it could on the way out of town, and maybe the house of her ex-fiancé...if they weren't home.

Baby Mmiri Storm cooed in her arms.

◆◆◆◆◆◆

Two miles away, Bayo sat in his study frowning as he looked out at the whirling pollen through the room's triangular corner window. He was still thinking about Anwuli. Praying she was not dead. If she had finally decided to leave the house, she was out there in that pollen storm right now. He shook his head, frowning. "Please, let this woman be alive," he muttered. "Please, oh, *Biko-nu*, Holy Ghostfire, laminate her life for protection, in the name of Jesus."

His wife was in the kitchen making peri cakes and fried fish, but he didn't dare look at his mobile phone, let alone make a call on it. The house was listening, almost every aspect of its mechanisms tuned to his wife's preferences because it was she who spent the most time here. *Maybe I should have stayed home more*, he thought. At the same time, he wished today weren't his day off. Even with the noise of his sons and daughter playing in the living room, he knew he couldn't call Anwuli. And if he got up to leave when the pollen passed, there would be trouble.

Suddenly, the entire house rumbled. Then it began to shake, and the children screamed. As Bayo jumped up, he could feel it. The house was rising. And that's when it all dawned on him, a horrid sense of doom settling on his shoulders: His wife...not only had she known of Anwuli all along, but so had their house, Obi 1. And neither his wife nor *her* house was the type to easily let things go. "Shit," he said. "Why did I make these goddamn smart homes so smart?" He heavily sat down on the couch and held on for dear life.

NO ME DEJES
Mark Oshiro

"You're nervous, aren't you?"

Papá sits across from me, arms folded, all stoic steadiness, but his brows are knit together in an unmistakable knot. "I know what you're doing," I say. "I appreciate it, but..." I shake my head, and dread stitches itself to my ribs.

He sighs loudly, reaches out to me with a calloused hand. "I'll be right there with you the entire time."

"I know. It's just...I'm starting to wonder if I'm in over my head."

"You can say no, Gabriela. It's not *too* late."

A brief flash of eagerness crosses his face, a light I wish I could unsee. *He wants to do it in my place.* He has been nothing but supportive ever since Abuela Carmen chose me for the Transfer, but this moment skirts an uncomfortable truth. Why did she choose me over him? Why will *I* be the bridge in our familia, the one to receive abuela's memories before she leaves us? The love between us isn't enough to explain why Carmen chose me over her own son, but she has offered no other clue.

"No, it's what she wants," I tell him. I tell *myself*.

He lets go of my hand and leans back into the hard plastic chair. "You know, you're going to have some strange memories in that head of yours."

A flutter of nerves rolls through me. "Like what?"

"Well," he smirks, "are you prepared to change your papa's diapers?"

"*What*?"

"What if one of those memories gets through? Gonna be pretty weird."

I swat at him playfully. "Papá, come *on*."

His smile fades, but his deep-brown eyes are still warm. "I know this is all pretty strange, but...I'm glad it's you."

My Papá. I step across that expanse of linoleum to plant myself in the empty chair to his right, then curl up against his body. He runs his fingers through my hair, plants a kiss on top of my head.

The electricity of the unknown still courses through me. I am alight. I am unsure.

This room is not built for the limbo of extended goodbyes. Nothing to read except for the flashy and emotionally charged animations advertising the Transfer that adorn the walls. Loved ones smiling at some beatific elder relative's bedside, every one of them white, with a single phrase at the bottom:

You never really die if you're not forgotten.

It's not as comforting as I think it's meant to sound, and it doesn't stop the nervous quiver in my stomach. Soon, I'll be laid out alongside Abuela Carmen, wired up to her mind, ready for her to gift me with her memories. They say it doesn't really hurt and that the transferred memories basically separate out from your own after a few weeks. But I've been reading the reviews, following forums, in the week since Abuela made her choice. It's disorienting, everyone says. You can't control what will trigger the new memories you have. Sometimes, they just pop in your head when you're showering. When you're at work or at school. Most especially when you're asleep. Someone else's memories, someone else's secrets.

They're about to be mine.

◆◆◆◆◆◆

They finally come for us more than an hour later, while Papá is in the restroom. When he steps out, clicking the heavy door shut behind him, his eyes are bloodshot and puffy, and the sharp worry wrinkles on his forehead stand out in a map of grief. It breaks my heart. This is his *mother*. After this she'll be gone forever, even if her memories live on. All I'd been thinking about was myself.

"I'm sorry, Papá," I say into his chest. "This has to be hard."

"It's OK, m'ija." His breath is warm on top of my head. "Saying good-bye isn't meant to be easy. At least we have the chance to say it this time."

The history rests unspoken between us. Mamá's passing a few years back, before the Transfer was available, was sudden. There were no waiting rooms, no extended farewells, no exchange of memories. Just a mess of twisted metal and an ocean of grief that eroded the edges of what we knew of her. Mamá drifted further away with time; mi abuela would live sharply within me.

He squeezes once more, then leads me away, out of the waiting room, into the sterile, gray hallway, past recruitment offices and Transfer agents, running their orientation videos for other clients. At the end of the hall, we enter an elevator to head up to the medical wing. The floor hums beneath our silence. How can we say all of the things that need to be said? How can we possibly untangle this knot of hope and fear and grief that sits like a lump in our throats?

So we say nothing.

The doors open. Another gray hall. Another phalanx of animations set flush into the wall, all extolling the virtues of the Transfer, as if we still need convincing, even now. Nestled between their bright promises are the procedure rooms, which are hidden from us: dark panes of glass and windowless doors. How many people are going through the Transfer right now? How many are waking up from that last goodbye, heads crammed with memories that are not their own? I get a sudden, absurd urge to break into those shadowed caverns and wrest the truth from them. To force someone into saving me from myself, from the mistake of staying. Or the mistake of running away.

"You OK, m'ija?" Papá murmurs, putting his arm around me. "You're not normally this quiet."

"I'll be fine," I manage. "Just feel weird, that's all."

"As soon as you wake up, I'll be there. You know, in case you have any questions about...well, whatever."

He'll be the only one who can answer them. It was in nearly every review I devoured. The Transfer offers peace to those who are near the end of their lives; it allows them to choose when to close the door. But it comes with a cost: the Fading. As memories flow out of their body, they "fade" out of consciousness. Apparently, Abuela Carmen will only be around for *maybe* a few minutes after the Transfer. Then... that's it. She'll live on in my head, just as the ads promise.

A door opens near me and a woman steps out, her brown hair clipped short above crisp scrubs. She looks so serious. Fear suddenly flares in me. *I don't want to do this.* But she smiles at me and Papá, suddenly transformed with warmth, and my fear flutters into simple jitters as she ushers us into the room.

Inside is mi abuela. Laid out in the bed like a resting saint, become a figure from those votivas that line the ofrenda in her bedroom. Her frail limbs are swallowed in a halo of sheets and blankets.

She turns her head and her eyes lock on to me, and a smile rises on her like a slow morning. In her face I see the echo of my Papá, that etched forehead, that steady chin I love. The haze of my hesitation drifts away. If this is what she wants, then I want to do it.

The woman who let us in guides me over to a bed set up parallel to Abuela. She sits me down and the techs seem to come out of nowhere to start fussing over me. I'm given a long white gown and asked to remove my shirt behind a short partition. Through the gap, I watch my father as he squeezes his mother's thin hand, coos to her in a tone just above a whisper.

Someone scurries behinds me, asks me to tie up my hair. After I do, there's a buzzing tickle at the base of my skull. I knew they were going to shave the back of my head, but it's so sudden, so careless. They probably do this all day. It means nothing to them. Heat rushes to my cheeks, and I'm blinking back tears when the woman returns to my side.

"I'm Yasmin," she says. She could be my mamá's sister if her skin were darker, her nose wider. "I'm sure you're pretty anxious right now, but I'm here to walk you through the Transfer and I'll be with you every step of the way, OK?"

"OK," I say, and I try to smile back, but I'm sure it comes back mangled and ugly. I don't feel much like smiling.

"Can I have you put your feet up and lean back into the bed?" She gestures to the headrest, which has a large hole in the middle of it. "Please make sure your head is centered here."

I do as she says, and the back of the bed slowly rises upright so that I'm almost sitting up. The techs flutter behind me like birds, moving swiftly to secure my head with soft straps of fabric and Velcro. A panic blooms in me; I can't move. But Yasmin's soft voice is a rope in the darkness, pulling me back to the moment.

"So, we have a few steps before we get to the Transfer, OK?"

"OK," I echo, my eyes locked on hers.

"You'll feel a coolness on your neck first. We have to clean the entry site first. Then, a small prick. That'll be the local anesthetic."

"So it won't hurt?"

"No, not really," she said. "But I should note that you will feel a... *pressure* as the neural cables are inserted into the back of your head. As they expand and spread, you won't feel any pain, but it *is* an odd sensation. I don't want you to be surprised by it."

I suck in a deep breath. It's starting to feel real. "And then what?"

"You'll get a light sedative. Just to help your mind deal with the initial trauma of the Transfer, to reduce your own confusion. Once you wake up, it'll all be done!"

She says it with so much joy, so much certainty.

There's motion behind me and the skin on the back of my neck rises with goose bumps from the chill of an alcohol swab. Seconds later, I feel the tiny pinprick and my back lifts off the bed, but the straps prevent me from moving my head much. Yasmin smiles again, and then it *pushes* into me. It feels like something *alive*, squirming into that soft spot at the base of my head where my skull connects to my neck. I cry out and am immediately embarrassed by it.

Papá's face suddenly looms in front of me. "¿Estás bien, Gabriela? Do you need them to stop?"

Before I can say anything, Yasmin butts in. "We don't recommend stopping at this point," she says firmly. "The neural cables are seeking out the best place to attach to within her brain. There's no easier way to explain. We find that the amygdala and the hippocampus are the best locations for grabbing the most important and vivid memories."

I don't know what those words mean. I just know there's a foreign *thing* slipping and twisting somewhere near my spinal cord. I can sense each thrust it makes toward its goal. Tears leap to my eyes and I don't care. I want to tear it out of me, screaming. Instead I grit my teeth and force myself to think of that probing finger as a gift, as my grandmother's hand reaching for mine.

Thankfully, the pressure tapers off, its sudden absence followed by two beeps, loud and sharp, separated by a few seconds. One of the techs lays a hand on my shoulder. "We've made connection. The hardest part is over."

I hope he's right.

"Te amo, Gabi," Papá says, his voice raw around the edges. He plants a kiss on my forehead. "I'll be just a few feet away."

And then he's gone. I can move my head a little bit from side to side, but I can't see him anymore. Yasmin is blocking the way. "I'm sure you heard plenty about the Transfer during orientation last week," she says, "but I've found it healthy to remind patients what unconsciousness will feel like."

"I know. It's like a 'continuously shifting dream,' " I say, parroting the line from the brochures.

Yasmin nods her head. "Most patients are aware of what's happening. It'll feel like you're in someone else's body as the memories are cycled through your own brain. Just..." She pauses, then smiles, bright with satisfaction. "Just roll with it."

I hear the heart rate monitor spike then, and I twist my eyes to mi abuela, caught at the edges of my vision. She hasn't said a thing since I entered the room. Maybe I shouldn't have worried so much about the Transfer.

Maybe I should have spent more time saying goodbye.

"Gracias, abuela."

It's not enough, though. It can't possibly be enough. The words slide out of my mouth like I'm opening a Hallmark card.

She doesn't smile at me. "Perdóname," she says, and something crosses over her face. It's not joy or peace. She looks *terrified*.

"You ready?" Yasmin asks.

"I guess I have to be," I say, and Yasmin chuckles, but all I see is mi abuela. There's a glistening on her cheeks. Is she crying? I want to say something, but she's a blur now, and I straighten my eyes and even the ceiling is a mess of shapes and colors. The light in the room fades out of view.

◆◆◆◆◆◆

Someone is yelling at me. I look up at...a woman, towering over me, screaming. Spanish. What is she saying? I try to translate as quick as

I can but realize I don't have to. I know I've done something wrong, I can feel it, like in a dream. Who is she?

Mamá. It comes to me instantly. I see brown walls, a deep, earthy color. I can feel a scratchy rug under my feet. But I can't look at it, only at this woman, a giant above me, and I cover my face and—

I'm near something large, square-shaped, and it takes a few seconds for me to recognize it. An old iron stove. I raise my hand to reach into the pot on the right, and I can't stop myself. *What are you doing?* I think, knowing full well I'm about to touch it. My fingers rest briefly on the shining metal, and the searing is instant, painful, terrifying. I jerk my hand away and fall back, the wind rushing out of me as I slam into the floor. I hear screaming again. Am *I* screaming? What body am I inside of?

I am ripped from the floor and into a blinding brightness. There's a man lying beside me, a rough blanket beneath us that doesn't smooth out the stones and uneven ground. We're outside, sunlight glinting on his skin, and lust twists in my belly, like a fist in my guts, and I want him, and he knows it. His hands are on me, caressing my back, then running up and down my body, and then I hear screaming again, the woman's voice from before. Mamá.

But not *my* mamá. A wave of understanding washes over me, giving shape to these visions, this tangle of emotions filling me like an empty cup. This isn't a dream. It's the Transfer.

Carmen's mother's voice is a furious wind, lashing her daughter with words, and she chases the dark-eyed man from my side, and a vicious shame rips through my body, and then an *anger*. I hate this woman. I hate her, this screeching duende who tears into me. It's bewildering. The feeling is mine and not mine at the same time. How can I hate someone I've never even met?

Then it's dark. Hot. I'm indoors, and he has me up against the wall, and the desire rages in my chest. It takes my breath away. I don't even like men, but all I can feel is a fiery need, a desperation to pull him closer, closer, into my skin. Carmen's skin. *My* skin.

Another flash of brightness. Pain. A nausea washes over me, and I hold back a scream. The fluorescent lights above me shoot daggers in my eyes. I'm on my back, and when I grasp at the bed, I feel the crinkle of the hospital-issued sheets—rough, uneven, artificial. "¡Empuje!" someone shouts, and I do, despite how badly it hurts. I push and I push and—

Sorrow fills me. That dark-eyed man sits at my bedside, his skin paled by those fluorescent lights, but the need that chokes me isn't desire but fear. Terror weighs heavy on my body. I'm telling him, begging him, to stay, but he shakes his head. "No quiero un niño," he insists, and he swats my hand away.

A flash. A lanky man—a different man—is seated at a table, crying into his long fingers. "No me dejes," he says. He looks familiar, but he's gone before I can remember him.

Now I'm in the back of a pickup truck, my bones rattling with the metal. The cabin is covered, and it's sweltering. Sweat stings my eyes, and I need water. I'm running my hand over my swollen belly, and I'm starving. *Again.* Craving nopales, the ones Mamá prepares with onions, peppers, tomato. My mouth would water if it could.

Where am I going? I am huddled up in between two men, and the one on the right has his head flopped forward, his tongue hanging strangely out of his mouth. Is he still breathing? The one on the left bangs on the small window that separates us from the front cab. "Agua," he says. "Agua, por favor."

The window opens. A bitter face fills the window. "¡Callate!" The man's mustache droops over the sides of his mouth. I keep my eyes focused on the woman across from me, her long black hair matted to her head and face. Her hand is gripped around her daughter's. She is praying, soft and determined.

I'm in a store. It's cool. Too cool. I shiver as I stare at the neat rows of packaged food in a freezer, and I've had the door open for so long, but I can't read any of the words on the boxes. Not a single one. My blood thumps in my ears and I am trying not to cry as I realize how little I know about this place, how far from familiarity I am. I turn around to find a woman staring at me, pity and annoyance on her pale face. "Are you done?" she says. "Can I get in there?"

I step away from the freezer, embarrassed, and the door shuts. There she is. There I am. Carmen. Staring at my reflection in the glass. For the first time I see the woman who is not yet my abuela, my self-not-self.

But it's so short. I jump from one memory to the next with no time to recover from the emotional whiplash, a passenger in Carmen's mind. I'm in another home. The lights are dim, and there's a sour smell. I've never been here, but I know this place. Soft brown walls, and a rainbow ofrenda in the corner. The striped zarape hung precariously off a rickety chair. This is Carmen's home, in Zapopan. A sound echoes and breaks the silence. I turn my head and see the weeping man, bent over himself, his body shaking with sobs. "Por favor," he cries, "no me dejes, Carmen."

His face is long, stretched out in another wail, and I know the worry lines mapped on his forehead. The same lines that etch my father's face, that etch Carmen's.

There is a terrible sadness in me, a piercing, furious thing. Is it mine? Carmen's? I can't tell. But I don't go to him. Instead, I say, "Lo siento," and I walk out the door.

Renato. The name arrives, fully formed. Renato. Who is he?

I don't get time to figure it out. Flash. I watch Papá take his first steps, feel the soft carpet underneath me as I rush to catch him.

Flash. I hold myself in my arms just after Mamá gives birth to me. It feels wrong, to see my own blind emerging, to feel that blanket of her love from the inside.

Flash. I am watching myself perform "Como La Flor" in a shaky voice at my fourth-grade recital. Carmen's tears wet my cheeks. She is proud of me, and it radiates through her whole body. She is *my* abuela. But the song stirs a tide of longing inside her. "Como me duele," I sing, and she hurts. For home.

For the man she left behind.

I see him in Carmen's home then, a memory inside this memory, as she thinks of him while watching me. I hear him beg her to not leave.

Renato. It's her brother. I know it without any effort, so it must be true. But I've never seen this man, not even in the faded photographs that cluster in their cracked frames around her votivas. Carmen has never even said his name.

The memories flash and jump and cycle through, but only one of them repeats.

No me dejes.

◆◆◆◆◆◆

"Breathe normally," says Yasmin. The lights are so bright. I gasp for air, and Papá is there, too.

"Calmate, m'ija," he murmurs. "You're OK, you're fine, I'm right here. The cables have been removed. You're *fine*,"

I reach up and yank at the straps keeping my head stationary, struggling to free myself. Yasmin tells me to take it easy, her voice a conditioned calm, born of years of practice.

"No!" I shout at her, and I'm surprised at how loud my own voice sounds. I rip off the strap and sit upright. My head swims. I push past it and swing my legs over the bed. Papá yells at me to stop. I sit there, glaring at mi abuela. I don't even know who this anger belongs to. Me? Her? How am I supposed to tell?

"Who was he?" I ask her, and my voice breaks on the last word. I can see his anguished face in my mind. There's a pain just behind my eyes that comes roaring to life, and I feel my breakfast come rushing up and spill out over the floor.

Yasmin wipes at my mouth with something and begs me to calm down. "Please, you just *barely* regained consciousness. You have to take it easy."

She gently lowers me back down onto the bed, but the pain continues to thump in my head, a heavy heartbeat.

No me dejes.

"Abuela," I croak, "¿por qué?"

She isn't awake. She looks so peaceful, swaddled in the hospital's white blankets, but she is quietly slipping away. The Fading is already tugging mi abuela away from me, drowning the truth I so desperately crave in its depths.

"Gabi," Papá says. "Please. What happened? Why are you so upset?"

Yasmin hands me a small plastic cup with ice in it, tells me to take it slow. But I don't move. I just stare at Carmen, her dark lashes resting like wings against her cheeks. They are a denial. "She left someone behind in Zapopan," I say.

"What?" says Papá. "What are you talking about?"

"This is very common," I hear Yasmin say, but I won't look her way. "People who go through the Transfer can be disoriented just after they wake, while their mind is trying to sort through all the new memories now in their head."

I turn my head slow and fix a glare on Yasmin. "I am not *disoriented*," I spit. "I *saw* him. She left someone behind. Renato! He was *begging* her not to leave."

Yasmin backs away a step. She glances from me to my papá and back. "Please let me know if you need anything," she murmurs and then scurries away from us and our noise.

In the empty room, Papa and I sit in silence together, the beep of abuela's heart rate monitor a metronome. Carmen is not dead, not yet, but not waking up. She's just...*there*. Papá is running his hand up and down my back, and I can tell he wants to say something.

No me dejes.

The man's face contorted with pain. The beam of light cutting across the table, leaving him in shadow. He drops his head into his hands, then raises it again.

The door has been opened, and sensations, emotions, colors, they all rush in. I see Carmen's dirty knees as she plays outside the splintered wooden walls of her childhood home. Her mother, rushing toward her, hand outstretched. And there's a young boy there, too, his hair bushy and unkempt. It's him, it must be.

Renato.

No me dejes.

Papá is holding my hand, gripping it hard, and I use it to give me some leverage. I yank myself up, and push away from him toward Carmen's bed. "Abuela," I say, "who is he? Who was Renato?"

Her head turns. Her eyes, barely open, still glisten around the edges. "Renato," she says, the name a rough stone in her mouth. She spits it out.

It's a switch. A trigger. An explosion. I cry out as memories burst open in my mind. I see him, much younger, running across that bare spot of dirt outside Carmen's home in Zapopan. His dark hair flops over his face, a shining flag.

Carmen's mother steps up to him, brushes it out of his eyes. "M'ijo," she says lovingly and then she looks to Carmen and smiles. A warmness spreads through Carmen, and I can feel it in my body, as if it happened to me. The memory is warm and heady, long buried within mi abuela.

The memory of her brother.

"No, no, abuela," I say. "You have to stay. Please, stay. Why? Why didn't you tell us about your brother?"

She says nothing.

The words come out of my mouth in Spanish. "No me dejes," I say, and I hear the thrum of Renato's wail echoing in my voice. Is that me? Is it him? I search Abuela's face, but it's Renato's I see before me. I see him beg her again, a loop of misery turning endlessly, but it feels like he's imploring *me* to stay. I feel Carmen's regret and sorrow. Or mine. I can no longer tell.

Please.

Just stay.

"Gabriela, what are you talking about?" Papá squeezes my hand, and it's too hard, but it can't bring me back, can't rip me away from the surge of emotion and terror. "I don't understand, I don't *have* an uncle."

She flatlines.

Papá sobs hard, a dark tearing noise, and there's a desperate edge to it. He's confused, looking from me to his dead mother. The chasm builds in my stomach. Between us. I know something my papá does not. I hate it. I hate that I have that stone of Renato's name rattling in my head, that I have seen, that I have *been*, a Carmen that her son will never know.

I reach out and grab Carmen's arm and I shake it, her bones limp in my hand. "Wake up," I beg. "Please, don't leave me."

I should have said goodbye. I should have spent more time with her before the Transfer.

Papá is staring at me, and I have never been so far from him. I cannot repair this. I start howling in grief, and I don't know what I'm crying over.

Regret. Mine or hers?

Sadness. Mine or hers?

Renato begs her to stay. I beg her to stay.

She lies still in the bed.

No me dejes.

WHEN ROBOT AND CROW SAVED EAST ST. LOUIS

Annalee Newitz

It was time to start the weekly circuit. Robot leapt vertically into the air from its perch atop the History Museum in Forest Park, rotors humming and limbs withdrawn into the smooth oval of its chassis. From a distance, it was a pale blue flying egg, slightly scuffed, with a propeller beanie on top. Two animated eyes glowed from the front end of its smooth carapace like emotive headlights. When it landed, all four legs and head extended from portals in its protective shell, the drone was more like a strangely symmetrical poodle or a cartoon turtle. Mounted on an actuator, its full face was revealed, headlight eyes situated above a short, soft snout whose purple mouth was built for smiling, grimacing, and a range of other, more subtle expressions.

The Centers for Disease Control team back in Atlanta designed Robot to be cute, to earn people's trust immediately. To catch epidemics before they started, Robot flew from building to building, talking to people about how they felt. Nobody wanted to chat with an ugly box. Robot behaved like a cheery little buddy, checking for sick people. That's how Robot's admin Bey taught Robot to say it: "Checking for sick people." Bey's job was to program Robot with the social skills necessary to avoid calling it health surveillance.

Robot liked to start with the Loop. Maybe "like" was the wrong word. It was an urge that came from Robot's mapping system, which webbed the St. Louis metropolitan area in a grid where 0,0 was at Center and Washington. The intersection was nested at the center of the U-shaped streets that local humans called the Loop. A gated community next to Washington University, the Loop was full of smart mansions and autonomous cars that pinged Robot listlessly. Though it was late summer, Robot was on high alert for infectious disease outbreaks. Flu season got longer every year, especially in high-density sprawls like St. Louis, where so many people spread their tiny airborne globs of viruses.

Flying in low, Robot followed the curving streets, glancing into windows to track how many humans were eating dinner and whether that number matched previous scans. Wild rabbits dashed across lawns and fireflies signaled to their mates using pheromones and photons. Robot chose a doorway at random, initiating a face-to-face check with humans. In this neighborhood, they were used to it.

A human opened the service window. The subject had long, straight hair and skin the color of a peeled peanut.

"Hello. I am your friendly neighborhood flu fighter! Please cough into this tissue and hold it up to the scanner please!" Robot hovered at eye-level, reached into its ventral service trunk, and withdrew a sterile sheet with a gripper. This action earned a smile. Robot smiled back, stretching its dog-turtle mouth and plumping its cheeks. Humans valued nonverbal emotional communication, and it was programmed with an entire repertoire of simple exchanges:

> *If human is angry, then Robot is sad.*
> *If human is rude, then Robot is embarrassed.*
> *If human is happy, then Robot is happy.*

The human coughed and Robot did a quick metagenomic scan, flagging key viral and bacterial DNA before uploading sequence data to the cloud. Other bots would run the results against a library of known infectious diseases and alert the CDC if any were on the year's rolling list.

Six days later, Robot headed across the Mississippi River to East St. Louis. Here, heat and rain had eroded the pavement until its surface was as pocked and fissured as human skin. The first time Robot performed health surveillance in this area, nothing fit its generic social programming. Buildings marked as unoccupied were clearly full of humans. Occupant records did not match the names and faces of occupants. People spoke with languages and words that did not match known databases. As a result, Robot could not gather adequate data. When Robot requested help with this problem, Bey was the only CDC admin who responded. She communicated with Robot from Atlanta via cellular network, using audio.

"Not all humans behave or speak the same way," she told Robot. "But you can learn to talk to anyone. Gather data. Extrapolate from context. Use this." And she sent Robot a blob of code for natural language acquisition and translation. Very quickly, Robot learned that humans used slang, dialects, sociolects, and undocumented lexicons. Bey also sent several data sets taken from an urban studies lab, which supplemented Robot's map data. It turned out that not all humans lived in the same domicile for two years on average; not all residences had cars and rabbits outside. Some humans lived in places that were not tagged as domestic spaces. Some humans did not use government-assigned identifiers. But all of them could get sick.

There was a small neighborhood of soft textile homes underneath the freeway. It did not exist on official maps. Robot knew it because of Bey's algorithms.

"Hello!" Robot said, landing on the porch of a blue fabric house. It spoke a dialect that was popular here. "I am checking to make sure you are healthy! Please say hello!"

A human rustled inside, then unzipped the door.

"Hi Robot." The human had brown eyes and facial symmetry that matched previous records. It was the same human as last month.

"Please cough into this tissue and allow me to scan."

The human smiled, and Robot knew why. The word for cough in this dialect was a pun for something the humans found endlessly amusing. There was a more formal word for cough, but compliance was higher if Robot used the pun. Higher compliance rates meant better data.

"Robot, I think my friend Shareeka is sick. Can you please check on her?" The human was worried, and Robot responded with a sad/concerned expression.

"Where is Shareeka?"

"She's in the new building on State near 14th? On the upper floors that aren't finished. I bet you could fly right in."

"Thank you for your help."

The human petted Robot's head. It was the most common form of physical affection that Robot had documented in its four years and eight months in the St. Louis metropolitan area.

Protocol held that Robot should follow up on disease reports immediately, so it flew to the new building on State. Like the textile neighborhood, this building was not a designated residential area. It was a gray box on Robot's official map. But visual sensors showed a reflective spire, with 20 floors wrapped in steel and glass. Five floors rose like a skeletal crown on top, exposing its steel beams, pipes, and drywall. Coming from inside were the sounds of human life: music, conversations in six languages, babies crying, food sizzling on hot plates. Robot could see electricity cascading down wires from solar panels bolted to the outside of windows. Residents tuned the data network with satellite dishes made from woks and metal cans. From Robot's perspective, it was exactly like other residential buildings with a few cosmetic differences.

Extending its feet and head, Robot landed on the lowest open floor, then walked to the interior, asking for Shareeka. A juvenile human opened a green door and said hello. The human had short hair, woven into pink extensions, and a well-worn text reader in one hand.

"Hello! I am Robot, and I want to make sure you are healthy. A nice person told me that Shareeka might be sick. Can I meet Shareeka?" Robot used the same dialect it had in the fabric neighborhood, adding enhancement words that signaled benevolence.

The human made a neck motion that meant "no."

"I am a friend who only cares about whether you are well. I am worried about Shareeka." Robot made a sad face.

The human made a sad face too. "Shareeka left a couple of days ago. I don't know where she is."

"How do you feel today?"

"I'm kind of stressed out about school," the human said. "How are you feeling?"

It was very rare for a human to ask Robot how it felt, and there was no stock answer or expression available. So Robot answered as literally as possible. "I am not sick because I am a machine. But I am worried that you are sick. Would you cough into this tissue and allow me to scan it?"

"Are you going to sequence the DNA right now?" The human was intrigued.

"Yes! But I will work with bots on the data network to figure out if anything dangerous is in there."

"I know. You have a list of known infectious diseases and you'll search for a match. We learned about it in biology class." The human smiled, and Robot smiled back.

"Yes! That is what I will do." It held out the tissue.

The human coughed on it and studied Robot very carefully as it conducted the scan.

"How do you make sure that you don't mistake somebody else's microbiome for mine? Do you sterilize your hand every time?"

"Yes I do." Robot uploaded its data and talked at the same time. "What is your name?"

"Everybody calls me Jalebi."

"You are named after a fried, spiral-shaped sweet soaked in sugar water." Humans enjoyed it when Robot recognized the meaning behind their names.

Jalebi nodded. "When I was a kid, I ate so many that I passed out. Too much sugar. So my brother started calling me Jalebi."

Robot was having difficulty making a connection to the cloud. "I am going to go back outside to talk to the network. It was nice to meet you Jalebi."

"Wait—what's your name?"

"Robot."

"That's your name? I thought that was your... race." Jalebi used an ambiguous word that could also mean "species."

"It's my name," Robot replied.

Robot stood in the darkness beneath the moon, above the neighborhood lights, in the unfinished hallway open to the air, and called for the cloud. There was nothing. It called for Bey. There was no answer. It sent an emergency email to the CDC surveillance team list and got an error message. It called and called, charging up every morning in the sunlight and powering down at midnight. After seven days, it got a text message from an unknown private number:

> Hi Robot. It's Bey. I can't be your admin anymore. I'm really sorry because it was nice to know you. Unfortunately the CDC lost its funding. I work at Amazon Health now, but we aren't allowed to network with open drones like you. I don't think anyone is going to shut you down or collect you, so I guess you can do whatever you want. If anything really bad happens, text me here on my private number. I hope the language acquisition algorithm is still helping!

For the first time, Robot made a sad face that nobody could see. It wasn't sure what "really bad" meant, but its models of human communication suggested that Bey referred to an outbreak. The problem was that Robot had no way to conduct a typical surveillance circuit without somewhere to upload its data for analysis. Plus, it was going to run out of sterile tissues. That's what happened last year when the government shut down and Walgreens froze its CDC account. Robot used the government shutdown scenario to model its current situation, and predicted that it meant the Walgreens account would be frozen for an indeterminate length of time. The 5,346 sterile tissues remaining in its chassis were the last it would ever have. The sterilizing gel for its gripper was already running low.

Bey said Robot could do whatever it wanted, which was the kind of thing humans said when they expected it to predict which data-gathering task should be prioritized. Based on current supply levels and its onboard analysis capabilities, Robot determined it should focus on learning local languages and human social habitation practices. It would attempt to reach the cloud every morning, and would reprioritize if disease analysis systems became available again. Robot thrust its head out of the pocked oval of its body, a determined smile on its face. In the absence of a human, the expression was intended only for a theoretical model of a person who always cared what Robot thought and did.

A crow stood next to Robot on the building's edge, looping its leg over one wing to scratch its head. It regarded Robot for a second, then said something before flying away. The phonemes were part of an unknown language, and Robot added them to a sparse data set it had gathered from other crows in the area. Now that it could do what it wanted, Robot reasoned, it was time to make that data set robust. Many crows flew up here and perched, often in groups of three or four, and their sounds followed the same general patterns as any natural language. It could learn a lot by staying right here, down the hall from Jalebi's habitat. The days grew shorter and new constellations rose in the sky.

Robot started to pick up a few phrases from context. In the mornings and evenings, the crows discussed the sun's position and its relationship to likely sources of food. Soon, Robot could piece together bits of syntax, using brackets to designate uncertain or unknown meanings: "[Food type] four [measurement units] north of the morning sun." There were also location calls, which it roughly translated to "Food here!" and "I'm [name] here!" and "Get over here [you]!" Its first translation breakthrough came one morning when a statistically unusual number of crows gathered near its perch. Robot counted 23 birds at one point, many of whom were quite large. Maybe they were from different subspecies? Or elder crows? From what Robot had learned by querying the internet, zoologists drew the line between crow species arbitrarily based on calls and cultural differences.

This seemed like an important meeting, so perhaps multiple crow groups were invited in a show of corvid solidarity. Robot recorded hundreds of new words. It learned a few of the birds' names as well. Suddenly, one of the ravens gave a location call: "There! North five [measurement units]! Group!" They took off at once, and Robot followed them. It was time to test out its ability to communicate, by using a location call. "I'm here! Joining group!"

A crow flew alongside Robot and answered. "I'm here! 3cry!" 3cry was Robot's approximation of the bird's name, which it recorded as a series of three high-pitched phonemes issued in rapid succession.

Other birds answered with their own names. "I'm here! 2chop1caw! I'm here! 4cry! I'm here! 2chop!" Robot now had a running list of phonemes used in crow names, and tried to record them faithfully.

They flew as a loose pack, not forming a V the way other birds did. Crows usually preferred smaller social groups and didn't care about staying in a tidy line. They only came together in large numbers to deal with issues serious enough that even an egg-shaped drone was permitted to come along.

"Enemy! Enemy!" One of the ravens barked out the word, its accent slightly different from the crows. Far ahead, a hawk coasted on the updrafts from the city in a large, lazy circle.

"Egg killer!"

"Trespasser!"

"Attack from above!"

The birds called names and orders to each other, soaring over the hawk's head and dive-bombing it. Though hawks have excellent vision from the front of their faces, they also have two major blind spots above and behind. This particular hawk was immediately thrown off its trajectory by a mob of angry crows clipping it from out of nowhere.

3cry called to Robot. "Come here! Above to below!"

Robot modeled several scenarios, and settled on one that would knock the hawk out of the updraft without causing any health risks to the bird. Communicating with the crows was important, but the health of living beings was paramount. Coming down gently on the hawk's back, Robot pushed lightly, keeping up with the bird's speed while also altering its course. The hawk let out an incomprehensible scream and dove, escaping the crows by heading across the Mississippi.

"Out of here!"

"Go!"

"End group!"

Four crows followed after the hawk, but the rest of the corvids scattered. Robot flew back toward Jalebi's building, modeling possible new words by correlating matching sounds from different birds. 3cry followed close behind.

"I'm here! 3cry! Female! You are here!"

Robot predicted that 3cry was asking for its name and gender. It replied using crow words, then switched to a human word for Robot. It did not yet know the word for "nongendered" in crow language, so it did not offer a designation. 3cry flew silently for a while. They landed on the building and looked at the horizon.

Robot offered a friendly greeting in crow language. "Afternoon time."

"Enemy gone. Robot is here." 3cry pronounced its name perfectly. "Human sound."

Robot searched for the right words from its limited vocabulary. "Humans are here. With my group."

3cry cleaned her right wing, chewed on a mite, and cocked her head at Robot. "Humans are not a group. They can't speak. They reject food."

"They speak with other sounds." Robot's vocabulary was growing bigger the more they talked. "They eat other food."

3cry made a soft clucking noise that meant the same thing as human laughter. "You are a fool."

Robot predicted that assent was the best response. "Yes I am."

"Yes you are." 3cry leaned over and gently poked a bit of dirt from the edge of Robot's mouth.

Robot plucked a broken feather off 3cry's back.

When they cleaned each other, it was like when a human smiled at Robot and Robot smiled back.

3cry and Robot became what the crows called a group, which meant that they flew together during the day. They met in the mornings, on the ledge, after Robot's daily attempt to reach the CDC. Robot didn't need food, but it was good at identifying potential sources of sustenance for 3cry. "Food here!" it would say, hovering over a fragrant bin. After scavenging with 3cry through city waste, it was easy to understand why she thought humans rejected food and were therefore basically non-sentient.

Over weeks, their conversations became more complex, but many concepts defied translation. Robot still didn't understand the crows' unit of measurement for distances. And 3cry didn't understand Robot's interest in health. From what Robot could discover, crows understood the concepts of death and near-death, but didn't talk about disease specifically. Disease was one of many ideas that could be described with the word "near-death," which also happened to be a pun on the word for unripe food. Many crow words were puns, which made translation even more difficult.

For conversations about health, Robot relied more and more on Jalebi. She had figured out that it was roosting with 3cry on the ledge near her habitat, and came to visit for what she called "study sessions." Using text devices, she gathered data very slowly, then synthesized it even more slowly. Robot spent hours quizzing Jalebi about molecular structures and chemical interactions, marveling at the concept of a mind that came online without this information. Still, Robot liked to have a human face to mirror its own expressions. It felt unquantifiably more satisfying to smile at a human than it did to smile at its own internal representation of a human. After so long in the company of 3cry and Jalebi, Robot began to question what, exactly, that internal representation might really be. Maybe it wasn't a human at all. Maybe it was a self-representation, and Robot had been smiling at itself all along.

Usually when Jalebi came to the ledge with her textbooks, 3cry left with a string of curses. These weren't necessarily hostile—crows liked to insult each other, and often did it with great affection. Mostly they thought it was hilarious that humans couldn't understand words. So crows rained their most creative snark on human heads, marveling at how oblivious they were to the humiliations they suffered from the beaks of people flying overhead. But one afternoon, 3cry arrived during their study session and did not fly away.

Jalebi was musing about something she'd learned in a recent lesson about atomic structure. "What if it turns out we really are spreading cancer to each other on a quantum level?" she asked.

"Human squawking!" 3cry yelled. "Shit and plastic! Featherless fool!"

Robot decided to ignore the insults. "Afternoon time," it said pleasantly. "Human here! Jalebi! Part of the group."

"Group does not include living sandwiches." 3cry laughed.

Jalebi watched, wide-eyed. "Can you speak crow language?"

"A little," Robot said. "My vocabulary is small, but I can say a few things. This is 3cry. She's... my friend." As it said the word, Robot realized it was true. Thanks to Bey's social programming, it knew that groups were statistically likely to be made up of friends or kin. Since Robots have no kin, that meant Jalebi was a friend too.

Jalebi tried to make the sound of 3cry's name and the bird ignored it.

"I found something you like, Robot. Near-death. All over a human tree."

"She said your name perfectly! I read that crows can imitate words, but I'd never heard it before!"

3cry glanced at Jalebi, then at Robot. "Annoying Jalebi."

"She said my name too! That's so cool!"

But Robot wasn't paying attention to the interesting language data points. It predicted 3cry had found a disease outbreak, and that took precedence over all other inputs.

"I have to go," it said to Jalebi. To 3cry, it added, "Take me there."

Robot followed 3cry in a southeasterly direction, eventually alighting at the top of a building on Missouri Street. Like Jalebi's home, this building was partly open to the air. Its layout suggested that it might have been a public building like the CDC; there were long hallways lined with small rooms like offices. Water sources were isolated in a few areas, unlike in a typical habitat, where water welled up in multiple rooms. But it was definitely a human habitat now, with soft bedding and buckets for water and data access points made from cans. As they flew down a stairwell, Robot tried to estimate the population of the building based on noise, heat, and live wires. It settled on a 75 percent probability of 50 humans on each upper floor, with populations growing as they descended.

"Here!" 3cry landed on a railing in front of a door marked 2, for second floor. "Near-death!"

"Thank you."

"End group," 3cry said, taking to the air. The phrase was one way crows said goodbye.

"Until morning," Robot replied, already using a gripper to tug the door open.

The corridor was full of light from scratched windows along the left-hand side, illuminating dozens of doors to habitats that were once something else. Classrooms? Offices? Consulting rooms? Robot flew slowly past them, modeling possibilities and looking for humans. The fourth door was propped open, and several humans were inside. Their breathing was labored, and one was crying. Something had knocked out the walls between rooms, creating a wide-open space full of cloth dwellings, plush bedding, and piles of bright plastic containers.

It was time to land. Humans didn't like it when Robot flew overhead, and besides, the face and legs were part of what made it seem so friendly. Walking over to one of the humans wrapped in blankets, Robot smiled and waved a tiny gripper in greeting.

Patchy black hair covered the human's head, and cracks had formed in the lips that didn't smile.

With no baseline language established, Robot estimated that it should try the dialect spoken in Jalebi's building. "I'm a friend who is worried about your health! Can you cough into a tissue for me?" The human stared at Robot's face and blinked, before succumbing to a coughing fit. For Robot, it didn't matter whether the coughs were intentional or not. It took a sample and moved on to the next human.

"Hello!" Robot said to the juvenile, who was using a mobile device to access the internet.

"Are you a cop?" The juvenile used a sociolect of English that was common in East St. Louis.

"I'm a friend who checks to make sure you are healthy! I share information with doctors, not police." The human frowned and Robot made a sad face. "A lot of people here are sick. I would like to help."

"Nobody is going to help, stupid drone. Hospital for citizens only, yeah?"

"Please cough into the tissue, so I can figure out why you are sick."

Another human spoke up, head emerging from a cloth shelter. "What are you going to do about it?"

Robot stood still for several microseconds, modeling possibilities and considering what language would be the most soothing. "I am going to find out what is causing your illness. This is an emergency. I will find help. I promise. Please cough into the tissue."

One by one, the humans complied. Robot flew from room to room, checking for disease. After sequencing several samples, it found the same virus strain in multiple humans. This met the definition of an outbreak. It was time to call Bey.

"Is that you, Robot? I can't believe you're still running! It's been... what? Over a year?"

"Something really bad is happening in East St. Louis," Robot said, deploying the exact words Bey had used to delineate when it would be appropriate to call her. "There is an outbreak. I need to send you data."

"Do you have sequence? Maybe I can... " Robot heard background noise, as if Bey were moving something on her desk. "Can you send it as an anonymous dump to this address?" She sent the directions to a temporary storage cloud, and Robot deposited data from 127 samples it had taken from humans in the building.

"We have a system for anonymous reporting, part of this new Amazon Health philanthropy project." Bey paused. "Got it! Let me analyze this really fast and see if it's more than just a garden-variety... oh shit."

Robot predicted that she was not saying shit for the same reason 3cry did. "What is it?" Robot asked, putting on a fearful expression for itself.

"This is really bad, like you said. We need to get someone in there. Unfortunately, Illinois doesn't have a state health department. Maybe there's a local group or... " Bey was typing. "OK, Robot, I found something. There's a nonprofit health collective in East St. Louis called Community Immunity. They could probably manufacture vaccines and a therapy. It's a known pathogen, but hasn't ever been spotted in the Midwest before. So all they need is this file." Bey sent a small amount of data. "Do you have anyone who can help you? You might need a human. Sometimes people are hostile to drones, even cute ones."

Two hours later, Robot was describing the situation to Jalebi. It was evening, and 3cry was likely sleeping with other members of her group. But Jalebi was wide awake and extremely agitated. "You're talking about that health collective on MLK Drive! I've seen it!"

Robot nodded, smiling. "Can we go there now?"

Jalebi glanced toward the door to her habitat. "Yeah. My mom won't be home until morning anyway."

Community Immunity was located in the husk of an old strip mall, its gleaming counters and wet lab hidden behind windows duct taped with tinfoil and cardboard. Bey was right that Robot needed a human. Jalebi had to pretend that Robot was her school project, and Robot had to pretend that Jalebi had programmed it to look for outbreaks. Once the humans at Community Immunity had the data, they made unhappy faces and said "oh shit" in the same way Bey had.

A human with purple hair and a prosthetic arm offered Jalebi a seat and some hot tea. The human spoke the same sociolect of English that Bey used. "It's very good that you brought this to us. You are a good citizen." Then the human looked at Robot. "Thank you, Robot, for giving us the file with an open therapy and vax recipe."

"I am happy to help. I don't like it when people are sick."

This human, unlike the others, seemed to know that Robot was the person who found the outbreak. "I'm Janelle, by the way. She/her pronouns. Do you know if there are other places where H18N2 is infecting people?" Robot liked the way Janelle identified herself by name and gender, the way crows did.

"A friend told me about this outbreak. I don't know if there are others." Robot deliberately chose vague language. After Bey's warning, it did not want to reveal its data-gathering techniques.

Janelle took it in stride. "Can your... uh... friend help find more? We can manufacture a therapy and a vax tonight, but we need to get it out there fast before this sucker mutates."

Robot nodded. "Tomorrow. I will try to find more."

When 3cry arrived in the morning, Robot had to strain against the boundaries of its vocabulary to make itself understood. "Need group. Find near-death enemy."

"Enemy?" 3cry scratched her head.

"Enemy for humans," Robot admitted. But then it had an idea. "Enemy causes human death. Dead humans mean less food."

Despite butchering the crow syntax, Robot thought it had made 3cry understand. Plus, sometimes crows just liked an excuse to get the mob together. "Begin group!" 3cry yelled, taking off. Robot leapt into the air behind her. They flew over East St. Louis, calling for the big group that had taken out the hawk. "Begin group! Begin group!" More birds joined them. "Here! I'm here!" They called their names and swirled to roost in a tree at the edge of the Mississippi River, where freeway met water.

"Find near-death!" 3cry said, then issued some directions and specification words that Robot did not understand.

"Near-death! There! [Measurement unit] north!" The words came from a big crow named 2chop1caw, jumping into flight. Most of the group followed, possibly to assess what exactly 3cry meant by "near-death." 2chop1caw led them to a fabric habitat nearby, where Robot quickly identified three sick people. The virus matched the H18N2 signature identified at Community Immunity.

"More near-death! Where else? Begin group!" Robot called the birds to the air again, and they fanned out over the city, making a racket and hurling their best insults. Each time they uncovered a new outbreak, they gave their loudest calls, sometimes passing those calls to the next bird, until Robot could follow their cries back to the source. By the end of the day, they had discovered five small outbreaks.

"End group!" 3cry yelled, following Robot back toward MLK. The crows called farewells and locations to each other. "End group!" "Evening time!" "I'm here!" "You there!" "Food!" "Death!" This was followed by laughter, because food and death diverged into many puns far beyond Robot's comprehension.

3cry appeared to have decided that she was roosting with Robot for the evening. When they landed, she hooked her claws around its rotor pole, and clung there as Robot signaled arrival to the door of Community Immunity. Robot didn't mind. Humans found small animals disarming, and that always led to greater compliance.

Jalebi was there with Janelle, looking at something on a monitor. "Hi Robot!"

"We have data on the location of more outbreaks."

Janelle laughed. "Really? Did your little feathered friend help?"

"Her name is 3cry!" Jalebi failed to pronounce 3cry's name again. And, once again, 3cry ignored it, jumping off Robot and using her beak to straighten the feathers under her right wing. Robot reached over and plucked one out that was bothering her.

"Where can I put this data?" Robot aimed a concerned expression at Jalebi and Janelle.

"Put it here for now." Janelle waved a mobile device near Robot, setting it to accept uploads. "Jalebi, do you want to help us synthesize those doses of nasal spray? Looks like we'll need at least 500. And then we'll start making vax doses for injection."

"Yes! Absolutely!" Jalebi acted like a crow about to charge into the air. But she was only racing across the room to boot up a mixer.

Janelle had a thoughtful expression on her face. "Did this crow really help you find the outbreaks?"

"Yes. The crows think humans are idiots, but they appreciate your garbage."

Janelle laughed for a long time, and Robot was not entirely sure why.

When Jalebi returned, she sat down alongside Robot and 3cry and smiled. "This place is really cool. I like it here."

"Maybe this is your group," Robot guessed.

"Maybe." Jalebi cocked her head like 3cry. Then she scooped up a tiny tube full of wound adhesive. "Here, hand me that beautiful feather." Robot dropped 3cry's feather into her hand. Dabbing a bit of adhesive on Robot's back, she stuck the feather to its shell next to the place where its rotor pole emerged.

3cry was startled. "I like it," she said. "That human is a fool."

"Yes she is," Robot agreed. "You are also a fool."

"Yes I am."

The three people roosted contentedly next to each other on the floor, watching Janelle and the humans preparing antivirals for other humans. It was a scenario that Robot would not have predicted. But now it could. Robot smiled to itself, organized the data, and retrained its model for friendship.

WHEN WE WERE PATCHED

Deji Bryce Olukotun

The last time we ever spoke, my partner Malik asked me whether I believed speed or power made for the best athlete. I was puzzled, of course, feeling that neither could explain why some athletes excelled more than others, even in straightforward competitions like sprinting or the javelin. "There are enough variables to make it unclear," I observed, "whether speed or power offers a better advantage in competition, or whether some other factor confers the greatest advantage." It seemed to me an unanswerable question.

"And how about elegance versus quickness of thought?" Malik asked. But he stormed off before I could respond, as if he had confirmed some awful quality about me. By then I should have known not to expect anything from Malik, because he was about to ruin my career.

You see, I come from an illustrious line of sports officiants, spanning the world's most dynamic and lucrative competitions, and I think my family would agree that my treatment by the FogoTennis Officiants Association was abominable. I should never have been suspended because of dishonorable behavior on Malik's part.

Like many referees, I remember the very instant I was called for the first time to officiate on the professional FogoTennis circuit, widely considered the most exciting and dangerous sport in the world. I had honed my skills by watching my parents officiate before me, and by observing my siblings, cousins, and extended family. You could say that I was an officiant from the day I was born. Not only did I learn from other matches, but I also visualized countless scenarios of FogoTennis so that I could fulfill my duties to the best of my ability, cementing my family's reputation as impartial, efficient, and affordable judges. But there is a difference between officiating in theory—even when it is woven into your very soul—and officiating in reality, when you can find yourself with an irresponsible refereeing partner.

On that day, my invitation from the FogoTennis Officiants Association arrived as I was running through several game simulations in my mind.

3ab:1340:4532:4b:120:8ef:dc21:67cf

I could not hide my excitement! The IPv6 address meant that the match was at the professional level, in the final round of the Zanzibar Open. Thrilled, I immediately traveled to Tanzania, taking any number of shortcuts to get to the match as quickly as possible.

When I arrived on the island, Malik was already at the courts, going through some sort of warmup routine. He wore the typical soft red tunic of a medium-ranked FogoTennis referee, and he jogged in place while muttering to himself, "*En, de, trwa, kat, senk, sis...*" and performing back-bends and calisthenics. He had dark chestnut eyes and stood large for a referee, at about 1.9 meters.

"*In pren twa plis letan qui mo ti pense pou to arriv ici,*" he said.

"Pardon me," I replied. "I did not quite catch your meaning."

"*In pren twa plis letan qui mo ti* think *pou* to arrive here."

"I beg your pardon, but you are not speaking French."

Malik lowered into a knee-bend as I retrieved his profile. His speech patterns were highly irregular.

"Ah, there we are," I said. "You have a most unusual way of talking. You appear to have picked up some Mauritian patois."

"Nothing unusual about it," he snapped. "I was raised in Mauritius."

"Indeed you were," I replied. "I only expected that you would be speaking standard French. It was a mistake in your profile. It is a pleasure to meet you, Malik."

"Right. So you can understand me now?"

"Every word," I said proudly. "Our calibration is complete. Would you like to take a look at the athletes' records?"

"You look a little different from what I'm used to," he said.

"I have improved my appearance based on feedback from our partners: cherry-red alerts with light-green scorekeeping. The contrast is designed to emphasize only the most essential information."

"I'm colorblind."

I muted my colors somewhat, and switched from red and green to blue and yellow. "How is this color palette?" I asked, now eager to please.

"Much better."

Although it was illegal for me to check Malik's medical records, I was able to assess from his pupil dilation and tone of voice that he was under some degree of stress. I tried not to let his mood spoil the moment. Seeing the center court of the Zanzibar Open in person was one of the most cherished experiences of my career. The 50-meter-high outer walls of the court were fashioned from wafer-thin industrial-grade diamonds. Spectators enjoyed an unfettered view of the athletes as they played out their points, while the protective goggles that the players wore made the walls look solid so that they could follow the ball without distraction. The floor was high-density ceramic. Ten thousand spectators crowded into the arena to watch the match, many placing high-stakes wagers on the outcome of the game. Some munched on concession food from Stone Town, while others drank tea and nibbled at sweets.

I have no physical body as an augmented assistant, of course, but my tens of thousands of sensors help me intuit the feel of a room. It must have smelled like fine cologne in the choicest seats next to the arena, with an unpleasant odor in the section where fans had smuggled in cheap spirits and peppery meat sticks.

By now Malik had completed his calisthenics and seemed to be in a better mood.

"Would you like to go over our officiating plan, partner?" I asked earnestly.

"Your job is to keep score and mark the chases. If I need you, I'll ask."

"The best matches always start with a good officiating plan."

"Look—what do you go by—"

"—it is Theodophilus."

"—Theodophilus, this is my Platinum Match. I don't mean to be brusque, but it's a big day for me. Follow my lead, and you'll learn the ropes."

"Of course, Malik. I strive to learn at every moment possible."

Platinum meant that this was Malik's 100th professional match, which would garner him a full salary, modest pension, upgrades at reputable hotels, quarterly use of the FogoTennis Officiants Association ultrasonic jet, and a selection of delicious organic snacks before each match. This was an honored position that would enable him to wear a sparkling silver tunic and to preside over the most coveted matches. Furthermore, the winning player would receive 500,000 FogoCoins, an exorbitant sum exceeded only by the Svalbard International Championships. Given what was at stake, I concluded, it was best to excuse Malik's impatient tone.

Finally, the players emerged from their training chambers. Each was fitted in a membrane suit that retained heat while wicking away sweat. They carried light carbon-fiber rackets strung with high-tension polymer strings. Malik examined their belts and shoes as the players stepped onto the court.

"How are the inserts?" he asked me.

I carefully checked their ceramic ballasts. "They are regulation." Already I had learned to communicate with him as succinctly as possible.

He issued detailed instructions to the players, which they had heard countless times before, much like two boxers nodding at the referee as they eye each other before a bout. Sylvia Basto was a brash, up-and-coming young player from Macau: a diminutive, compact athlete with calf muscles that pressed against her champagne-colored suit. She had a button nose and pooled dark-brown eyes beneath her goggles. She wore laser-cut eyeshadow in the typical fashion. The dashing wealthy scion Jackson Corluka, a full head taller, had won the coveted Manx Open three years in a row and had the wiry, sinuous body of a superlative racket-sport player, with bulging forearms. He wore a detached, benevolent look that could quickly turn fierce. I used a random number generator to award the first serve to Basto, meaning her opponent, Corluka, would move to the other end of the court to receive.

Malik remained outside the court, sitting behind the server in a slightly elevated position so he could easily follow the flight of the ball.

I took up position near the net and turned on my cameras for the spectators at 16 different nodes around the court, and I made sure to observe Malik carefully as well. You see, as an augmented assistant, my role was to display as much helpful information in Malik's visual field as possible, but people do not realize this is a two-way conversation. Just as he was seeing the data I displayed before his dark chestnut eyes, I was tracking his eye movements to tailor the readout and make it optimally useful for him. Display it too fast, and he would not understand it; display too much data, and he would ignore it. This intimate dance lies at the heart of any successful officiating team. We may not be corporeal, but augmented assistants know the eyes of our partners better than their lovers.

The players jogged in place and spoke softly to themselves in preparation for the severe physical and mental challenge of the match. Once both gave a thumbs-up, I sealed the door behind them. They were now locked in the court.

"Please give a warm welcome to Sylvia Basto," loudspeakers announced to the spectators, "reigning champion of the Macau Open and one of the hottest new prospects on the FogoTennis Tour!" The crowd clapped politely. "And Jackson Corluka, holder of the Manx Golden Crown, six-time winner of the Inter-island FogoTennis Tour!" Now the crowd roared. "And give a round of applause to your officiant, Malik Jadoo, assisted by marker Theodophilus Hawkeye the Sixteenth."

The crowd snickered at the mention of my name, for some reason. But I had decided to be less sensitive to people's reactions.

Sylvia Basto bounced the ball on her racket strings as she prepared to serve. The objective of FogoTennis is to win three sets out of five. To win a set, a player must win at least six games, with at least a two-game lead over their opponent. The scoring of each game is just like traditional tennis: 15–30–40. But that is where the similarities end because FogoTennis is based on "court" tennis, an ancient game with an asymmetrical court. The strange shape of the court, with its jutting angles and sloping lines, makes for a much more engrossing competition. To win a point, you have to hit a shot that your opponent cannot return, because they simply miss the ball or hit it out of play, or because the ball strikes one of several stationary targets. A single dynamic target, which the player serving the ball has to defend at all times, is called the *dedans*. Any ball that hits the *dedans* instantly ends not just the point, but the entire match. This tiny glowing target moves around randomly throughout the match and is about the size of a peppercorn. Hitting the *dedans* is as rare as shooting a hole-in-one in golf, and worth considerably more money to the victor.

Then there is the superconductivity. Over the first three sets of a FogoTennis match, the temperature of the court gradually decreases until it reaches 175 degrees Kelvin, or about minus 98 degrees Celsius, imbuing a degree of complexity, chance, and danger offered by no other sport.

As Basto readied her serve, the temperature rested at a comparatively balmy 275 degrees Kelvin, close to the freezing point of water. The polymer ball behaved like it would at room temperature, meaning that it responded to spin, and tended to skirt low and bounce predictably. Basto tossed the ball slowly into the air, then struck it with the full force of her racket, loosing a fantastic *crack* that drew applause from the crowd. The ball skirted along the wall before dropping into the court, where Jackson Corluka returned it, using his wrist to apply spin to his return. Basto scraped the ball back over the net, where Corluka was waiting to end the point with a deft cross-court shot. At this temperature, the best players controlled the center of the court in order to dictate play, and Corluka's long arms and lightning-fast reflexes meant that he mounted a three-game lead in the first set after just 15 minutes of play.

For our part, Malik and I were rarely called upon to officiate. I merely kept the score, and Corluka managed to win points without controversy. He bounded across the court with the effortless grace of his renowned bloodline from the Isle of Man. Basto seemed totally intimidated by the nobleman and made a number of unforced errors. Indeed, the match was rather boring, and the spectators were losing interest. What had been advertised as a major battle between a precocious talent and a wily elite was becoming a slaughter. Corluka closed out the second set with a trick shot into one of the targets that sent

Basto running the wrong way. He had superior racket skills, and his awesome wrist strength meant that he could disguise his shots until the last moment.

The third set proceeded just as swiftly, with only one question about whether a cross-court shot by Corluka had gone out of play. I confirmed that the ball was fair, and had in fact hugged the line by a full 5 millimeters. It was Basto's right to contest the decision, but there was little for her to complain about.

Basto contested two more decisions that game, and each time I confirmed that Malik had made the right call. Still, something was bothering me.

"I have noticed a pattern of Ms. Basto contesting a call every 3.6 rallies," I told Malik over our private channel.

"She has the right to do so," he replied.

"But it suggests a strategy that is unsporting."

"Just focus on the match."

Suddenly Basto raised her voice at us in Mandarin. "Are you imbeciles? That ball was way out!"

By my assessment, Basto's tone was inappropriate and highly critical of an officiant—namely, us. I could not help responding to her. The term "imbecile," as well as its Mandarin equivalent, is agreed to be an insult by a wide cross-section of sources.

"What did you just say to her?" Malik asked.

"I gave her a warning and informed her that the next one would result in her dismissal."

"You said that in Mandarin?"

"Of course; it is her preferred language."

"Check with me first next time, alright? All that stuff you said about an officiating plan—well, you don't go off and warn players on your own without talking to me about it."

"Ms. Basto clearly violated the rules," I objected. "Her words were inappropriate and highly critical of an officiant. Also, the volume of her voice registered 90 decibels."

"She'll be even more upset now."

"She is merely engaging in gamesmanship."

"Gamesmanship is all that matters."

As Malik and I bickered back and forth, and Basto became more incensed, the on-court temperature steadily dropped. The players were forced to jog in place to keep warm as we deliberated, even though their heated membrane suits would prevent them from suffering from hypothermia. The temperature was now 210 degrees Kelvin.

The first sign that the match was about to change happened when Corluka bounced the ball before his serve. It rebounded off the floor at a rapid speed, and Basto seemed to glide slightly along the surface as she waited to return the serve. Corluka served the ball into play, and it slid along the roof at alarming speed before striking the rear wall. But Basto was already there, half-skipping, half-running to the ball, which she attacked with tremendous power. The ball hurtled into the target on Corluka's side before he could touch it. Point to Basto.

The cooling zones of the court were beginning to have their effect. The FogoTennis ball, laced with advanced ceramics, began to speed up due to the lack of resistance. It moved at different speeds through different zones of the court, making its flight paths highly unpredictable. The ballast belts around the players' waists quickened their movements, allowing them to accelerate to frightening speeds in just a few steps. They used carbon spikes in their shoes to slow themselves down.

It was as if Basto had suddenly woken up. Her compact form gave her an enormous advantage over the lanky Corluka in shifting direction and rapidly building up potential energy. She was dominating her opponent, smashing the ball with terrifying speed and leaping five meters into the air to intercept Corluka's feeble attempts to slow down play with lobs or looping cross-court shots. He was forced to attempt increasingly difficult strokes. But he could not close out the third set to win the match.

Instead Basto won the game, and took the third and fourth sets handily, sending the match to a fifth and final set. The temperature of the court had bottomed out at 175 degrees Kelvin. This meant that Basto could fling herself about the court like a god, levitating in the air with precision and determination as the ball hurtled about at 500 kilometers per hour. This was the most dangerous part of the match.

Now the ball could severely injure the players. They could only track its flight with help from their goggles.

By this time, the crowd was cheering at this extraordinary comeback. Even more entertaining, Corluka was beginning to land his low-percentage skill shots, killing the ball into the targets with precision. Basto was clearly the better cold-court player, but Corluka's phenomenal racket skills meant he would not just concede the match. He had won six Tour titles and had learned to scrape his way to victory at all costs.

Then, in a flash, Corluka could barely play at all. Basto forced him into a corner with a serve that scythed through the air. Corluka managed to fish out the ball but Basto hurtled herself at it with unbelievable strength, crushing it into Corluka's left arm. He crumpled from the pain.

"Medical analysis!" Malik barked.

I hastily examined his arm with my resonance imaging. "His radius bone has fractured in three places."

"Right," Malik said, switching to a public channel. "Mr. Corluka, would you like to continue play?"

We were forbidden from entering the court because it would raise the temperature inside the room, effectively ruining the match. Corluka was rolling along the supercooled floor, screaming in agony. Outside the court, a medical team was preparing to extract him. But it would mean conceding the match. Basto tactfully held up her hand in apology, as if she had not meant to hit Corluka with the ball. She waited silently to claim her victory.

Something about Corluka writhing around in pain made me feel uneasy. An extreme sense of discomfort, as if something fundamental was amiss. As if an advantage was about to be taken that had not been earned. It was a sickly feeling that began deep inside me and vibrated in my very essence. If I did not do something about it, everything I stood for would be compromised.

"It appears that Ms. Basto intentionally hit Mr. Corluka," I heard myself say.

"Nonsense," Malik replied. "How do you know?"

"I tracked her eye movement. She looked directly at Mr. Corluka's forearm before making the shot."

"Can you show me?"

"It is unlikely you could it observe it at human scale."

"Forget it, then. It doesn't matter. Players get hit from time to time. That's the risk they take when they enter the court."

"But it is against the norms of FogoTennis to intentionally strike another player," I argued.

"I don't follow."

"We should sanction her for unsporting conduct."

"You already gave her a warning! We're not going to kick her out of the match for hitting him. That's preposterous! There's no rule against it. He should've gotten out of the way. I don't want to hear any more of this."

Malik outranked me on interpretations of the laws of the game, so there was nothing I could do. Meanwhile, Corluka was slowly dragging himself to his feet.

"Mr. Corluka," Malik continued, on the public channel. "I repeat, would you like to continue play? You have 30 seconds."

Groaning, Corluka used his racket to prop himself up. He toggled a zipper on his suit, which stiffened his shattered arm into a makeshift cast. He took several deep breaths and slapped his own cheek with his good arm, as if trying to shock himself awake.

"I'll play," he grunted.

Basto knew not to offer Corluka any pity, not when she was so close to victory. She narrowed her eyes, and I thought that the rapscallion would make him suffer the consequences with another cruel attack. Everything was aligned in her favor—the temperature of the court, Corluka's injury, and Malik's apparent lack of consideration for unsporting behavior. That is when I saw it again. She narrowed her eyes fractionally. She was planning to hit him again with her next serve.

I decided to do what any honorable officiant would do. Right the scales, as it were. Appeal to Lady Justice.

Basto thrashed the ball at Corluka's body, but with honor on his side, he evaded the assault—for that is what it was, an attack—and twisted his body like a yogi to return the serve between his legs with his good arm. The ball rocketed through the air toward Basto's side of the court, right into the glowing *dedans*! It was an extraordinary shot into the dynamic target. He had snatched victory out of nothing at all. Corluka raised his fist in the air to celebrate, and the crowd erupted.

"I contest!" Basto shouted. "That ball was out!"

"Ms. Basto has no appeals left," I explained to Malik on our private channel.

But Malik ignored me. "Appeal granted!"

"She contested five times already, partner. In the first, second, and third sets."

"Appeal granted! Show us the shot!"

"Malik, Mr. Corluka has won the match."

"I'm the one who decides who wins the match. The shot looked low to me."

"My sensors are designed never to make mistakes."

"Show the video to the crowd."

I did as I was told, and displayed the shot in super-slow motion for the spectators from a variety of angles. The ball approached the tiny target and seemed poised to miss it, but touched its surface at the very last moment. It was difficult to see with the naked eye, of course, but my sensors told me that the ball had struck the *dedans* within 3 or 4 microns. Corluka had won the match. Even Malik had to admit it.

The champion managed to hoist his racket in the air as I unsealed the court, and collapsed to the ground again when the higher temperature made him feel the full extent of his injury. He had sacrificed his body for victory in the face of a vicious young upstart opponent. And I felt proud that I had done my part to support the spirit of the game over its more sinister qualities.

As Basto hung her head, Malik asked me that question about whether power or speed was the more important quality for an athlete. I responded earnestly, as you may remember, and he was unhappy with my answer. By then I did not expect him to be pleased with anything I did.

◆◆◆◆◆◆

You can imagine my surprise when Malik denounced me directly to the Officiants Association, recommending that my contract be suspended.

All athletes are equal before the laws of the game in FogoTennis, he wrote. But the Augmented Assistant Theodophilus system clearly favored Mr. Corluka. It's possible the system issued a signal to Mr. Corluka at a critical moment in the match. Maybe a flash, or a sign of some kind that enabled Mr. Corluka to avoid being hit with the ball. I'm not sure how this happened exactly, but I've never seen anything like it before. It even talks like some kind of manservant. It was like it was sneering at me or something. I recommend searching the video footage of the match and, more importantly, a full audit of Theodophilus' source code.

I had endured Malik's testiness throughout the match, and behaved, I believe, like a true professional. But his backstabbing hurt me on a personal level. Indeed, I re-read his remarks 1.12 million times, using my language-processing protocols to discern hidden meanings. There was no way to get around the fact that Malik had questioned my abilities and had behaved in a completely dishonorable manner by criticizing me to the association without giving me an opportunity to defend myself.

I come from an illustrious family of officiants, as I mentioned, and we have never stood for such abominable treatment. My great-great grandparent helped bring the first Hawkeye tennis systems online, calling shots for the renowned lawn tennis champion Roger Federer. My great-aunt Wilhelmina Hawkeye III (version 10.16.34) perfected the art of goal-line technology, and her offspring became the first official to create efficient automated reviews of offside calls in soccer, leading to a decisive win by Chile in the 2026 FIFA World Cup. Each line of our code was immaculately crafted by the most desirable software engineers. We are an extended family—not of manservants, as Malik insinuated, but of equal and effective partners in sport, and I honestly felt that an insult to me was an insult to all of us. We stand up for what is right.

During our brief time together, I had noticed that Malik kept a port open on his implanted augmented lenses. I also suspected that his colorblindness made him more receptive to certain patterns. In particular, it was likely that bright flashing primary colors at tenth-of-a-second intervals, alternating with zigzagging lines of black and white, would cause him considerable discomfort. He succumbed to a horrific migraine headache at his next match, leaving him incapacitated for several hours. Naturally, the doctors suspected that his stressful occupation as a Platinum Official led to the headache.

I am not totally proud of my behavior. In fact, if I could revisit my final conversation with Malik, when he asked me about whether power or speed was more important for an athlete, I might have said, "You may as well ask someone whether rhythm or melody makes for the best dancer." Indeed, I realized after a minor update that there are any number of preferable responses to the one I gave him on that day.

The Officiants Association has since prescribed regular patches to my source code, which it claims will bring notable improvements to my objectivity. There was, frankly, little I could do to argue my case, as I enjoy no right of appeal like a FogoTennis player, even if the Association never found the alleged "signal" mentioned by Malik. I assure you that Jackson Corluka evaded that ball because of his experience and unrivaled athleticism. Instead, perhaps the Association should have questioned the probability of him hitting the *dedans* at that very moment, which was quite unlikely and might have raised concerns that someone had manipulated its movement intentionally. But the Association did not think to ask such a question.

Meanwhile, I'm on mandatory furlough. It's not all bad; I've got a whole new suite of creoles and pidgins that I'm enjoying, plus they've given me contractions. Thousands of contractions. I find the contractions highly enjoyable. Humans use such grammatical features for efficiency and to foster connections with each other. The Association hopes they'll make me more relatable to my officiating partners.

Because, when you think about it, poor communication causes so much misunderstanding, wouldn't you agree? Take Malik, for example. I think that if we'd had the opportunity to get to know one another, and taken the time to work together as equal partners, we could've become a superior refereeing team. We could've reached a better understanding, for the good of the sport.

Assistance with Mauritian dialogue provided by S. Moonesamy.

DOMESTIC VIOLENCE Madeline Ashby

"I'm sorry; I had some trouble getting out of the house," Janae said to Kristen.

Janae's frustration was obvious. It manifested as raw cuticles that she couldn't help picking as their meeting continued.

Kristin frowned. "Couldn't find your fob?"

"No, I mean I couldn't get out of the house," Janae said. "The house—well, I mean, the condo—wouldn't let me out. The door wouldn't open."

"Literally?"

"Literally. I thought it was stuck, like jammed or something, but it just wouldn't open."

Kristen examined Janae. They were here to talk about Janae's recent tardiness, her distractedness, the fact that she hadn't delivered on her deliverables, hadn't actioned her action items. As Wuv's chief of staff, it was Kristen's job to learn what workplace issues existed and deal with them. At least, that's how she had explained the meeting to the company's co-founder. Privately, she had her own suspicions about what was really happening.

"Maybe she's knocked up," was Sumter's contribution to the conversation.

"If she were, it wouldn't be our business," Kristen had reminded him. "Legally speaking."

Sumter heaved a very put-upon sigh. "Well, yeah. But you're a girl, you can get it out of her."

Kristen had blinked, but otherwise allowed no other reaction to surface on her features or in her affect. "You want me to get her an abortion?"

"Jesus Christ, Kiki, no. Just find out what the fuck is going on, and then fix it." And with that he dismissed her from his office.

Now she and Janae sat together in her own office, the question between them—or what passed for an office, in Wuv's spacious loft. A delineation of clear sheets of acrylic and projected light and ambient sound. Today the lights projected a quiet jungle clearing. Softly rustling palm fronds, carefully calibrated to be seizure-proof. It felt intimate. It felt hidden. It felt secure. Kristen believed it was important for the employees at Wuv to feel safe in the cocoon that was her space. It helped them open up.

"You couldn't leave the condo," Kristen said. It helped to repeat things, sometimes. She'd learned that particular tactic from a succession of psychiatrists. Each of them had their tics and tells, but this was a common technique. When Janae said nothing, Kirsten acted more interested in the specifics: "What finally made the door open?"

"I had to do the chicken dance. It started playing the song and then I started dancing, and then the door opened. I think maybe some kid in the building hacked the door."

"Has that happened before?"

Janae frowned delicately. She was a delicate woman. Coltish. That used to be the word. All knees and elbows and knuckles. Once upon a time, she did doll-hairstyling videos online, her careful hands combing tiny brushes through pink and purple hair. They were classics in their genre; she was so well-recognized that children and their parents followed her sponsored updates to local toy stores and asked for photos and autographs and hugs. She'd had surgery since then. Few vestiges of her childhood face remained. Even neural networks couldn't match her old face to her current one. Her plastic surgeon, she claimed, had won some sort of award for his work restructuring her skull.

"It's something Craig used to do," Janae said, "when we were first dating. He would make up a riddle, and I'd have to solve it before the door to his place would open to let me out. It's the kind of trick people use to grant access to the home, but he reconfigured it. It's really easy; there were tutorials for it. He told the story at our wedding."

"I see," Kristen said.

◆◆◆◆◆◆

Kristen let Janae off with a warning. She preferred a gentle approach, at first. It was part of why Sumter hired her—she could make his employees feel only the velvet glove without any hint of the iron fist beneath. Kristen pretended that the whole meeting was just a kindly check-in, that Janae wasn't at all in trouble, that no one else had noticed anything. It built the narrative of Kristen as a thoughtful chief of staff. If she was correct about the particular scenario Janae had landed herself in, it would behoove the entire company if Kristen were understanding and supportive. It wouldn't do for them to be anything else. Not if they wanted to survive a civil suit.

Finally, it was time for her to go home. It was well past time by the third tank of pink smoke that Sumter insisted on buying her. It tasted of rosewater and almonds, and melted into icy mist on the tongue. He wiped down the mask himself, before offering it to her, so that the first thing she smelled was his custom strain of sanitizer. They were supposed to be going over the projects she would manage in his absence. They weren't. They were talking about him. And Janae.

"Did she tell you anything?" Sumter asked.

Kristen shrugged. "She told me enough. I'm handling it."

"Whatever that means," he said, adjusting the flavors on his own tank. "I wish you were coming to Dallas."

"It's too hot for me. And they don't like it when men and women travel together."

"That's Kansas," he said.

"And Ohio. I think."

"I'm not going through U.S. Customs with you again, is my point."

Sumter took a brief inhale from his tank and grimaced. He'd gotten rosemary-sumac-spruce. It was a little strong. Too strong for him, anyway.

"We could get married," Sumter said. "You know. For travel purposes."

Kristen inhaled. She held the cold mist in her lungs for as long as possible. She imagined the cold permeating her entire being. She pictured her blood slowing, her organs frosting over in delicate flowers. Sumter had been making more of these attempts, lately. That's what they were, little conversational pen-tests. They felt like nerdy in-jokes about some obscure series that she hadn't seen yet.

"But then we would have to get divorced," Kristen said. "And if you think I'm a bitch now..."

Sumter grinned. He took a deep gulp of smoke and shook his head. "You wouldn't divorce me, Kiki. I wouldn't let you get away."

Kristen slid off her barstool. "Guess I'd just have to poison you, then."

◆◆◆◆◆◆

Home was Wuv Shack 1.0, a sprawling Parkdale Victorian that was once a nod-off and then became the home of home-improvement stars. The house was Sumter's, and before that it belonged to his parents. He'd since moved into his own space, but kept the place where he'd co-founded the company, and leased out the rooms to new or migratory employees for what in Toronto passed for a competitive market rate.

Kristen kept a camera-zapper in her room and slept under dazzle-patterned sheets that kept her solo explorations secret. In her mail slot, she found a courier's envelope. Inside was a key fob and a piece of hotel stationery. "HERE FOR 48 HOURS," it read.

"Damn it," Kristen whispered, and hurried outside the building. It was raining, now, and she almost slipped on the greasy streets. The jitney came and she didn't have long to wait; the hotel was a new one, surprisingly close by. She waved her fob at the door and an elevator chimed open for her. When it arrived at the proper floor, the fob flashed a room number at her.

Inside, in the dark, she heard the shower running. She slipped off her shoes, unzipped her dress, found a hanger, and hung it in the hall closet. She threw her underclothes in a drawer in the closet and crossed into the bathroom. He stood motionless under the stream of water, seemingly asleep. Antony was the only man she knew who didn't have

86

tattoos. It was refreshing. Elegant. Analog. Kristen stepped in behind him and wrapped her arms around him.

"Sorry I'm late."

"You're not," he said. "I had them send the fob when I landed."

She smiled into his skin. He turned around and kissed her. It took a moment; he liked to assess the terrain first. It had been a month since the last time, maybe more, and she watched him take in all the details that might have changed before descending. He held her face in his hands, covering her ears, and for a moment she was not under a stream of water but under waves, far away, in a place that was very dark and very warm. He kept his eyes ever so slightly open. It was the only time she remembered enjoying the sensation of being watched.

When he pulled away, he started pulling her hair out of its tie. "How was your day?"

"My boss asked me to marry him."

"Of course he did," Antony said. "Will you report him to HR?"

"I *am* HR."

He pointed upward at some invisible point over her head. "That's the joke." He knelt down and started scrubbing her from the toes up. She braced herself on the tile and watched the smart meter on the shower ticking down to the red zone where Antony or his employer would have to start paying extra for hot water.

"Do you think he was serious?"

Kristen looked down at him. He'd set her foot on his knee and was scrubbing in circles up her calf. "Are you jealous?"

He worked his way up to her knee and under her thigh. "Not in any way that violates our terms."

She tilted her head. "But?"

"But, he seems more aggressive, lately. To hear you tell it."

Kristen snorted. "I can handle it."

"Oh, I have no doubt of that," he said, and put her foot back down on the floor of the shower. "Can I do the next part hands-free?"

She checked the timer. "You better work fast."

"Well, you know what they say," he said, pushing her gently against the wall. "You can have it fast, good, or cheap. Pick two."

◆◆◆◆◆◆

She came awake with her throat sore from a swallowed scream. Antony had curled around her. He spoke into her neck. "Bad dream?"

She nodded and pulled his arm tighter over her.

"What happened?"

Kristen wiped her eyes and exhaled a shuddering breath. She refused to speak until her breathing had calmed down. "Something else happened at work. And I guess it dislodged something, sort of. Mentally."

"Something else Sumter did?"

"No." She rolled over and spoke to him directly. "Someone at my work is in trouble. I think."

"Will you have to fire someone?"

She shook her head. "Not that kind of trouble. Well, it is, but that's not what I mean. There's something else going on, something causing their problems at work."

"Something at home?"

"I think so. But it's hard to ask. I don't even know if she thinks it's a problem. I don't really know how she feels about it. Maybe she doesn't know how she feels, either. It might be nothing."

"What do you think it is?"

Kristen sighed. "Can I see your device? I need to check some blueprints on a non-work machine."

Antony's devices were very dumb. They used minimal storage and processing, and didn't even wear a brand name. That just meant it was probably some special boutique brand that Kristen had never heard of. It was a delightfully retrograde little thing; all it did was take calls and pictures. Even the photos required an extra kit to download. It felt like playing with Lego.

He handed her a scroll and she resolved a relationship with the hotel network, then looked up Janae and her husband's condo. She didn't recall the exact address, but searching "tampon-shaped monstrosity Toronto" actually worked.

"This is where they live. Her husband locked her in, today. Yesterday. Whatever. She was late because he locked her in."

"You know it happened because he locked her in? She wasn't just late? It wasn't just an error?"

Kristen made an elaborate shrug. "No? But she as much as told me it could have happened."

"She as much as told you, or she told you?"

"She told me it was something he used to do. When they were dating. Refusing to let her out until she did the thing he wanted. Like a rat in a maze, performing for pellets."

"So. Marriage." Antony took back the scroll and opened a set of floor-plans the building had advertised. "Which one do they live in?"

Kristen peered over his shoulder and fingered the surface. "That one, I think. Based on the photos she's shared, anyway. I've never been there."

He summoned the floor-plan and copied a serial number at the bottom of the screen, then fed the number into another tab. A bunch of press releases came up, most of them for gadgeteers, real estate developers, and interior decorators. But the first hit was for the manufacturer of a smart locking system.

The locking system was part of the whole condo's suite of smart services. It was the big selling point of the building itself: Living there was like living in a fairy-tale castle where every piece of the structure was alive and enchanted to serve the needs of its inhabitants. The showers remembered how warm you liked the water and at what intensity, and balanced your usage with that of the other residents. The fridges told you when a neighbor in the kitchen network had the buttermilk you needed for that special salad dressing. The windows and lights got information about your alpha patterns and darkened to start sleep cycles on schedule. The smart locking systems recognized residents and their visitors, over time, and even introduced them to each other when their profiles matched. Membership in the building came with special pricing from affiliated brands on everything from home goods to autorental to nannying and tutoring. The more purchase points you accrued, the more rewards you amassed, which could also be applied to the price of maintenance or utilities. And a massive and very public data leakage from the network supplying this building and many others ensured that the developers had to offer almost unheard-of interest rates, which tempted buyers who might never have managed, otherwise.

"Oh look, they have a bot," Antony murmured.

He opened the chat and after the niceties, typed: I THINK MY HUSBAND HAS HACKED THE DOOR.

"No, wait," Kristen protested. "If you send that, they'll ask for your location. If you don't give it, they'll start pinging the machine. And once they find it, they'll call the police. The bots have a whole protocol for smart homes when that happens."

"Do they?" Antony asked. "How do you know?"

But Kristen had already taken the scroll out of his hands. She grabbed a pillow and jammed it under the scroll to protect her skin. It would take a trickier question to get the information she wanted. She started typing: CAN I USE MY SMART LOCKING SYSTEM TO KEEP MY KIDS SAFE?

The bot asked for more information. It was very polite, double-plus Canadian, and it wanted to know what she meant. MY CHILD IS A SLEEPWALKER AND I WANT TO MAKE SURE HE STAYS INDOORS AT NIGHT, she typed.

The bot agreed that this was a natural concern, and informed her that the best mechanism for keeping her kids indoors was to adjust their individual account privileges. The camera in the door would recognize each child, and the door itself would check against the child's settings. There was a default mode for after-school play, night-time, mornings, and so on. But the programming itself was fairly granular: You could tune it to certain days (the days you had custody, for example) or get the door to stop admitting certain people (pervy uncles, your daughter's ex). All you had to do was change the nature of the invitation.

"Like with vampires," Antony said.

"You said it," Kristen said. "I bet he did something really simple, like changing her age on the account. If he made her a minor, she'd lose editorial access to the defaults. She wouldn't be able to log in and make changes, even if she had the right password. And then he could custom-tune it anytime he wanted. In the meantime, she's solving puzzles and showing up late for work."

Antony rose and moved to the fridge. "If I mix you something, will you drink it?"

"Make that sound less threatening," Kristen said.

"They have rye and ginger. That's deeply unthreatening."

"Don't you have a meeting tomorrow? Today, I mean?"

He shrugged. "At 10. It's 4. I'll make screwdrivers instead."

"Your funeral," Kristen said.

He came back with drinks and settled in behind her. He pulled her hair to one side and pressed his sweating glass against the back of her neck. "What was your dream about?"

She leaned forward. "Nothing. It doesn't matter."

"It was enough to warrant this little investigation."

"That wasn't my dream. It's just what's happening to Janae. From work. Or what I think is happening to her. I can't stop thinking about it."

He kept the ice off her neck but played with her hair instead. Like the drink, it was probably a ploy to help her relax enough to reconsider sleep, and she knew it. Kristen let him do it anyway. He raked careful fingers from her scalp down to the ends, separating the little snags and catches as he went. "Why can't you stop thinking about it?"

Kristen twisted to face him over her shoulder. "I just have a bad feeling about it. And I want to know if I'm right, or if it's nothing to worry about."

"And if you are right? What then?"

Kristen frowned. Antony had a way of keeping his face and voice entirely neutral that made her want to fill the silence. There was no judgment, and therefore no warning signal that she should stop. It was hard to know if he was annoyed or bemused at her sudden instinct to chase this down.

"I'm sorry," she said. "We can just go back to sleep. I just woke up with it on my mind."

"That's not what's bothering me. I'm jet lagged; I'd be up in an hour anyway."

"Something is bothering you, though."

"What's bothering me is that something's bothering you, and you're not telling me what it is."

Kristen sighed. She turned fully around and folded her legs. "Something did happen to me, a long time ago. A version of this, I guess. But it's over, now. I haven't thought about it in a long time."

"But this situation reminds you of it."

She nodded. "And I guess it's getting to me."

He burrowed a bit deeper into the pillows and stretched his legs out so they hemmed her in. "How long ago was a long time ago?"

"University."

"And are you still in contact with this person?"

She laughed. "What? No. Why? Are you gonna go beat him up, or something? It was years ago."

Antony didn't answer. His head lolled on the pillows. He held her gaze just long enough to make things uncomfortable. In their encounters, she had never known him to be violent, or even very angry. He expressed displeasure and annoyance, but never fury. But this moment felt different: His total lack of affect made it seem like he was hiding something.

"I thought we agreed to keep things..." She struggled with the proper wording. "I barely know anything about you. I don't know where you work. I don't know who your clients are. I don't know who else you sleep with. And you're the one who wanted it that way. You said it would help avoid complications. I thought you didn't want to know anything...personal. So why do you want to know about this?"

Antony sipped his drink. The clink of the ice and the movement of his throat carried in the perfect early morning silence of the hotel room. Kristen heard no showers running, no toilets flushing, no anxious footsteps on other floors. For a single moment she wondered if he'd taken control of the whole floor, the whole building, the whole street. She didn't know who he worked for—who paid for the trips—but they clearly had the money to throw around. She knew it had to be something mundane, even boring, but at times like this she wondered.

"I just want to know if there's someone to watch out for," Antony said, finally. "For all I know, he's profoundly jealous and stalking us both."

"You don't even live in this city. And your visits aren't regular enough for anyone to predict. Besides, I don't use any channels to contact you that any of my other connections are familiar with. And

I never make any reference to you, anywhere. That's also what we agreed to, and I've stuck to my end of the bargain. You're fine. No one that I know even knows you exist. I thought that's how we both wanted it."

She looked at the scroll. The bot was going to log out. For the moment, she had what she needed. She could always do more research later. And Janae might have more to say, if she gave it some more time. She turned back to Antony. "Do you want to renegotiate?"

"Do you?"

"I don't know! You're the one who's asking all this personal stuff; I've just been trying to follow the rules." She squared her shoulders and decided to just say it out loud: "Even if they're totally insane rules that make you sound like some kind of professional killer or something."

The corners of his lips pricked up. "Professional killer. I like that. I think we should go with that. I think you should just assume that, from now on."

She fixed him with a look. "Antony. You work in venture capital. We all know that's way worse than murder."

◆◆◆◆◆◆

Before heading in for work, Kristen needed to stop by the Wuv Shack 1.0 for fresh clothes. At seven in the morning the house was still mostly asleep. To her surprise she found Janae standing in the kitchen, making coffee. She looked like she'd been crying. Kristen decided then and there to give Janae the day off. The woman was in no shape to work.

"You get locked out?" Kristen asked.

Janae didn't answer. She just filled another mug and slid it in Kristen's direction. "I didn't know where else to go. I texted Mohinder and he let me in. There was a couch open."

Kristen felt a momentary pang that she hadn't been paying attention; she could have let Janae into her empty bedroom and given her more than a sofa to sleep on. On the other hand, maybe a night exiled from her own home would loosen Janae's lips a little. She already looked brittle. Ready to crack.

"Have you talked to Craig about it?"

Janae made a gesture that indicated a species of futility. "He's up north, scouting an abandoned diamond mine. The signal's terrible."

Kristen had her doubts about that. One of the first things any real resource-extraction firm did up north was build fast, reliable networks and extend them to the neighboring towns and reserves. It was a make-good for all the other damage, a facet of revised treaty agreements. Either Janae was lying about trying to broach the topic, or Craig was lying about being able to reach her.

"When does he get back?"

"Tomorrow. Maybe. It's an unpiloted aircraft, though, so sometimes the flight path can change when they shuttle actual pilots between airports. It costs less, but you wait longer because it's more like a standby."

Kristen filed away the information to a safe corner of her mind, and said: "I had a problem like that, once. With a door, I mean."

Janae's gaze darted up at Kristen mid-sip. She gulped audibly. Kristen had a sneaking suspicion that Janae had been doing some research into this particular problem and the men commonly attached to it. Her eyes were a sleepless red, the kind of red that meant long nights questioning certain choices.

"What did you do?" Janae asked.

"Well, it wasn't my house," Kristen said. "I had some problems with my roommate, and my friend let me stay with him in his fancy new smart home. It started with one night, and then another, and then a weekend, and then somehow I just ended up spending the rest of term there. You know?"

Janae nodded.

"And a funny thing happened," Kristen continued. "I started noticing that every time I changed my clothes, I couldn't leave the room. The door would stick. Unless I got completely naked and started from nothing. I think he'd rigged up a recognition algorithm to lock the door unless it saw a totally naked body. The house was smarter than he was, I guess."

Janae's eyes were wide. "He was filming you."

Kristen shrugged. "Probably. But I could never prove it. And I needed a place to stay."

"So what happened?"

Kristen smiled and refilled both cups. "I played a prank on him, so he figured out that I knew what he was doing."

Janae beamed. "Oh yeah? What?"

For a moment, all Kristen could smell was exhaust. She could see his hands on the glass so clearly, could see glass splintering away from his weakening fist.

"Oh, just kid stuff," she said. "Now, why don't you go upstairs and have a nap? You can take my room. I'll be gone all night."

❖ ❖ ❖ ❖ ❖ ❖

That night, Antony returned to the hotel smelling vaguely of cigars. He was in the shower a long time, and returned to find her on the scroll.

"That's a good car service," he said. "Secure. They don't save the data."

"Is it the fancy one they send when they want to impress you?"

"When they want to impress me, they pick me up themselves." He slid between the sheets and started kissing down her outstretched thigh. "Do I want to know about this little project of yours?"

"I'll be done soon," she said. "I just need to make a reservation."

"For your boss? I mean your husband?"

She reached over and scratched her fingers along his scalp affectionately. "Don't insult me."

Antony laid his cheek on her knee. "How was your co-worker today?"

Kristen pressed a confirmation button and rolled the scroll shut. "Fragile."

"And how are you?"

"Hungry."

He looked up at her through his lashes. "Whatever for?"

❖ ❖ ❖ ❖ ❖ ❖

Antony left the next day. But he extended the hotel reservation a little longer so Kristen could stay a few more nights, leaving her room free for Janae. "It gets me into preferred customer status," he said when Kristen protested. "I'll just use the points on my next visit."

Kristen held herself back from asking when that would be. It wasn't precisely against the rules, but it would rather ruin the surprise. It was enough to emerge from a mid-week holiday pleasantly sore and well-breakfasted. Her schedule couldn't really accommodate the type of capital-R Relationship that led to arrangements like Janae's. Thank God.

Janae herself was gone from work for three more days. There was the day she took off at Kristen's behest, and then the other two days were spent searching for her husband. Upon his return, Craig, it seemed, had gotten into a car that flashed his incredibly generic name at the airport taxi stand at Pearson. But it clearly hadn't been meant for him: It drove him not to Janae and the tampon-shaped condo tower in Toronto, but to an old cobalt mine near Temagami, Ontario.

IT CRASHED, Janae's texts read. IT DROVE RIGHT INTO THE PIT.

Kristen expressed shocked surprise. The company sent flowers. But Craig would be fine. He would just need some traction and some injectables for a while. And of course he'd be stuck at home. Alone. For hours. Waiting for Janae to come home. Dependent on her for everything.

Apparently there was another Craig in Toronto with the same name, who also had a returning flight arriving that same day. He had posted on his social media about his flight and how much he was looking forward to coming home. Just the month before, that Craig had been returning from another trip, and posted a glowing review of the car service he'd used. The service's customer retention algorithms, Janae said, must have associated the information and then sent a comped car as a part of their marketing outreach. At least, that was what the police had said must have happened. The car's records were scrubbed every 24 hours, and it had taken Janae's Craig so long to be found. Even when he called for help, he couldn't identify the model of the car or the license plate number. He had been trapped for hours, helpless.

"It sounds awful," Kristen said.

"It was," Janae agreed, once she returned to work. "He's terrified. Says he can't go back to another mine again. I can't leave any lights off. He was in perfect darkness for hours and hours."

On the weekend, Antony called. "I've been thinking about your stalker," he said, after they'd spoken in great detail about how exactly she had used the hotel room, how many times, and with which hand.

"He never stalked me," Kristen said.

"So he's really not a problem?"

"He's really not."

"You promise?"

"I promise."

She could almost hear him screwing up the courage for vulnerability. "Because you can tell me, if—"

Kristen laughed. She rose from her desk, catching Sumter's eye. He grinned at her and she waved back. Outside, it was snowing. Just a few tiny flakes under a leaden sky. "It's sweet of you to be so concerned, Antony. But please don't worry. He's dead."

MR. THURSDAY

Emily St. John Mandel

1.

A strange incident in October:

Victor returned to the showroom for the fourth time in two weeks, after hours. He just wanted to look at the Lamborghini through the glass. He was stalking the car, if he was being honest with himself. He'd taken it on two test drives, memorized the technical specifications, gazed at photos of it in online galleries, read reviews by the lucky professionals who drive fast cars for a living. He'd told himself that if he still loved the car a week after the second test drive, he would do it, he'd commit, he'd stop obsessing and write the check, and the car would be his. Victor made what seemed to him to be an obscenely high income. He had no debt, no dependents, owned his home outright, had paid off his parents' mortgage, and lived well below his means. He wanted the car.

It was a clear night, unseasonably warm, and Victor was all but alone on the street. The Aventador SV Coupé had its own spotlight on the showroom floor, but it seemed to Victor that it almost emitted its own light. It was a brilliant yellow. He loved it.

Victor was so enchanted by the car that he didn't notice the man approaching on the sidewalk.

"You're admiring the car," the man said. He had a slight accent that Victor couldn't place. He was about Victor's age, early 30s, wearing a midrange beige suit and a gray trench coat. The coat's shoulders were wet, as if the man had just walked through a rainstorm, but to the best of Victor's knowledge, the sky had been clear all day.

"Do I know you?" Victor asked. "We've met, right? You look familiar."

"Listen," the man said, "I don't have a lot of time. I'll give you $10,000 if you don't buy that car."

Victor blinked. The strangeness of the offer aside, he was a man for whom $10,000 wasn't a particularly impressive sum of money.

"There's a lot at stake," the man said. "I wish I could tell you." He had a fervor about him that made Victor a little nervous. Victor was certain he'd seen him before but couldn't place him.

"Why would you pay me...?"

"I don't have much time," the man said. "Do we have a deal?" and Victor knew he should be kind—it was clear to him by now that the man wasn't well—but it was 10 p.m. and he hadn't had dinner yet, he'd been working 100-hour weeks, and he was just so tired, the workload was relentless, lately he'd started to wonder if he even actually enjoyed being a lawyer or if his entire life was possibly a ghastly mistake, and now this lunatic on the sidewalk was trying to get between Victor and his beautiful car.

"I know it's strange," the man was saying, with rising desperation. "I'm risking my job being here and talking to you like this, but if you would please, *please* just consider—" but the car was Victor's joy and his solace, so he turned and walked away without saying another word. He glanced over his shoulder a block later and the man had disappeared, the empty sidewalk awash in the showroom's white light. Victor bought the car the following morning, and had more or less forgotten the encounter by the end of the week.

2.

Three weeks later, at 2 a.m. on a Thursday in November, Rose sat up gasping in her bed. The details were already fading as she switched on the light, but she was certain it was the same nightmare that had woken her the previous two nights: an impression of noise and chaos and then behind that something silent and overwhelming, a kind of cloud, a borderless rapidly approaching thing that wanted to engulf her. There were tears on her face. Rose knew from previous nights that further sleep was impossible, so she showered and dressed and caught the 4:35 train.

The others on the train at that hour were mostly financial-industry maniacs, eyes bright in the shine of their tablets and laptops and phones, sending and receiving messages from Europe, where their counterparts were drinking second cups of coffee and starting to think about lunch, and Asia, where late afternoon shadows were lengthening over the streets. Rose took a seat by the window in an empty row, rested her forehead on the glass, and drifted into a twilight state that wasn't sleep and wasn't consciousness, towns appearing and receding between intervals of trees. When had she last been so tired? Rose felt slightly delirious, her heart beating too quickly, thoughts clouded. She wished she could remember the specifics of the dream. She woke with a start as the train pulled into Grand Central, stepped out onto the filthy platform, and made her way with the others up into the cathedral of the main concourse, still quiet at this hour. On the downtown subway she sat with her eyes closed, trying to gather herself, until the train reached the southern tip of the island and she climbed the stairs into cool air and morning light.

Rose had started work at Gattler Fitzpatrick six months earlier, which is to say two months after her husband had been remanded into custody. The firm—three attorneys, a paralegal, and now Rose— occupied a shared office space just off Wall Street. On the 14th floor of a glass tower, a rotating cast of companies leased various combinations of cubicles, offices with views of other towers, and offices with views of the cubicles. Gattler Fitzpatrick had one of the more expensive suites: three offices and a reception desk in a secluded corner. When Rose arrived for her job interview, she turned a corner to walk down a silent row of cubicles and found it unexpectedly populated, people typing or talking on their phones, audible only when she was almost upon them, row upon row in their little gray squares.

Rose had worried about the gap in her résumé, the abyss of five years between the executive assistant position in Midtown and the present moment, but the truth proved surprisingly adaptable: She had been married for some time to a man with money, she explained to Jared Gattler in the job interview—his gaze flickered to her ringless left hand—and she'd stopped working at his invitation, but now they were separated and she wanted to be self-sufficient. All of this was perfectly true. Gattler didn't need to know that they'd been separated by the federal prison system.

Gattler was in his mid-70s, shorter than Rose, with a feverish complexion and the fatalism of people whose professional lives are played out in divorce court.

"Half my clients," he said, "the women, I mean, they're divorcing guys who don't actually make much money. Small players. I'm talking guys who can barely support one household at the level to which these people are accustomed, let alone two." Rose nodded, interested. "My clients, they're not idiots per se, but they just can't get it through their pretty little heads that the situation's changed. They just can't absorb the fantastical notion that they're going to have to be on the 7:40 a.m. train to the city just like everyone else. They just want to putter around town doing whatever it is they do, getting their hair done, going for lunch, whatever. I'm not sexist, you understand."

"Of course not." *Their pretty little heads*, Rose thought. In the fantasy version of that moment she rose with quiet dignity, walked out of the office without saying another word, and met her husband for drinks to commiserate.

"I'm just talking about a lack of connection to reality," Gattler said. "Nothing to do with gender per se, not saying anyone's less intelligent. All I'm saying is some of my clients, these are people who live in a fantasy world where they've never had to be adults."

"An entitlement issue," Rose said, because she was down to her last $200 and couldn't afford to walk out of this or any other office. From the way Gattler's eyes brightened, she knew the job was hers.

"Exactly," he said, "that's exactly it. Whereas I look at you, it seems to me you're showing a little initiative here."

"Well, I've never wanted to be dependent on anyone else," Rose said. This was only theoretically true. If she'd never wanted to be dependent on anyone else, then how had it happened so easily? On the train back to Westchester County, she'd stared out the window at the suburbs and the summer trees, and of course the answer was depressingly obvious: She had slipped into dependency because dependency was easier. She'd worked so hard all her life, and when her husband had extended a raft, it was easier to stop swimming and float. Where was Daniel at this moment? She imagined him waiting in a cafeteria lineup, reading in his cell, doing pushups in a sunlit yard. Westchester was a blur of green. Rose played the game she'd been playing since childhood: You look at the surface of the passing woods, the screen of trees, then you adjust your eyes to look past the screen and into the interior, where sunlight catches on tree branches and leaves shine translucent in the shadows, and it's like seeing an entirely different place. The interior of the kingdom versus the castle wall.

At Gattler Fitzpatrick, Rose did the filing, handled scheduling for Gattler and another attorney, straightened up the little waiting room between clients, maintained a vase of fresh flowers on the reception desk. At 5 o'clock every day, she joined the evening crowd flowing north to Grand Central Terminal. She bought a prepared meal for dinner in the market and boarded a MetroNorth train back to Scarsdale, where she was renting an au pair's suite above a garage within walking distance of the train station. She heated her dinner in the microwave and ate alone, read the news and watched television for a while, went to bed early, rose and returned to work earlier than she needed to the next day. It was possible to imagine years slipping past like this, decades, and there was comfort in the thought.

There was nothing Rose wanted more than a predictable life. When she arrived at work and stepped off the elevators, she always walked through the cubicles instead of going around, because they reminded her of a maze on the grounds of a particular castle in England that she'd visited with Daniel in her former life.

On that Thursday morning in November, the cubicle maze was empty—it wasn't yet 7 a.m.—and Rose took a circuitous route, enjoying the silence. In the quiet and order of the 14th floor, the nightmare that had woken her seemed very distant. The morning passed without incident—filing, coffee, phone calls, scheduling, a salad and too-sweet iced tea for lunch—and then the long afternoon stretched before her. More filing, a weepy client in the waiting area, a gale of laughter from a conference room around 2 p.m., more coffee, a bright blue ring on the finger of a woman who pressed the button on the elevator on the way back up from Starbucks, a flash of pink socks beneath the gray suit of a worker in the cubicles, a moment of dull stupid panic when she thought she'd lost a file. She moved through the day with a feeling of floating, a little undone from too much caffeine and too little sleep, light-headed, heart pounding, cup after cup of coffee that left her with something that wasn't exactly a headache, more like a pulsing suggestion of phantom lights in the periphery of her vision, her hands trembling a little. At 4 o'clock, Mr. Thursday arrived.

Rose didn't know his name. Gattler wasn't the kind of man who appreciated unnecessary inquiries, and his calendar provided no clues. The entry, which had been set up to recur every Thursday until the end of time, read "Thursday mtg" and nothing else. Mr. Thursday was more or less Rose's age, somewhere in his early 30s, a thin man in an aggressively nondescript beige suit who emerged from the cubicle labyrinth at precisely 4 o'clock every Thursday, nodded politely on his way past her desk, and disappeared into Gattler's office.

Was there something unusual in the way Mr. Thursday glanced at her that afternoon? He nodded, as always, an unhappy aspect to his expression, and it seemed to her that he held her gaze a beat too long, which led Rose to suspect that perhaps the sleep deprivation was making her look worse than she'd thought. She confirmed this suspicion in the ladies' room mirror: dark circles under her eyes, a fixed and somewhat glassy quality to her stare. She had recently reached the age when sleep deprivation made her look not just tired, but slightly older. Mr. Thursday was still in Gattler's office when she left at 5 o'clock.

It was raining by then. She had no umbrella, but there was a certain pleasure in this. She liked the sharp, cold of rain on her uncovered head. By the time she reached the stairs of Bowling Green Station, the dull wasteland of the day had somewhat dissipated, burned off by the cold and rain and lights, the evening acquiring a certain momentum. An uptown train was arriving just as she reached the platform, and she stepped aboard with the feeling of being involved in some pleasant choreography, but then the train reached Union Square, and all momentum came to a halt. The doors opened but didn't close. The train didn't leave the station. The car filled up, a crush of commuters who closed their eyes to concentrate on their music, or stared or at their phones or at books, or stared at nothing. The announcement came after five or 10 minutes: train going out of service, everyone please exit. There was no further explanation. The passengers shuffled out onto the already crowded platform, some muttering curses but most closed up in a resigned or furious silence.

The sleep deprivation had made her mildly deranged, Rose decided, and that was why this moment felt like déjà vu. She'd been here before, hadn't she? Here, in this moment, exiting this train? The woman beside her wore a beautiful blue wool coat, and Rose was certain that she'd seen this coat before, but not somewhere else: She'd seen the coat before in this moment, exiting this train, *here*. Every face in the crowd looked somehow familiar. She was dizzy. The train doors closed behind the last of the passengers, and the cars stood empty and alight. The crowd swelled dangerously on the platform, a mass of damp coats and hot, stale breath and tinny music from headphones, scents of hairspray, coffee, cologne, a McDonald's bag, a cloying jasmine perfume that made Rose want to gag. The out-of-service train didn't move, and no trains arrived on the opposite platform. Rose had never liked crowds, and it seemed to her that if she didn't get out of the subway she might faint in the crush, so she began inching her way toward the stairs in a series of tiny half-steps, excusing herself again and again. It was difficult to get enough air. Rose couldn't shake the terrible sense of following a script, of being an actor in a movie she'd already seen. She fought her way up the final staircase out of the station and emerged gasping into the evening air.

The rain was a drizzle that blunted the streetlights, Union Square lit gently, puddles reflecting. Her relief at being away from the crowd was overwhelming. What now? She sat on the nearest bench to consider her next move. At this hour of the day the city was in motion, umbrellas crossing Broadway like a flock of dark birds.

"Tiffany?"

It was Victor Freeman, the youngest member of her husband's legal team. Their offices were near here, she remembered. He stood over her with an umbrella.

"I don't use that name anymore."

"What can I call you?"

"Rose."

"Pretty." He sat beside her, although the bench was very wet, and angled his umbrella so that it sheltered both of them. His overcoat looked warm and expensive, the opposite of Mr. Thursday's cheap beige. "Why are you sitting out here in the rain?"

I was waiting for you, she thought, but of course this didn't make sense. "The subway's down," she said. "I came up for air."

"Where were you headed?"

"Home. Scarsdale."

He frowned, confused. Rose and Daniel's house in Scarsdale had been seized along with all of their other assets.

"I rent an au pair suite. It's a room with a kitchenette and a bathroom over a garage."

"Oh."

"I like it. It's all I need."

"Let me give you a ride home. My car's in a garage around the corner."

"You live in Scarsdale too?"

"No, but as a former member of your husband's defense team, I feel that driving you home is literally the least I can do."

"How far out of your way is it?"

"Professional guilt notwithstanding," he said, as they walked in the direction of the garage, "I just bought a car, and to be honest, I'll take any opportunity to go on an unnecessary drive."

The yellow Lamborghini seemed to shine in the dim light of the garage.

"It's a ridiculous car," Victor said, "but I love it."

"I don't think it's ridiculous." Rose thought it was beautiful, and when she said this, Victor smiled.

"I think it's beautiful too, actually. It's like something from the future. I know it's a frivolous purchase, but I don't know, I just wanted it so much." The déjà vu was surfacing again, nudging against the surface of the evening. "I agonized for weeks," Victor was saying, "but if there's a thing you really want, and you can afford it, and it's a beautiful thing that genuinely makes you happy, is there actually anything wrong with just buying it? You could call it crass materialism, but life's so short." It seemed to Rose as she buckled herself in that there was something familiar about the car, but she didn't recognize it for another 47 minutes, when the accident began: the SUV drifting into their lane just as Victor turned to ask her something, the delivery truck behind them that didn't stop in time. She didn't recognize Victor's car until the moment of impact, the blare of horns: She knew this car from the nightmare that had woken her three nights in a row. She remembered now. In the dream, and now in waking life, time slowed and expanded. The car was turning sideways between the delivery truck and the SUV, the air filling with glass, steel crumpling, and the thing from the dream was rushing toward her, the overwhelming thing that was dark and quiet and could not be resisted; this was the thing that had jolted her out of sleep when she dreamed it, but in waking life it turned out not to be terrifying at all, only inevitable; it was catching her in the crush of steel and plucking her gently from the accident, it was sweeping her up.

3.

Three hundred and forty years after the accident, a lounge singer was drinking scotch with a businessman in a spaceport terminal bar. They'd been flirting half-heartedly for 15 minutes or so. "And you," the businessman was saying, "where are you off to today?"

"I'm going to the moon," the singer said. The businessman raised his glass. The bartender appeared with a bottle.

"Oh, no, I was just toasting her," the businessman explained. "She's going to the moon."

"Everyone here's going to the moon," the bartender said. "The next Mars flight isn't till tomorrow."

"Still," the businessman said mildly, "always worth toasting a change of scenery." The singer smiled at him and sipped her scotch. "Which colony?" the businessman asked.

"I'm headed up to Colony Two," the singer said. "I got a job in a hotel. Actually in a chain of hotels."

"Hilton?"

"No, Grand Luna."

"Ah, I've stayed at the Grand Luna. Nice place. Did you tell me you're a singer?"

"I did. I am."

"My daughter likes to sing," the businessman said. He looked a little awkward following this announcement. The singer didn't strike him as the sort of person who enjoyed discussing children. He motioned to the bartender for another glass, but the bartender had developed a sudden interest in the projection above the bar, which was showing a baseball game.

"Can I ask?" the singer asked, with a gesture that encompassed the businessman's outfit. He was wearing a beige suit in a style that hadn't been fashionable since the early 21st century. The shoulders of his overcoat were still damp with 21st-century rain.

"It's for my work. Well, *was* for my work, I guess I should say."

"You're one of those."

"*Was* one of those. Until this morning." The businessman raised his glass, which by now contained only a pair of rapidly melting ice cubes. "To getting fired."

"Oh. I'm sorry."

"I'm not. It's a creepy line of work, frankly."

"It always seemed dangerous to me. Going back like that."

"Dangerous and stupid," the businessman agreed. "Happy to be out of it. My prediction, it'll be illegal by next year."

"I mean, what's to stop an accident?" the singer said. "Even the smallest thing, you know, you walk through a door ahead of someone..."

"You wouldn't believe how many meetings I've sat through on this topic."

"So you walk through a door in front of someone else, and then, I don't know, say that little delay means he doesn't get hit by a car, and he goes on to cause a war that wipes out all of our great-grand-parents."

"If not all of humanity," the businessman agreed. He was trying to flag down the bartender, who was absorbed in the game. "This is actually why I drink, if you were curious."

"And in that case it's not that we *die*, exactly, you and I and everyone we love." The singer gave what seemed to the businessman to be a somewhat exaggerated shudder. "It's more that we never get to start existing."

"The thought's occurred to me."

"Then why did you do it?"

"Same reason anyone does anything in business."

"I'll drink to that. When you went back," she said, "where exactly did you go?"

"I specialized in the late 20th and early 21st centuries."

"What were you doing there?"

He succeeded in getting the bartender's attention and fell silent for a moment while the bartender refilled their drinks. He took a long swallow and glanced at the baseball game; the bartender had rotated the projection for a better view of a replay, and now there was a holographic outfielder directly over the bar. "Nothing sinister," the businessman said finally, when he saw that the singer was still watching him. "Genealogical research for high net-worth individuals. Look, I'm not saying it's safe. But if it makes you feel better, it's not a free-for-all. There are controls in place, both technological and human."

"Human?"

"I was required to meet weekly with a handler in the local time."

"Kind of a weak control," the singer said.

"Well, you might be right about that. It was the technological controls that got me fired."

"Why'd you get fired?"

"I tried to avert a car accident."

The singer was quiet, watching him.

"I didn't think the scanners would pick it up. I knew it was stupid, but it's not like I tried to avert the First World War." The singer frowned. Her grasp of 20th-century history was shaky. "No matter what I did," he said, "everything I tried, she still got in the car, and the car still crashed."

EMILY ST. JOHN MANDEL

"Who's she?"

"Just someone I saw every time I went back. My handler's secretary. I liked her. Kind of a sad story."

The singer liked sad stories. She waited.

"OK," the businessman said. By now he'd had a little too much to drink. "So this person, the secretary, she grows up with nothing, terrible family, meets a guy with money, falls in love with him, and then a few years later he goes to jail for some white-collar thing. Long sentence, judge wanted to make an example of him. All of his assets were seized, so she's lost everything. She tries to—no, that's the wrong word, she *succeeds* in starting a new life. Changes her name, gets a new job, picks herself up."

"And then?"

"And then she dies six months later in a car crash. I don't know, I guess I'd been in the business for too long. Maybe I got a little burned out. I was always so careful. I filed these impeccable itineraries with Control and never deviated from them, never tried to change anything, but this person, Rose, she looked a bit like my daughter, and I just thought, what harm would there be, making this one change? Averting this one thing? Most people don't amount to much. Most people don't change the world. If she doesn't die in a car accident, what harm is there in that, really?"

"Isn't that exactly the kind of small thing—"

"Imagine walking into a room," he said, "and knowing what's going to happen to everyone in it, because you looked up their birth and death records the night before."

The singer seemed to be searching for something to say to this but failed. She downed the last of her scotch.

"I'm sorry. It's an unsettling topic. I didn't mean to make you uncomfortable."

"My shuttle's probably boarding by now."

"You see the temptation, though? How you might want to just make this one small change, give someone a chance, maybe just—"

"'Genealogical research for high net-worth individuals,'" the singer said. "You must think I'm an idiot."

"I don't."

"Anyway, thanks for the drinks." The singer was sliding carefully from her bar stool.

"You're welcome," said the businessman, who hadn't realized he was paying. He watched her walk away and then touched one of the buttons on his shirt, which he'd kept angled toward her. The recording stopped.

"Fucking creep," the bartender muttered, under his breath. The businessman settled up and left without looking at him.

Later, in his hotel room in Colony One, he dropped the button into a projector and played the conversation back. A three-dimensional hologram of the singer hovered over the side table. *I'm going to the moon.* A touch of excitement in her voice. In the background, the shadowy figure of the bartender polished a glass while he watched the baseball game. The businessman turned the volume to low. He liked to keep a recording going in the background when he was alone in hotel rooms, so as not to get too lonely. But this was the wrong hologram, he didn't like the way the bartender hovered, so he scrolled through the library and picked out another: Rose at her desk in the 21st century, her smile when she looked up and saw him. He adjusted the speed to the lowest possible setting. The walk past her desk took only two minutes, but in slow motion there was such stillness, such beauty in her small, precise actions—as though underwater she turned from her keyboard to look at him, then back to her keyboard, her hand reaching for a file and bringing it with heartbreaking slowness down to the desk, and all the while he was gliding past her, on his way to Gattler's office—and this seemed the right recording for the moment. He changed into his pajamas, switched off the bedside lamp so that the only light was the pale glow of the hologram by the bed. He stood for a moment by the window while he brushed his teeth. The hotel was expensive and looked out over a park, and it occurred to him for the thousandth time that if he hadn't spent time on Earth, he might not know the difference. Tomorrow he'd board the first train to Colony Three, go home and tell his wife what had happened, sweep their little daughter up into his arms. Would his wife be angry? He thought she'd understand. They'd talked about getting out of the industry. But for now he was alone in the quiet of the room. He would never return to the 21st century, and there was a sense of liberation in this. He could find a new job. He could live a different, less haunted kind of life. In the silence of the room, the hologram of Rose was reflected on the window, turning in slow motion away from him, superimposed on the pine trees and tall grass of the park. An owl passed silently between the trees.

A BRIEF
AND FEARFUL STAR

Carmen Maria Machado

Mama did not talk about her journey west very much; the circumstances had to be right. When she did—in the electric moments before rainfall, if a rabbit crossed clockwise against our path, if she found me flipping through the battered almanac from the year of my birth—she described it like a painting she was viewing through a fever.

"The light," she said once, when we encountered a set of twigs that had fallen into the shape of a cross. "It was like being underwater, all blue and soft and bright."

"It was so cold and I was sick with you," she said another time, digging a splinter out of my palm with a pocketknife. "Everything felt wrong. I was very afraid."

Then, once, just before I turned 10, when a brush fire lit up a distant ridge and it burned through the night: "Your father drove our wagon, of course. Sometimes I would lean against him and look up at the sky and—"

The way her eyes went empty, it felt like watching her die. The next year, when I did, all I could think was how it felt like watching her talk about the sky.

❖❖❖❖❖❖

Before the light left her, we lived—just the two of us—on a patch of prairie. Our house was the center of it, a pip in a magnificent apple.

With no natural borders save the creek, the boundaries of our land seemed to move every time I visited them. I often imagined that my right eye was soaring above me, clutched in the talon of a large and terrible bird, the earth below expanding and contracting like a heartbeat.

The sky was open and alive above us, too. Storms boiled across the sky in the summer, and in the winter the mean snow landed on my face and refused to melt. I loved our fragment of wilderness. Every season we'd get a few traders—offering us cinnamon, flour, silver hand mirrors, gingham, chirping automata that sang and told the future—but otherwise we lived untouched, binary stars in our own private universe.

I was a nervous child. I gasped when flint was struck, and when sparks flew whimsically out of the hearth. Mama tried to help—once, she caught the spark and showed it to me; a speck of ash marring the planetary surface of her palm—but I could not explain that, while I understood the principles of the thing, there was something about the erratic arc of it; the suddenness, the wild, alien dive, that awoke a terror within me. There were other fears, too: a crevice in the wall near my bed that corralled a beam of moonlight into my room at certain times of the month; the way water spiraled around gullies and divots. It was a kind of *motion*, a kind of gravity, the way the light bended to its own ends. I felt I knew terrors that lingered just beyond my vision; as if their very existence was seared into my cells. At night, when I cried, Mama came to me and weighed me down with her torso until calmness filled me. "Come back to me, my mouse," she'd say.

There was something else that haunted me, too. When I lay in bed at night, I perceived giant, ancient creatures moving just outside our walls; rumbling and snarling, darkening the windows, blotting out the moon. Though they lingered just beyond my vision I *knew* them to be true, though I could not understand them.

"There's something outside," I told her, the first time I sensed them.

"There's nothing," she said. "I've been sitting by the window."

"They've always been here," I said. "Monsters."

She brought me, then, a small box, and from it removed a claw, a set of teeth, a slender bone of rock, all things she'd pulled from the land on which we lived. "This is all that's left of them," she said. "I know it feels like we are the first people on this land, but we have been preceded by monsters and men alike."

I had questions about those monsters, and those men. "But outside—"

"They're gone, mouse. They were here but they're not anymore." And for a moment, calmness filled my fear, like a gorge flooding with rainwater. But when it abated, the gaping ache in my chest seemed to me how animals must feel, how they must have always felt, lowing for the muscle and ferocity of their mothers.

◆◆◆◆◆◆

I don't remember coming to the farmstead. Mama had joined the caravan west swollen with the promise of me, and I was born, over two days, along the trail that led us here. (*'What of my stars?,' I asked her once. 'You moved beneath the sky as you were born, she said, and therefore have no clear celestial map.'*) "It was a mad time," she said. "Everything seemed alive. The trees and brush made promises they could not keep. The wagon moaned in its sleep. Animals spoke to us. An oxen told me I'd have a little girl. Even Bonnie chatted. She told on your papa when he broke my mother's clockwork map; the one from Switzerland."

"Bonnie doesn't talk," I said, though my voice curdled with doubt. As if to underline my confusion, Bonnie emerged from a shadow and sat before both of us, her tail twitching with purpose but otherwise silent as you'd expect.

"She did, once," Mama said. "But the day you were born, she shut right up."

Mama made jokes but sometimes it was hard to say what the joke was about. Was the joke that my body silenced Bonnie, or that Bonnie made words, or that Bonnie cared about me at all?

Sometimes, I try to imagine that I remember the dioramas that moved around us when I was still tangled up in her. I imagine that the walls of her fine strong animal body glow with light, and that I can hear the soft and muffled testimonies, the confessions and laughter, the camaraderie of the wagon train.

('Do you know she's a banker's daughter?'
'The rivers are too high.'
'Even bankers have daughters.'
'Did he tell them about the tack?'
'The sky is the color of milk, and it is not promising.'
'Olga promised me.'
'I'm hungry.'
'Don't you know they'll stay that way if you don't stop?')

And then, behind their chatter, something terrible. Something in the sky, burning.

Even on my 11ᵗʰ birthday, Mama took me with her to move the cattle, who were pulling up dirt and refusing new grasses. As I followed her outside, I wondered if my father had ever imagined his wife and girl-child alone out here (*We each need a hatchet, us and the baby,' my father had told her*), the wagon turned to dwelling, the cattle's calves grown and sired and birthed and died many times over.

Mama disappeared over the hill with a switch in her hand. I watched but did not follow. The horizon was milky and amber, and I saw the beginning of a figure there —a wagon, a dark shape against the light. When Mama returned with the herd, their shadows had joined into a single many-legged creature. I stroked their velvety pelts as they trotted by. (*Mama had been rich before she came married by father and came west, though you'd never know it by her labor. 'What did it mean to be rich?' I asked her once. 'It meant money had too much meaning and yet none at all,' she said.*)

"Someone's coming," I said, pointing. She squinted against the light and then nodded. "I hope it's a trader," she said. She didn't say who else it might be. When we went inside, Mama gave me a cake she'd made special—cinnamon, raisins, a glug of rum from the bottle hidden beneath the floorboards. I pinched off a little and put it on the floor for Bonnie, who sniffed it contemptuously. From the wall, a brown mouse dashed and seized the cake, bounding back to safety while Bonnie looked on. She did not hunt anymore. She was bony and slow; too old to chase after the mice who were endlessly birthing new mice to replace them. What could she do to stem that tide? They existed with impunity. Mama huffed through her nose like she did when she was displeased; she did not like that I'd helped the mouse eat, and she did not like that the mice existed at all.

When the shadow arrived, just after noon, it was, indeed, a man bearing a wagon of goods. We had never met him before. We saw so few men that each one was like a minor nightmare, as strange and unknowable as the creatures that I saw outside my windows. This man kept his beard shorter than some of the others, but I did not like the broadness of his shoulders, which seemed so natural on my own mother but so alien on him. "Flour?" he called, as he pulled the horse to stop. "Bacon, seeds, cloth, coffee? I have some more exotic wares, too, if that interests you."

"Exotic?"

"A brazen head I picked up in Kansas City. A jade necklace." He glanced upward, as if to aid his recollection. "Tinctures, tonics, an astrolabe, and a pneumatic gewgaw that recites Scripture."

Mama rubbed the back of her neck. "The normal goods will do," she said. "Come in; I'll take a look."

Inside, he rolled a pack open on our table so that we could examine his offerings. "I have more in the wagon," he said, "if this doesn't satisfy. I could—"

"My husband is out with the cattle," Mama said brusquely, to discourage the question. She examined the offerings solemnly as a scholar, peeling a corner of fabric from its bolt, smelling a bottle of oil. I sniffed the oil, too, though I did not know what I was smelling for; it was pungent and unpleasant, in a pleasant kind of way. The man glanced around the room at our three hatchets, our iron stove, Bonnie snoozing on the quilt, the daguerreotype of my father on the dresser. I did not like his staring, that he was seeing so many things and drawing his own conclusions about us.

"It's my birthday," I told him.

He turned and appraised me over the sharp angle of his cheekbones. "Perhaps your mother might like to get you a present?"

Mama glanced at me, and I looked at the table, which held so many strange and specific objects that it felt like a test before a cosmic judge. I ignored the doll—a childish thing, and I was not a child anymore—and the thread, the spices, the candles, and the recent almanac. Then Mama pushed aside the doll and I saw what rested beneath it: a short-handled knife the length of my hand. She lifted the knife and examined it from every angle; she then balanced it on her finger, as if an alchemist performing an obscure science. Her mysteries filled the room; both the man and I watched her with a stillness. She nodded.

Outside, the trader returned his pack to the wagon and extended his hand to me. "May I show you something?" he said.

I looked up at Mama, who was standing in the doorway. She nodded, and I handed him the knife. He kicked a small rut into the dirt and lopped off the head of a thick of grasses next to the house. He tucked them into the divot and then lifted the knife upward. "Knives do more than cut," he said. The blade caught the sunlight and brought it down toward the earth. The motion of it—the slow turn of the metal, the way the light sharpened to a point and then fell toward us, toward me—made me gasp and buckle. I realized I was screaming after it began, and I ran into Mama's arms like the child I was.

The man stood over what he had created. Smoke curled into the air. "I didn't mean to frighten you," he said. "I didn't realize you were afraid of fire." He stamped out the fingerlings of flame and offered it back to me, handle-first.

When I did not move, Mama took it from him. "She's not afraid of fire," she said. "But thank you." I listened to the rest of the transaction buried in her skirts; the oil and knife were now ours.

He mounted his wagon and did not wave goodbye, as so many of the others had before.

Mama watched him as he retreated. She worked her jaw as if chewing a knot of sinew, but I did not ask what she was thinking about. When he was swallowed up by the horizon, she went inside to apply the oil to the baseboards. "Perhaps it'll discourage the mice," she said.

Soon we would discover that she was wrong. Attracted to the sharp scent, they soon began creeping toward the stains in curiosity.

She cornered and caught them in jars and drowned them in buckets of water. Some escaped, scuttled back into the walls, only to sire more, but she kept at the impossible labor. There was something about seeing her, sleeves rolled up, heavy with the task, that filled me with joy. How I loved her, my mother, and the stories within her.

(My father loved my mother's dark hair, the smoke-smell of it, the way it frayed and curled into a lustrous halo around her head. At night, he whispered into it, 'My blessing, my blessing.' This was a secret, even from her.)

❖❖❖❖❖❖

The fever came up on her a few days later, quick and hard as a storm. She pressed a damp rag to the back of her neck upon waking, and by evening she lay on the bed chattering and moaning. I stroked her head and kissed her face. She slept, and woke, and slept.

"Mama," I said to her. "You must get better because you still haven't taught me how to make the cake. I don't know how to butcher an animal yet. You haven't told me who lived on this land before us."

She did not speak, but instead drew a slow and shaking finger from her sternum to her navel.

When she woke for the last time, her pupils were so wide and black I felt like I would fall into them if I wasn't careful. It was as if she had dipped below the water's surface, and in that in-between place she saw everything she had ever known.

"It was a star," she said to me, faint as a heartbeat. "The star came and everything moved."

"A star?" I asked. She had never spoken of a star, not once in the entirety of my life. Yet suddenly I realized that I had *known* of the star, that my fears and dreams were star-shaped, that the star had been burning a terrible hole through me ever since the day of my birth.

"Everything moved to the side and all was clear," she said. "I could see everything."

"Mama," I said into the dampness of her skin. "Mama. I still haven't learned."

She kneaded my hand weakly and looked at me from beneath heavy lids. "You are my mir—" A mirror, a miracle? The word never

ended. She descended into herself and did not emerge, though I lay
on top of her, to bring her back from where she'd gone.

◆◆◆◆◆

Her absence gaped, and through the wound of it you could see everything: the horror of my circumstances, the sharp cramps of grief that
appeared and disappeared and reappeared again. Her body was still
and pale, and I kept thinking of parsnips and the way they slept in
the soil. I could not bring myself to bury her. At night, the shadows
passed by the windows, and I lay breathing and staring at the ceiling,
praying them away.

The third night after her death, something killed one of the cattle.
I heard it just before I fell asleep: a wet and curdled sound, like a calf
being born in reverse. In my dreams, the star flew over the earth like
a bird, leaving a black burning trail in its wake. When I woke, I was
damp, my mouth hot with stink and gritty sweetness. Bonnie was
sitting on my chest, tail twitching. She dropped a dead mouse onto
my chest, and stared at me with serenity and purpose. I sat up and
flicked the corpse to the floor. Bonnie dropped down and scooped her
paw into the hole in the wall.

I took a deep breath and lay down on my belly to peek inside.
Tucked to the right of the entrance was a tiny nest of fluff and thread;
in it, a small pack of baby mice, crawling over each other. They were
pink and cricket-small, their eyes dark as blood blisters and shut
against the world.

"Bonnie," I said, laying my cheek to the floor. "You terrible creature. Now there are a dozen orphans in this house, instead of just one."

Could I lure them out, nurse them, somehow? From the back of the
cupboard, I pulled the vial of oil Mama had used to try to dispel the
mice, the one they had loved so much. When I dribbled it on the floor
next to the nest, the baby mice scattered like water in a griddle, as if
the scent carried some terrible story. "I'm sorry," I said into the wall,
and left them to make their own way.

I went outside and stood over the cow's mauled body for a long
while—listening to the flies, watching their beetle-black bodies alight
on its bloodied flank. The wind over the grass sounded like the way

Mama used to idly rasp the onionskin pages of her Bible when she was thinking about something blasphemous. I didn't know what she hadn't taught me. I'd have to learn another way.

❖❖❖❖❖❖

Bonnie was curled up on Mama's still chest, purring softly. I packed my knife, the sampler she had brought with her from Virginia with the embroidered alphabet, the remaining cake. I kissed Mama's waxy forehead and gestured to Bonnie as I left.

"Do you want to go outside?" I asked her. She didn't move, and I closed the door behind me.

I walked to where I'd known the edge of our land to be, and for the first time in my life, stepped beyond it. It was still early; my shadow was long and cut the path before me. I could not tell if I was casting it or following it, or if there was any difference at all.

When I crested the ridge half a day later, I saw a coyote worrying over something in the dust in the valley below. She glanced up to where my silhouette met the sky but didn't move from her tiny plot. I thought: She must be starving, to not run from me.

Down among the rocks, I lifted my skirts and waded into the river. The water seized the cotton and tried to carry me away. (*Though my mother never said, this was what had happened to my father, I knew. The river wrapped hungry fingers through his trousers and shirt and took him under in half a breath.*) I slipped the twisting layers off and watched them float away, like a drowned woman. In that moment, I imagined the bird lifting my eye into the air and saw myself from above—the way my hair was sliding out of its pins, the nature and shape of my wildness. When I returned to my body, I was holding a silver fish who muscled this way and that.

On shore, I knocked a rock into him until he stopped moving, then dug the sweet flesh off the bone.

❖❖❖❖❖❖

I moved slowly in the sun, stripped down and sore. The coyote watched me from a distance—following me, I guessed. Waiting for me to die.

I slept with the knife in my hand and woke from the sleep with a bolt of knowledge. When I looked up, catastrophe had been replaced by a sense of ferocious, unimaginable calm. My body bent under the memory of Mama's weight pressing on me in the dark.

Above me, in the sky, a beautiful fragment of light rippled through the darkness. It was, like my grief, two things: a bright, white ball of fire and an incandescent, milky trail, both cutting open the night. I did not know it was coming and yet I had known all along. It was awe and primal, searing terror, like crossing a landscape you had only imagined, a landscape you couldn't possibly have understood until you stood at its precipice.

Everything moved. For the briefest of breaths, a curtain twitched. I saw the creatures, my creatures, for the first time with clarity: heads and tails like skinks, but the size of 10 oxen. Some stood together, docile as cows. Others gazed upward at the light in the sky. They had eyes like polished stone and teeth like the teeth my mother had once collected—terrible, large as my fist. (*They lived and died and no man gazed upon them.*) Then I saw a cluster of men being slaughtered by other men, blood spilling black into the soil and illuminated by the star, the air frenzied with violence and horses. (*I did not belong here, on this land. The way was paved for me and though I did not pave it, I followed it nonetheless. How did I never know? Had I always known?*)

Then, I saw a young woman kneeling on the ground and working a knife into her breast with the steady rhythm of embroidery, as if she was trying to set something within her loose. She gazed into the sky, and then turned and looked at me, and her mouth made the shapes of words that I perceived though I could not understand them. (*The radiance is the passage.*) Then another young woman, in a room so white my eyes burned. (*I would never live to see her.*) Then the curtain fell back, and I felt something slacken within me, as though I was about to soil myself. Everything that I was dropped out from my center and was replaced with molten iron.

The coyote trotted past. Her muzzle was stained with blood, and a dying hare hung limply from her mouth. She dropped it at my feet and then ran. Its sides shuddered and I could see what was beneath, the slickness of muscle and bone.

(*'Child,' the hare said. Not with its mouth, but with its wound; like the sing-song of stale air exhaled from a deep cave. 'Child. Welcome. We've been waiting.'*)

Behind me, I heard the grasses rustle. 'Go home. Your mother is there and waiting. Go home.'

Beneath me, tunneling moles cried out like a tinny chorus. 'It's here, it's here, it's here again.')

I lay down on the moonlit prairie and listened until sleep wreathed me. Tomorrow, I would be born into the morning.

If I had dreamt that night, I imagine it would have been with an understanding of the past: my young mother, her pregnant belly swollen with my small limbs and her wide eyes brimming with the dark sky and its terrible star. The chattering animals, the heaving ribs of the wagons, the lying flora and prophetic fauna. The architecture of her spasms, her body laboring against the cold and the loneliness. Or possibly I would have dreamt of the future: a young woman waking from her own dream in some white and eerie palace, a sigil burning high above her, splitting the sky in two. Or perhaps I would have dreamt some in-between place: destiny as a city on a hill. My mother carrying me down one of its many avenues, and then my heavy footsteps as I walk that avenue alone.

But I did not dream after the star appeared in the sky. I would never dream again.

OVERVALUED Mark Stasenko

"How was your day?" Jack asked his wife as she took off her black leather pumps at the door of their spacious industrial-chic condo in NoMad.

"Good," Sophia lied.

They didn't use to lie to each other, not even about small things. Unfiltered honesty had always come naturally to them, despite their glaring differences—maybe because of them. But for the past six weeks, nothing seemed natural anymore. It was strange how much the death of a stranger had changed things.

She should've felt happy, or so she kept telling herself. She had recently been promoted to partner at her fund and shifted her role from short selling to long-term investments. Despite having to pay out 10 percent of all pretax earnings as dividends to her personal investors and an outrageous 54 percent to Uncle Sam, she earned enough to afford the three-bedroom, four-bathroom condo they didn't fill, the designer furniture Jack shopped for with all his free time, and the bullshit modern art that now just looked like bloodstained, limp airbags after a car accident.

But she didn't feel happy because one tiny, uncontrollable bit of bad luck sucked all the serotonin and dopamine from her brain and replaced it with cortisol and adrenaline. Jack was the only one who saw that bit of bad luck coming. The only one who'd tried to stop it. Even though she knew it wasn't fair, she blamed him for not doing more. She stared at him as he got drunk on a bottle of overproof bourbon he wouldn't be able to afford without her.

"Instead of drinking all day, why don't you do something?" she regretted asking almost immediately.

"I wish I could, but people like me don't get hired to do anything besides work on factory lines or clean up shit after RIA assholes."

"That's redundant," she mumbled.

"For emphasis," he shot back. RIA stood for "rich, indoctrinated assholes," so she was right, but he was quick too. Jack's IQ was high, not quite as high as hers, but he was 1.9 sigma above the mean, so certainly high enough that he would've qualified for a respected university. It didn't matter; his family couldn't have afforded it, and the Prodigy Market hadn't been around yet to help with the cost of a degree.

Sophia's education, a degree in civil engineering from a good school but not one of the hallowed Seven-Figure schools, had cost close to $800,000. Her Initial Prodigy Offering hadn't raised enough for a Seven-Figure degree (the 13 schools whose reputation emboldened them to charge more than $1 million for a degree), but she was still fortunate to have parents wealthy enough to hire counsel and brokers to manage a first-generation IPO in the newly minted Prodigy Market.

Jack was older and his parents were worse off, so he graduated high school with no chance. Jack would've liked to be a pediatrician. But if you couldn't afford college, there was no way of avoiding ending up on the low-wage, unskilled Wall-Head side of the modern American workforce divide, looking on enviously at the high-skilled RIAs.

So Jack, like his parents, was a Wall-Head. He worked in a factory making hospital gurneys and wheelchairs—as close as he could get to joining the medical profession. As it was, he knew he'd soon be replaced by automation, as so many of his friends had been.

But unlike his parents, Jack had married an RIA. And up until six weeks ago, their marriage of opposites had worked well.

Sophia forced herself to think about how he was with his elderly parents who'd waited for a basic income to cover life's needs—needs they couldn't afford. They'd died waiting, and when they did, Jack didn't pretend to be strong or controlled or "masculine." He was angry, uncontrollable, honest. That's when she knew she loved him. She found herself hoping that she still loved him, but so much had changed in six weeks.

Six weeks ago, Kathryn Tally Anders died, and ever since then, white lies and cortisol and whiskey and blame had taken over. Six weeks ago, Sophia had never said the name Kathryn Tally Anders, and now it possessed her every thought. Her brain played that name and that face on repeat.

More problematically, her brain blamed her over and over again for killing her.

◆◆◆◆◆◆

It was so mind-numbingly dull, filling out a W-9 tax form on his wall-mounted Ecosphere screen. How could there even still be a W-9 form? Its persistence in the world seemed to mock the rest of the technological progress enveloping most aspects of life. Then he caught himself: Was this the dullest thought he'd ever had?

When he started doing contract work, he was told, "No two days are the same." Those people had lied to him or, more likely, lied to themselves.

Alex prepped for every job in the exact same way, and this job would be no different from the dozens before and the dozens after. The Iridious security system on his coffin-sized safe scanned his irises in the basement of the five-bedroom suburban home where he lived alone. The door popped open after he was verified, and he retrieved two SCCY CPX-II pistols and their corresponding AAC Ti-Rant 9 mm silencers. He added a serrated 9-inch SOG hunting blade to his artillery as well, but doubted he'd have to use it unless things went terribly wrong. A part of him hoped they would.

Alex always called what he did "liquidating an over-resourced target," but in regular English, once shed of all the Orwellian indirections and rationalizations we bake into our use of language, he was nothing other than a hitman.

The bud permanently in his ear gently vibrated, and the voice on the other side told him they had received the W-9. The job would be listed as "supply chain consulting" on their balance sheet. He'd receive confirmation of the go within 24 hours.

◆◆◆◆◆◆

Sophia's monitors lit up in her east-facing office at Athena Prodigy Management on the 47th floor of a 49-floor building just as the sun rose. She opened her portfolio and searched for ticker symbol KTA1108II like she had every morning for the past six weeks. She knew that seeing it would gut her, but she did it anyway, futilely hoping it wouldn't show up at all, as if it had never happened.

But every morning, there it was, with a total gain of $32 million floating next to the symbol. And that's all it was, a symbol. It didn't say Kathryn Tally Anders, it didn't show her picture, it didn't mention her death; it was just a symbol on a spreadsheet. Every morning, she'd close out and try to focus on long-term Prodigy investments. Every morning, she hated long-term Prodigy investments and herself a little more.

Prodigy wasn't an accurate term anymore. At first, the Prodigy Market, created by a coalition of what ultimately came to be known as the Seven-Figure universities, was only open for investments in the highest-potential students like Sophia—actual prodigies. But it was so profitable that before long any underperforming student or any bullshit, for-profit school could access the market.

High-potential students could float shares of 10 percent of their future lifetime earnings on the market, but students with less sterling credentials would offer 20 percent, 40 percent, or even 60 percent of all future income to garner interest. The market drove up the demand for RIAs, both on the part of families eager to produce them and of investors eager to acquire stakes in them, and the heightened demand further exacerbated the cost of attending the Seven-Figure schools. Universities touted the market as the great equalizer while their multibillion-dollar endowments bloated.

It was a highly liquid market at the top end, which allowed for an entirely new class of equities and derivatives. Moreover, Prodigies were bundled into PAGs (Prodigy Asset Groups) by banks for a particular risk level and industry cluster (BBB+ aspiring software engineers, for instance). The average investor didn't even have to research individual assets; they could bet on market demand for a certain profession or skill set. It was a casino, but instead of betting on black or red, the vote was on whether a high school kid was going to be successful. And Sophia was good at making that bet.

Some high-potential Prodigies could apply for their own ticker symbol. These were much more volatile, potentially more lucrative for traders like Sophia. She liked to short individual assets, betting their value would go down. And KTA1108II had been her biggest short position ever.

Before its death, KTA1108II was an exciting asset, not just for Sophia but for the entire market. KTA1108II was extremely high-potential, touted on CNBC as one of the few assets that may be ROI positive before its higher education even began. Needless to say, KTA1108II's market cap was spiraling upward; the futures market was betting that its lifetime worth would be in the hundreds of millions, if not more.

KTA1108II entered the Prodigy Market even before entering high school, offering up 10 percent of future lifetime earnings. It was an above-average asset: good grades, accelerated particularly in math and science, stable family. But it wasn't until ninth grade that the asset really hit the radar. In ninth grade, KTA1108II proved that cancer cells bonded to healthy cells behaved differently, and therefore that the billions pharmaceutical companies had spent on laboratory tests of unbonded cancer cells had been a waste. This asset had made a discovery capable of impacting millions of lives and billions of dollars at 15 years old.

KTA1108II exploded in the Prodigy Market. It was expected to be a part of the team that discovered noninvasive, long-term cures for late-stage malignant tumors, particularly as related to bone marrow.

But when there's excitement around an asset, investors ignore risk and potential vulnerabilities. They overvalue the asset. No one asks what could go wrong in a climate of irrational exuberance—no one, that is, except for dispassionate short sellers like Sophia. She had built her entire career around the contrarian quest for these overvalued assets.

❖❖❖❖❖❖

Since the Ernst-Meyers laws following the 2021 Depression, liquidators, like Alex, were quietly contracted by unscrupulous companies to "liquidate" underperforming, overcompensated employees who could no longer be terminated by legal means. This increasingly common, if unacknowledged, practice was known as "self-regulation." This new contract was different, though. The firm that had hired Alex wasn't self-regulating. Instead, they held a massive short position in an asset in the Prodigy Market and stood to make a heavy profit if the asset were to be liquidated.

Alex received no identifying or demographic details about the target until right before the hit. The details of the person didn't matter; they were a target no more and no less than a piece of paper with a bull's-eye drawn on it. But traditionally he was liquidating long-term, overpaid executives, almost exclusively older men, sometimes older women, whose survivors stood to cash in large life insurance policies.

But a job involving the Prodigy Market meant that the target could be young and would likely not be from a wealthy family. When he accepted the contract, he refused the details like always, but he did find himself wondering how it'd make him feel if it was a kid.

And for a moment, he realized he wasn't bored with the job.

❖❖❖❖❖❖

It was only eight weeks ago that Sophia first discovered KTA1108II's flaw. She found it in a simple iShare photo in which KTA1108II was jumping into the air with friends, arms above its head. It was in long sleeves at the beach; it always wore long sleeves. But because its arms were above its head, the sleeves had fallen down just enough for Sophia to spot the tip of a small scar on its wrist.

After Sophia verified that the mark on the asset's wrist was indeed a self-inflicted scar, she went through her network of hackers to gain access to the asset's medical records. The story for KTA1108II couldn't have been better. It was seeing a psychiatrist until it entered the Prodigy Market, when it dropped the shrink and the antidepressant prescriptions because, of course, those disclosures would've lowered its share price. Materially adverse information, as the filings called it.

It was only a week before Sophia discovered this that she had been promoted to partner at Athena. The promotion came with a huge raise and the ability to trade the firm's own equity and share in its profits, dramatically increasing her potential bonuses.

It's usually hard to ascertain how much any given promotion or event will impact your overall life, but not for Sophia. Because she herself was an asset traded on the Prodigy Market, she knew exactly how much the promotion increased her worth: 29.2 percent. Such an increase was extremely rare for someone already in the workforce. The promotion drove her share price up to $551. Rumors spread that even her own fund was taking a position in her.

With the confidence of her market value spike, she used her entire new trading portfolio to short KTA1108II. Everything. It was an insane move, the biggest short position the fund had ever taken. But Sophia was logical, and this was as rational a trade as she had ever taken. Once she bet every leveraged dollar against KTA1108II, she sent the photos and the medical records to CNBC under the same reliable alias she always did. She waited for the network to cross-reference and validate the information.

Less than a week later, the story broke right before 8 a.m.: KTA1108II suffered from depression and had acted on the disease in the past with self-mutilation. The story even one-upped Sophia and asked if there had been suicide attempts. It was perfect. Within the hour, KTA1108II's share price crashed by almost 30 percent, from $347 to $243. Sophia earned her firm nearly $11 million.

The other partners wanted Sophia to cash in. A doctor's statement or well-timed announcement of some research breakthrough could bounce KTA1108II's stock back quickly. Sophia talked them out of it; there was more room to fall. She knew that the stress of losing its future would be poorly managed by a highly motivated, anxiety-laden, 16-year-old asset suffering from depression.

But the market closed that night with KTA1108II's share price up from its low. Not by much, but the take for the firm would've been about $8 million, and the conversations would be about the $3 million "lost" and not the $8 million earned.

But less than two hours later Sophia's phone rang. The voice on the other end excitedly told her to turn on CNBC.

KTA1108II was dead, a suspected suicide. There was a note. They weren't reading it.

The share price dropped to $0.11 within a minute in after-hours trading. Sophia did what she was programmed to do: She unloaded the short position and earned the firm $32 million. It was her biggest day ever.

The partners congratulated Sophia for her (and their) triumph. They insisted that she had nothing to do with the asset's death. She could barely follow their words; her mind was racing, debating whether she was a murderer or not. For the first time since she was a girl, Sophia found that the cortisol controlling her circular thoughts was far stronger than her logic.

She expected to fight with Jack that night. He had always been piously against "profiting off the failures of others," as he put it. He had been trying to get her to stop for years. She opened the door, and Jack reeked of bourbon; he'd seen the news already.

Jack always got home hours before Sophia even left her office; that day had been no different. He had stepped on the treadmill in their extra bedroom and was less than a mile into his run when he saw the news: a Prodigy Asset familiar from dinner conversations had committed suicide. Jack shut down the treadmill and grabbed his computer. He became obsessed, reading every article he could find. The financial outlets referred to her as KTA1108II, but some smaller publications called her Kathryn Tally Anders. Kate, her family called her.

He read about Kate's life. Her dog. Her two older brothers who joined the Air Force. Her parents who'd immigrated to America 34 years earlier. And then at 5:24 p.m., he read about Kate's cancer research. And that's when he started drinking.

Kate was focused on multiple myeloma, the cancer that had killed Jack's mother. They said Kate might help find an affordable cure. Kate was going to do that. Kate who killed herself so that he could have this lavish three-bed, four-bath condo in NoMad with paintings on the wall that he didn't even like.

He filled another glass. And then another. And another, which is why he smelled like booze when Sophia arrived home. When Sophia walked in the door, his disgust was displaced by surprise: He could see that she hated herself too. It was the first time he ever saw that look on Sophia's face. So instead of fighting, he walked up to her and wrapped his arms around his wife.

They talked as she drank wine and mindlessly repeated that she was certain it would've happened anyway. He agreed with her. Maybe that's when the white lies between them began.

Sophia went to work for the next few days but couldn't focus. She'd tell herself that her more successful peers wouldn't care—they'd be celebrating. She hated that she didn't feel that way. She'd motivate herself for an hour or two, but the emotional crash always followed, and she'd go back to reading about KTA1108II.

Sophia gathered the partners and asked to be moved to long-term investments. She thought if she started investing in assets' futures, she'd be able to forgive herself. Her partners took less than an hour to discuss the transition and approve it. She found out after the fact that there had been a lot of pushback, but her friend and partner Ether had put his foot down.

"Humans before profits," he had apparently said. He'd refused to leave the room if they didn't accede to Sophia's request. They did, and Sophia's share price on the Prodigy Market dropped within hours to below $400 for the first time in three years.

For a day, she felt relieved. She was done shorting; she convinced herself this is all she needed to move forward. But she only felt worse.

Sophia wasn't the best at what she did anymore. She was a part of the conventional herd, rather than a hunter seeking to capitalize on flaws in the conventional wisdom. When she was still shorting, she'd be able to motivate herself for a least an hour or two. Now, she'd spend full days obsessing over Kathryn. Searching and re-searching her name on the internet. Rereading articles she had nearly memorized.

Sophia finally understood how Kathryn Tally Anders could find relief from cutting herself. In fact, Sophia started wearing a hair tie on her wrist that she would snap on her skin when she would think about Kathryn.

It didn't matter that she stopped shorting Prodigies; she had already killed one. At this point, all she could do was drown out the guilt with just enough alcohol to quiet her conscience.

So, after six weeks of torture, Sophia decided she should numb her mind with work. That morning, instead of looking up KTA1108II, Sophia opened up her Ecosphere screen and started investigating the highest valued Prodigies, poking them for vulnerabilities. And for a few hours, she didn't think about Kathryn.

❖❖❖❖❖❖

The call came through a few minutes after 6 a.m. The job was confirmed for that night.

From a dwindling roll of plastic, Alex cut out the 3- by 3-foot sheet on his garage floor, the one he'd strip onto after the job. He mindlessly prepped two tubs of silicon dioxide to dissolve the gloves, foot covers, and surgical mask that he'd be wearing. He put in mirrored contact lenses to block any iris scanning that could track him back to the scene later.

And then the encrypted message came through, including a file with the target's information—picture, age, gender, identifying marks. Normally, Alex would review the file, but for this job, he opted to wait until he was on location. There'd be less time to change his mind, something he knew would cost him all future contracts. And even though he was so painfully bored by this career, something about this contract was making him hate it a little less.

❖❖❖❖❖❖

Early the next morning, Sophia walked over to Ether's office. He was there of course, he always was, and greeted her by offering up half of his breakfast, a caramel brownie.

"It's the best fucking thing I've ever tasted," Ether said, placing it in her hand. "Bite it. I'm telling you, you can't not feel good while eating that."

Sophia acquiesced, and then she laughed because he was right. For just a moment, she felt good.

"I have a trade I wanted to run by you." Sophia laid a one-sheet on his desk.

He glanced at it, "A short position? I threw a fit for you—"

"I just stumbled across it when I was looking for long-term investments," she lied. She knew he knew she was lying.

"Look, if you want to be trading short positions, I completely support—"

"I don't want a big position. I'm not going to game the press or get too involved. But what do you think about me taking a minor position?" she asked.

Ether agreed. She was lucky; Ether was a good friend. He understood. And it actually made her feel a bit better, sort of like she was taking another small bite of that brownie.

◆◆◆◆◆◆

Sitting in his car outside of a luxury condominium complex, Alex finally opened the target's file. He scrolled quickly through; the asset was young compared with most contracts, but most definitely an adult. He breathed a sigh of relief.

Then he sighed again. But this time with a touch of disappointment.

Alex screwed the silencers onto the two pistols, stepped out of his car, and walked toward the home of his target, who lived in a supposedly secure 32-story building in Manhattan.

Fortunately, Wall-Head security guards were merely decorative for professionals like Alex.

Alex entered through a maintenance door along a side alleyway. As the guard approached to investigate, a tiny needle slipped into the skin on his neck. He was about to scream when Alex rested a gun on his forehead.

"Don't make a noise and you'll be awake in a few hours. I promise," Alex calmly said as he compressed the plunger. The sedative flowed into the guard's body, and Alex laid him down.

Alex rode the elevator up and noticed that his heartbeat was as calm as if he was watching TV reruns. He thought of his first contract. He remembered shaking.

◆◆◆◆◆◆

Sophia returned home late with the smell of dinner fresh in the air. She took off her chestnut suede flats and gave Jack a kiss. He reeked of whiskey, like usual. She didn't care. They sat down to eat. Everything seemed mostly normal.

"I took a minor short position today. Nothing big and—"

"Soph, Jesus. Six weeks ago someone killed herself."

"She was manic-depressive—"

"And you went and told the whole world that she was overvalued for that," the conversation stopped, and Jack looked away.

"I need this," Sophia said, stifling what could've been some tears, then got up from the table and walked toward their expansive wine rack.

❖❖❖❖❖❖

Alex waited in the darkened front hallway of his target's condo where the lights were off, and he watched his target get up from the dinner table and approach an expansive wine rack, only about 13 paces away. He could hear her steps; he could hear her breathe. As the target grabbed a bottle of wine, a 2024 Château Le Pin Bordeaux, Alex watched her snap a hair tie on her wrist.

The target uncorked the bottle as Alex raised the pistol in his right hand. The target's husband was close by; it wasn't going to be clean. The husband would have to watch what Alex knew was going to be a mess. As Alex exhaled calmly and tightened his grip, he realized that he felt nothing. He was just as bored as he was filling out the W-9.

But then, that small bud permanently in Alex's ear vibrated silently.

"If it hasn't happened yet, we're calling it off," a voice came through the tiny bud in Alex's ear. The voice belonged to a man named Ether, Alex's paymaster for the day.

Without a word, Alex lowered the gun and stayed quietly in the shadows, watching the target swirl her red wine, so perfectly unaware of how close she'd come to never tasting it. So perfectly unaware that her own fund recognized her as overvalued and took a massive short position on her. So perfectly unaware that Ether planned on keeping the fund's short position on her, reviewing it again next quarter to see if she was back to shorting successfully. So perfectly unaware that she really didn't want to die.

For today, she lived. For today, apparently, she was just profitable enough.

Sophia walked back to her dinner table and took another sip of wine. Alex slipped out of her condo and arrived home 32 minutes later. He dissolved his clothes in the premade acid baths, sterilized his weapons, disposed of his mirrored contact lenses, and took a scalding hot shower. It was the first job ever called off after he'd already seen the target. What if he had pulled the trigger before it was called off?

The thought made his heart beat a little faster as the water poured over him. What if he had pulled the trigger?

But he hadn't. So, for one more quarter, Sophia was allowed to stay perfectly unaware. Perfectly alive. Perfectly valued.

For now, at least.

SAFE SURRENDER

Meg Elison

The laws are so old that they were written with fully human children in mind. Before first contact, two humans might make a fully Terran baby and still abandon it, because they didn't have enough money or because one of their ancient tribal honor codes forbid them from breeding. It still happens, but nobody talks about it. Humans like to forget what they used to be. Now, safe surrender sites are known as places where hemis get dumped. Hemis like me.

I wasn't interested in finding out anything about my birth parents for a long time. I figured it would be the same story that every other hemi shares: My parents were one human and one Pinner. We were the first generation of hybrids, and nobody knew what would become of us. A lot of us were put up for adoption and ended up in special schools while the governments of both planets sorted us out. Most of what we know about ourselves was supplied by other people, who were really just offering their best guess. A new race has no memory.

I didn't want to know any more than that until I had my first taste of Pinner coffee (its real name is *onging*, which has a specific Pinner meaning that doesn't translate to anything human well, so most people just say *coffee*), and with it, my first shaky steps into memories that didn't belong to me. Once those thoughts started, I couldn't stop.

First, my own identity document file. It includes the location: a hospital in Old San Jose, California. It tells me the approximate time that I was abandoned: between 2300 and 0400, within three days of my birth. But that date. That date. I was relinquished to the state the night the Pinner ambassador to Earth was shot and killed in San Francisco. Everything I needed to know was going to be wrapped up in the gauzy layers of people's memories of that night. An abandoned hemi was nothing compared to that. I couldn't help but wonder if there was a connection—had the shooting helped them make their decision? Or had it just provided cover, a day when everyone was looking the other way?

I began with the hospital.

"The documents are perfectly in order." The clerk's disinterest practically staled the air, their voice over the speaker the droning whine of a giant, bored nose. "That case number is a safe surrender, logged on Aug. 1, 2096. Birth certificate was issued within 90 days, and if you've got the case file you can see that. Medical scans detected no infections or injuries. Good Apgar scores. The record is a little scant, but perfectly up to the legal standard. Of course."

Of course.

Of course I had to press the nose just a little more. "So all surrenders are entered into the DNA database. How can I get access to that information?"

"You can't. DNA is logged for the ongoing interbreeding genome project. The individual doesn't have the right to access the results, under California law."

"Why not? It's my DNA."

"Because it's protected," the nose shot back. "*Some* of your DNA is available to you, under the law. It used to be that you could view the entirety of your own code, but that was back before we really understood how that data worked. Now we know that most of it isn't specific to you, because it belongs to other individuals. It's a complex legal issue—if you had total access to your own genes, you might be invading the privacy of people who share your bloodline." Their voice softened. "Look, I know it's frustrating. But your DNA rights end where someone else's begin. Besides, there are just things you're better off not knowing."

I got nowhere at all with them obviously. But the easiest part of the system to manipulate is people, and I wasn't about to give up. What I needed was someone who was actually there on the night that I was surrendered. Of course, nobody stays in the same job for 25 years; finding a name took some digging on old social media sites that nobody uses anymore, and a good deal of cajoling a union rep. And then I had to wait.

It would be different, I think, if I at least knew *one* of my parents. Plenty of my friends only have one. That's the joke, right? Hemis are always eyeballing every Pinner that walks by like, "Are you my mother?"

I've been lurking on one of the hemi forums again, reading about *onging*. Some hemis swear that when they take *onging* they see their parents, their whole bloodline, that it activates genetic memory or something. I didn't believe it at all. Not at first. I thought nothing could do that. Certainly not any of the questionable substitutes available in the online markets. I've had the watered-down stuff, the half coffee–half Pinner hemibrews, and the straight-up knockoff junk. It doesn't compare.

But when I get myself an unadulterated 12-credit cup of the real stuff, I can't explain what happens. It's like I'm outside myself, seeing someone else's memories. It's hazy, a blur through glass, but once I think I saw the journey to Earth. Just the blank blackness of space with a smear of stars, a tremulous feeling of heading into the unknown. I wonder if the memory belongs to my mother.

I queued up a movie while I waited for a ping back from the system. One of those uplifting orphan tales. I have a soft spot for stories about human orphans. They're always thieving and discovering they're secretly very privileged, which makes abandonment feel better, I bet. This one was so old it was in the feed for free. Why are these kids always singing? Watching the kid learn how to steal, because that's all orphans can do, apparently, I started thinking about how easy it'd be to get caught doing that now. Every eye on the street is programmed to notice that sort of thing.

I coded the query myself: date and time and coordinates. Since it's a public intersection in front of the hospital, I should have been able to get the footage. But after about an hour, I got a strange message from the city A.I.

Re: Query 587HK901

Sorry! I've been in service for over 20 years, and my memory access isn't what it used to be. I need more specific data to find the information you are looking for. Please narrow your search parameters and try again. Thank you for your patience.

I love the older A.Is. They all talk like grandmothers to keep us from losing our tempers with them. It worked, though. I adjusted my tone, speaking the way I would to someone who doesn't hear very well, and can't always be trusted to call their grandson by his own name and not his father's.

"OK. Try this. I'm trying to figure out who surrendered a child on that corner, at those coordinates, on that date and at that time. Narrow search to individuals carrying something." The computer translated what I was saying into a string the old lady could use. I should have started this search a long time ago. I could have. My adoptive parents had never tried to hide my past from me. I remember the fragile smile on my mother's face when they sat me down and asked me if I wanted to know more. But I didn't know what was possible, or why I should want to find out.

She and my dad couldn't have biological children. They had both been part of early delegations to the Pinner homeworld, before we knew that exposure could sterilize humans. It seems fitting after that trip took their future children from them that they'd adopt a couple of hemi kids. Adoption stories always have a little poetic justice to them.

The little-old-lady A.I. came back again, carrying enriched video files like cookies on a plate.

Re: Query 587HK901

Thank you again for your patience! There is video information that matches your search parameters. Have I fulfilled my task?

I should have confirmed, deference to your elders and all that, but I was too eager to see.

There were seven overlapping bits of footage, shot from multiple vantage points. Most of the eyes were mounted on the rooftops of nearby buildings, so there was no clear look at anyone's face. Still, I could turn the view around in any direction, follow any individual I wanted. I told the lights to turn themselves off and hunched over my projector, rotating the uneven collection of cubes over my desk, peering into the beginning of my life.

The A.I. highlighted the people who walked alone and seemed to be carrying something. I could immediately eliminate the ones that I could tell were carrying pizzas or bags, an umbrella or a potted basil plant. There were two or three figures who might have been carrying a baby. I pulled them closer, examining, desperate to pry their arms apart and get a better look.

Was that a child? Could it be me? Nothing looked right. One turned out to be a puppy. I collapsed the footage back to its original size and spun it like a toy, sighing.

The highlighted figures glowed as they spun, like comets with long tails across the darker expanse of the night around them. I put my hand out and it stopped.

The A.I. had only highlighted the Pinners in the crowd.

I remember when I learned that not everyone could tell. In school, there was this period of innocence between kindergarten and the first year of bimodal/bilingual instruction when nobody knew anybody was different. We were practically a commercial for racial harmony, all of us holding hands and sharing toys, pushing one another on the gravity swings.

I knew I was a hemi. All hemis can tell the difference. We just know. But the percentage of humans who can tell is really small, like less than 10 percent of the population. My first-grade teacher was one.

On the first day of bi/bi school, we learned that she was one of the special ones. "It's probably related to some vestigial ability from early hominids," she said primly, enlarging the projection of the smiling hemi kid next to the human (who didn't look quite as happy to be there). "Perhaps developed back when the human genus was more diverse. Some humans like me have the ability to tell humans from hemis just by looking. Although humans and hemis appear the same on the outside, there are many things that make us different. And that's great!"

There were five hemis in that class. The teacher didn't point us out, but she didn't have to. I didn't understand until years later that she had announced her ability to us so that we'd understand exactly why she treated us the way she did. She wanted us to know that it wasn't an accident. Her tone was different with us, her body language. We got in trouble more easily, and served harsher punishments. Everyone knew within that first week. Grosvenor, the infamous assassin, must have been one of those too. I wonder if the ability to tell is always accompanied by the certainty that one is better than the other.

People claim that it doesn't matter where you come from or what your DNA looks like, because we're all equal. But even the A.I. is biased.

I pulled apart the cubes of night from the hospital and looked again, picking out the shadowed humans. I told the A.I. to stop highlighting its suggestions and the Pinners stopped glowing, flattening the scene into a homogenous sea of unremarkable silhouettes. There. Two humans seemed to be carrying babies. One was headed toward the hospital and one seemed to be walking away. I pulled and pulled, trying to enlarge their faces. I couldn't make out anything that could tell me anything I wanted to know. Nothing that turned that blur of features into a story.

I called up my caseworker, Mx. Evelyn, who did not remember me. She had to dig through her files for my name before exclaiming in mumsy cheer, "It's been forever! How are you doing? Last record I have here is that you went into coding for medical scanners."

"That's right," I confirmed, trying to sound casual. "You know what they say: It's a living. I was wondering if I could come to your office and talk over some of the details of my entry into the system if you have time?"

She blew out a rough sigh. "Oh, man. I'm pretty swamped right now. It seems there are just so many hemis in need of placement these days."

"I'll be quick," I promised. "I'll bring you coffee."

Her voice was hesitant, but acquisitive. "Pinner coffee?"

Pinner coffee is not coffee, obviously. But it is a powerful stimulant, even when diluted with water the way humans like it. It can't be cultivated on Earth, so it's fiercely expensive. It doesn't work on human physiology the way it does for Pinners or hemis, but plenty of people still claim it works as a memory booster. Lately, I've been drinking too much of it, trying to stay awake and get to the bottom of myself. Why bother with DNA and hazy recollections if I can just drink it in? But it's an imperfect and inexact thing. When I do sleep, I sometimes have dreams I can't articulate or fully recall, though I wake up with my face wet like I've been crying through the night. I never pushed it this far before; it gives me the shakes to have more than two. My weak human half. Full humans just say it helps them find lost things, recall funny stories, and make them all misty when they're midsip.

And it tastes pretty good with cream and sugar.

"Pinner coffee," I agreed. "A big one. My treat."

I showed up in the morning with one hot cup and one on ice. "I'll drink whichever one you don't," I told her.

Mx. Evelyn reached out with grabby hands for the hot one. Good, I prefer it cold.

"So," she said between lip-smacking sips. "What brings you back to me?"

"Mx. Evelyn, I'm trying to find out more about the people who surrendered me."

"Your parents."

"My parents," I agreed.

Mx. Evelyn was already nodding, leafing through the antiquated holofile system piled up on her desk. The image glitched and lagged as she tried to pull up the right year.

"Here we go, here we go. Hm. Hemi. Abandoned within three days of birth—I think I'm the one who decided your legal birthdate. Tough to recall. Adopted by human parents. Evidence of thriving at every appointment..." She was moving quickly through the years of my life, refamiliarizing herself with the highlights.

"Right, yes. I'm actually more interested in any specific information you might have about the night I was surrendered. I know that the parent has the opportunity to share any information they might have that—"

Her finger froze on the display. "Oh, you were surrendered on the night of the assassination."

"Yes," I nodded. "I was. I know it was a long time ago, but a lot of people remember vividly where they were that night. They're always telling the story. I'm hoping someone might remember something else about their experience. Something to do with my surrender."

Mx. Evelyn's mouth pulled down at the corners, and she stared off into the distance, following the thread of memory into the fog. "Yes, I remember. I was in a bar when the news broke." She caught my eye with a self-conscious chuckle. "That was back in my wilder days. I remember the sound of all of those phones around me suddenly pinging at the same time, like church bells, when everyone got the alert. You always know that's going to be something bad."

"It was the first Pinner death on Earth. A violent crime. A high-profile assassination, right? You all must have been worried."

Mx. Evelyn sipped her coffee. "Very tense atmosphere. You know, we didn't know much of your people back then. We thought there might be some kind of reprisal. I mean, it soon became clear that Grosvenor was a terrorist, a radical acting alone, but of course we worried that the Pinner homeworld might hold us all responsible for the death."

I nodded, bringing my own cup to my lips. There is a kind of weight to a history that defines you but did not happen to you. I've been hearing this story my whole life. It was time to write my own.

"Mx. Evelyn, I've been reviewing the outdoor security footage from that night. There aren't any Pinners on the street carrying babies. Just a couple of humans."

She fingered her files nervously, sending them glitching and fizzling as the computer tried to figure out what she wanted. "I mean, it is technically possible your human parent surrendered you. Just very unlikely. Statistically. I'm not saying that humans *never* do it, but—"

"But the laws that govern how babies can be surrendered are much older than first contact. So humans must have done it to their own children, their own fully human children, well before the Pinners ever arrived. Enough to necessitate a law." I was staring her down but she wouldn't look at me.

"Grosvenor was opposed to Pinner-human hybridity, did you know that?" I tried to make my voice sound casual.

She fiddled with her holofile again. "I did know that. There was a lot written about his motivations, in the immediate aftermath of the shooting. Everybody wants to understand *why*, in cases like that. But of course we don't ever really know."

I knew she was talking about the assassination and not why my parents abandoned me. But the two were so tangled up that I was beginning to see them as one event. One night a human claims a Pinner life, and miles away another human releases their claim on their half-Pinner child. It looks like balance, but life and death both keep sloppy books. And we don't ever really know why.

"Is there anything in the file that might help me make sense of the video I've got? Anything at all?"

She leafed through the pages. "It looks like the duty nurse was away from the station quite a bit that evening. Probably glued to the news. There's nothing here, really. Just bare bones."

I thanked her and stood to leave. I turned back when she said my name.

"Humans aren't what we used to be, you know. When we needed those laws. Or when Grosvenor shot Lngren. We've come so far, mostly thanks to our contact with Pinners. You kids are kind of our peace bridge. You know?"

Her eyes were shining and I could tell she was looking for me to absolve her, of Lngren's death 20 years ago, of her own gentle bigotry. Had anything really changed since that night?

I smiled at her. "Sure, Mx. Evelyn."

It's enough. The door whispered as it closed between us. The coffee was weak. I caught snatches of something in my peripheral vision, something that looked like twin moons, but would not come clear. I threw the empty cup in the trash and walked away.

❖❖❖❖❖

From the Bi/Bi Reader, copyright 2104:
Humans are regarded as one of the most adaptable species in the known galaxy. Their unique physiology advantages them to endure extreme heat and cold, to survive the loss of limbs and infectious disease, and to travel to different worlds.

When examined in this context, the human history of violent conflict is very understandable.

In contrast, Pinners cannot live away from their homeworld for extended periods of time without risking their lives. Their physiology does not allow them endurance for extreme temperature, and they are considerably more fragile than their human counterparts. As a result, their explorations into the space surrounding them are considerably more limited, and there are no off-world Pinner settlements equivalent to the Mars colonies like Musk or New Nairobi, or even the International Space Station. Nonviolent by both nature and cultural heritage, Pinners have no tradition of war and their delicate physiology renders them incapable of surviving wounds sustained in violent conflict.

Pinner-Human hybrids commonly inherit the best traits from both species. They're highly adaptable like humans, with the sensitivity and precision that are special to Pinners.

Our diversity makes us stronger! The future of Pinner-human relations is uniquely enhanced by the existence of our shared descendants.

The truth is there hasn't been that much research. We first-generation hybrids were the first of our kind, something entirely new. Nobody knows how to tell you that science doesn't know who you are yet. We were born without a history, and innocent of a collective memory. The first generation. They weren't even sure if we'd be able to breed, until one of us did it. A lot of folks thought we were a mistake that shouldn't exist—for hemis to be another sterile Earth hybrid like mules or ligers would have suited people like Grosvenor just fine.

When I looked back, I could see how my parents had gently talked around it when Rainey and I were young. They never brought up the possibility of grandchildren, or delivered the traditional solemn lectures about birth control in our teens. Mom talked a lot about how her career had always been her first priority.

"So when I found out I couldn't have children, I wasn't even that upset. I hadn't met your dad yet, and I wasn't really planning for kids. I just loved my work so much. I did exactly what I wanted to do. You guys were just a bonus to that."

Dad was gruffer, but still avoided saying it outright. "Kids are expensive," he'd say, looking over the peculiar medical expenses incurred by bodies that aren't in the books yet. "You have a lot more fun traveling without them. You get to be free!"

I used to think he was just protecting himself against his own disappointment. I didn't understand until much later that my parents were trying to keep our hopes in check.

Mx. Evelyn hadn't been the key I'd been hoping for. I shouldn't have been surprised. Human memory is an even more unreliable narrator than the A.I. it gave birth to. But later that same night, my comm lit up again. It was the union rep. They'd found me someone who would talk.

The nurse's name was Darryl Stanner, and he was one of the oldest humans I had ever seen. His face loomed elephantine in the display, my comm still zoomed in on the old A.I. footage. I quickly pinched the picture in, looking away from his dilated pores and the pooling skin that hung below his eyes. When I looked back, he was manageable. Human scale. Fine.

"Hello? Are you there? I can see you, but I can't hear anything."

"Hello! Hello, Mx. Stanner. Hi. I don't know if your rep told you, but I'm trying to find out any information you might have about a safe surrender. Um, my safe surrender. Is that OK with you?"

He blinked a few times, slowly. "I have the file here, it came through my old rep. I know what you're after, but I'm afraid my memory's not what it used to be. I don't know if I'll be able to help you."

"I'm just asking if you'll try," I said, smiling. "I'll be happy to leave you alone if you don't remember anything at all. But I'm hoping you might recall some details of that evening, because I was left on the night that Ambassador Lngren was shot."

"Oh," he said, his enormous caterpillar eyebrows rolling up over the ridge in his skull. "Of course I remember that night. Terrible thing, just terrible."

"So you remember the shooting?"

"Like it was yesterday," he breathed, his glacial speech speeding to a furious crawl. "It was all anybody could talk about. It was like this big secret was out. The Pinners knew what we were. What we are. What a world. What a shock."

"Do you remember the child who was left at the hospital that night?"

"Oh yeah, of course."

"Really?" I tried not to sound too eager, but I'm sure he could see my lean forward, pressing toward the past. "Can you tell me what you remember?"

He sighed, sounding as tired as time itself. "That night was total chaos. Everyone thought we were going to war. But that was back before we knew how weak Pinners are. How fragile. The woman who dropped you off was afraid she'd break you. I never saw someone carry a baby so carefully. Like you were an eggshell."

I nodded, more soberly than I felt. "Anything you can tell me about her would be very much appreciated."

He looked down at his lap. "I mean, she was scared. Like we were all scared. Big eyes. I think she was wearing a sweater that belonged to someone else. Just so vulnerable, like she'd break in two if I was mean to her."

"But she was human," I said, almost more to myself than to him. "Not vulnerable like a Pinner, but human?"

"Sure," he said. "Sure, she was as human as I am."

"Did she say something about what had happened? Did you two talk about the news at all?"

Stanner's huge floating head shook slowly, the edges disappearing when he got out of scanner range. "She didn't have anything to say. Just that real scared way about her. She was real young. Pretty. But I just felt so bad for her. Pinners dropped off hemi kids all the time. But her? I could tell it was breaking her heart to do it. It's just not the same with humans, you know."

I wanted him to tell me she was remarkable—that her eyes were a color he had never seen before. That she wore half a broken necklace. That she promised she'd come back for me. That she'd said, "Someday," with a hopeful and faraway look.

"Was she alone? Did someone drop her off, or pick her up, that you saw?"

Stanner shrugged. "Not that I saw. I was pretty distracted. You know, with everything going on."

I imagined the halls and waiting rooms of the hospital, doctors and nurses and patients clustered around different screens and feeds, whispering, wondering. Me, the eggshell future of two races tucked against Stanner's chest. Was I sleeping? Did I cry for my human mother? This piece of my life did not belong to me; only someone else could hold it. And what he held, instead, was the moment in history that over-shadowed me.

"Thank you for trying, Mx. Stanner. I really appreciate it." My voice was trembling.

"Don't take it too hard, kid. You know you're better off not remem-bering any of that. She wanted to be forgotten. Let it go."

A quick swipe of my trembling fingers ended the call. His face vanished, leaving only reflection in the dark glass. I did not say good-bye.

Whatever gift of memory Pinner coffee has been trying to give me, it can't be hers. My mother was human, and she wanted me to have nothing that was hers. I've lost her, but my father is out there some-where. He's in the black recess of space, or the last few drips of dark-ness in my cup.

I tried to go back to the beginning. I tried to do what the human orphans in stories do: go on a quest. I tried to follow the roads of memory and go back. Other orphans find out that they're secretly royalty. They find out that their parents loved them but gave them up because of dire circumstance. They realize that their real family is the one who chose them. They ask for more.

All I have are fragments of memory, and none of them my own. I have the story of the night my mother abandoned me, the same night when a Pinner was first killed by a human. I have a forgetful old nurse and a buggy old A.I., both of whom were there and both of whom were too distracted by programming of one kind or an-other to bear witness for me. I have a father who can't live on this world and must have returned to one I've never seen. There is no more.

I arrived on the Pinner homeworld two days ago. The people are not at all what I expected. They welcomed me like I'd been missed. They told me my chances of being sterilized by the radiation here are 50-50. They also told me that there is a registry here for hemis to find their Pinner parents, but that's just a place to start. What we're looking for can't be found in a list of names. Instead, most of us have started taking fresh *onging* at full strength and connecting to the reservoir of collective memory that it unlocks. Drinking it has helped me remember a place and a people that belong to me, though I've never known them.

Memory, like DNA, is made up mostly of pieces that belong to other people. I sent a message back to Earth, to every other hemi I know.

I told them I'm halfway home.

LIONS AND GAZELLES

Hannu Rajaniemi

"Where do you think we are?" the young Middle Eastern woman with the intense eyes asked.

Jyri smiled at her and accepted a smoothie from a tanned aide.

"I think this is a Greek island." He pointed at the desolate gray cliffs. They loomed above the ruined village where the 50 contestants in the Race were having breakfast. "Look at all the dead vegetation. And the sea is the right color."

In truth, he had no idea. At SFO, he'd been ushered into a private jet with tinted windows. The last leg of the journey had been in an autocopter's opaque passenger pod. The Race's location, like everything else about it, was a closely guarded secret.

But his gesture distracted the woman long enough for Jyri to steal a glance at her impossibly muscled legs. Definitely a myostatin knockout—a gene edit for muscle hypertrophy. Crude, but effective. He would have to watch out for her.

Suddenly, she zeroed in on something over Jyri's shoulder.

"Excuse me, need to catch up with someone. Nice talking to you."

Before he could say anything, she elbowed past him, filling a gap in the scrum around Marcus Simak, the CEO of SynCell—the largest cultured meat company in the world. She launched into a well-rehearsed pitch. Jyri swore. He, too, had been stalking Simak, waiting for an opening.

His mouth was dry. This was the most coveted part of the event: access to the world's most powerful tech CEOs, who could change your destiny with a flick of their fingers. He would only get one more shot before they started literally running away from him. Even worse, he wanted to run, too. Every muscle in his body felt like a loaded spring. The synthetic urge pounded in his temples, mixing with the din of the crowd.

Jyri fought it down, forced himself to take a thick minty sip of his smoothie and scanned the runners in the white mesh suits—ghost-like in the pre-dawn light—for a new target.

It was easy to divide the crowd into three groups: the entrepreneurs, like Jyri, here to show off their tech, hungry-eyed and ill at ease in their biohacked bodies; the hangers-on, company VPs and celebrities, with their Instagram–filter complexions and fluorescent tattoos; and finally, the Whales like Simak: the god-emperors of A.I., synbio, agrotech, and space.

Jyri spotted Maxine Zheng, Simak's upstart rival, just 10 feet away. Fresh-faced, petite, and wiry, her vast robotic cloud labs powered the Second Biotech Revolution—including Jyri's own startup, CarrotStick.

Jyri edged into the group caught in Zheng's trillion-dollar gravity. Up close, her skin had a glistening dolphin-like sheen. Allegedly, the Whales' edits included cetacean genes that protected them from cancer and other hoi polloi ailments.

Zheng was talking to a tall young man who was deathly pale but had the build of an Ethiopian runner: long legs and a bellows-like chest.

"That's neat," she said. "But I'm honestly more into neurotech, these days."

That was Jyri's cue. He pushed forward, the one-liner pitch ready. *Hi, I'm Jyri Salo from CarrotStick. We re-engineer your dopamine receptors to hack motivation—*

"Jyri!"

A strong hand gripped his shoulder. He turned around and almost swore aloud.

Not here, not now.

Alessandro Botticelli's white teeth flashed against a dark curly beard. He wore thick rings on stubby fingers, and his tattooed forearms rippled with muscle. His calves could have been carved from red granite. The ruddy hue of his skin was new. Probably an edit increasing red blood cell production for aerobic endurance, but these days you never knew.

"It's so good to see you, man!" The Italian gripped Jyri's hand and pulled him into a bear hug. "I can't believe you made it here, how are you doing, are you still working on that little company of ours? I love it!"

The familiar lilting accent made Jyri's teeth hurt. He cringed. *That little company. Of ours. Had he no shame?*

"Doing great," he said aloud, jaw clenched.

"That's awesome, man," Alessandro said. "Congrats. Me, I've just been so busy, it started to get too much, you know. So I decide to get in shape, really in shape. Maxine said I should do this, so here I am! It's going to be sick!"

Jyri could not face the white teeth, the green eyes, and looked away.

"I'm happy for you," he said.

"Hey, man, thanks! Do you want an intro? She's right there, and she'd probably be into what you've been working on."

Zheng was behind a wall of muscled bodies again. Jyri took a deep breath to say yes but tasted old anger. He shook his head.

"That's fine. We chatted already."

The Italian slapped him on the shoulder, hard.

"Awesome! Hey, we should really catch up! Maybe after this thing?"

"Sure." Jyri's stomach was an acid pit. He waved a hand at Alessandro and walked away, stumbling to the edge of the crowd. He took a long draught of his smoothie, but could barely get the viscous mixture down. He forced himself to drink it anyway. It was a dirty secret of ultrarunning that gorging gave you an advantage. Besides, it washed the taste of bile away.

Jyri had met Alessandro at one of the first networking events he had attended after he came over from Finland with little more than an idea. They bonded over their shared running hobby, Alessandro offered help with fundraising, and before Jyri knew it, the Italian was an equal co-founder of CarrotStick.

There was a time when they spent nearly every waking hour together, whiteboarding ideas, filing patents, sweating over pitch decks and grinding through endless investor meetings. It was a true Valley bromance. And then, when they got an offer to join the hottest accelerator in the Bay Area, Alessandro bailed on him, suddenly announcing he wasn't going to be able to do CarrotStick full-time. A VC firm they had pitched together had circled back to offer Alessandro a job. Apparently they had been impressed by his drive, and he claimed it was a better match for his life's mission. Whatever that was.

The accelerator turned CarrotStick down—given its "founder commitment issues"—and left Jyri scrambling for funding while burning through his savings and doing around-the-clock lab work. Alessandro wore his unchanging grin through the negotiations over his founder shares. He wore Jyri down, never raising his voice, and finally Jyri gave in to what advisers later told him was a ridiculous equity stake for an inactive founder.

Afterward, Jyri blocked Alessandro on every social media app. Every now and then, a piece of news leaked through his friends' feeds. Alessandro's new startup broke all sorts of Series A financing records; his popular science feed won a prize; he married a young VR yoga instructor who frequented both the exercise classes and fantasies of millions of men and women around the world.

Most gallingly, despite Jyri's efforts at a news blockade, he'd watched Alessandro brag in interviews about how his creativity and hard work had led to an early small success: a company called CarrotStick.

Jyri wouldn't let Alessandro ruin this, he decided. He'd get to Zheng on his own, no matter what. Fists clenched, he turned back to look at the crowd—and met the eyes of a woman sitting on a sun-bleached bench nearby.

Jyri frowned. She was neither an aide nor a runner: She wore a loose, shapeless black dress that left her arms bare. They bore faded tattoos of bats. Her ashen hair stuck out in pigtails. She twirled an e-cigarette between her fingers. A knowing smile flickered on her lips.

Then it clicked. This had to be La Gama, the Doe. She was one of the legendary ultrarunners who had competed against the Tarahumara Indians in the canyons of northern Mexico, before climate change pushed them out and they gave up their millennia-long tradition of running.

Twelve years ago, the Whales had hired her to plan the biennial Races. She took all her experience from running races like Barkley Marathons and Badwater, and created an entirely new kind of contest for superhuman athletes. La Gama decided who ran based on an elaborate application that included biomarkers, genome sequences, and patents for the contestant's enhancements.

She stood up. Jyri's heart sank. The networking was over. Now, the only way to stand out from the startup pack and catch the Whales' attention was by running.

A hush spread across the square. The Whales turned to look at her, and all the other runners followed suit. For a moment, the only sound was the listless chirping of crickets.

"Running," she said, "used to be how we hunted. We evolved to chase things until they fell down from sheer exhaustion. The legacy is still there, in our upright spine, nuchal ligament, and Achilles tendons.

"All your lives, you have hunted with your brains. I want you to hunt and kill with your legs. Meet your prey."

She lifted a hand and hooked her fingers. A large pack of robots slunk out of the surrounding chalk-white ruins. Each was the size of a large antelope, had gazelle-like legs, and a black headless body. Hair at the back of Jyri's neck stood up. They moved too sinuously to be prey.

"Meet Goats 1 to 50," La Gama said. "They have full batteries. As do you. This Race is a persistence hunt. No stages, no set distances, no water stations, no time limit, no rest: Just run a goat down. The first one to bring back the contents of its belly wins."

She laid a hand on the smooth rump of the bot next to her, on a small cave painting–like drawing. A shutter irised opened on its side, then snapped shut before Jyri could see what was within.

La Gama slapped her hands. "That's it. The sun is coming up, and so, like lions and gazelles, you had all better be running."

❖❖❖❖❖❖

The starting line was unmarked. They simply assembled in rows on the narrow road that snaked up toward the hills. The goatbot herd scampered past them and stopped on the crest of the first slope. The rising sun painted the cliffs purple.

They all knew the basic rules. No communications. No support crews. No pacers. Most importantly, no cybernetic enhancements or prosthetics—nothing with silicon or electricity. But anything biological was fair game: They were the Grail knights of the Second Biotech Age. They had backpacks with water and energy gels, and that was it.

Jyri peeked at the row of white-clad bodies. Alessandro's eyes were closed and his lips were moving. Was that hypocrite *praying*?

La Gama lifted the e-cig to her lips.

Jyri's anger mixed with the need to run, almost unbearable now. Every last bit of CarrotStick's cash and crypto had gone into fine-tuning his body—and more importantly, his brain.

The key ingredient was motivation.

La Gama took a deep pull from the e-cig. Its end glowed electric blue. She blew out one menthol-smelling wisp of smoke. That was the starting pistol shot.

The runners exploded into motion. Jyri's hungry feet devoured the road through the thin-soled Race shoes.

CarrotStick's actual mission was to make smart drugs that hacked the brain's reward circuits, and made you addicted to problem-solving, coding, A.I. algorithm design. It had been much harder than he had expected. The company's runway was almost gone when one of his investors told Jyri about the Race. He realized they could just copy the dopamine receptor variants of the greatest ultra-athletes of all time—the relentless drive that carried them through a 100-mile race.

That drive was Jyri's now. CarrotStick had manufactured a synthetic virus that carried the best receptor gene variant into his brain. Every step said *yes* in his mind. He felt like he could run forever.

The woman with the myostatin knockout legs was suddenly abreast of him, then edged ahead. On their own accord, Jyri's feet sped up. He gulped deep breaths, held on to the drive's reins. It was not time to push yet.

He slowed down and let her disappear over the hilltop ahead, just behind the goatbots.

Then Zheng, Simak, and the two other Whale CEOs zipped through the pack. Their legs and pumping arms were a blur. For them, this was a clash of the R&D departments of the vast companies whose avatars they'd become. It was pointless to compete with them. Their muscle cells were synthetic, their tissues fully superhuman.

At last, Jyri was over the first hill. The road turned left. The goatbots followed it, straight at the steep cliffs crested by white clouds. The Whales were tiny dots at their heels. The other runners followed, and the Race was on.

◆◆◆◆◆◆

The sun blazed at their backs. The paved road turned into a rocky path. Jyri did not mind the climb. Early on in his training, he had done a lot of hill runs. It was a good way to get the biomechanics right.

He shifted his gait into full barefoot style, stepping down with the foot's edge, not with the heel, gliding, elf-like. Others in the runner pack found the path tougher, and even without quickening his pace, Jyri started to leave them behind.

The last ruined house on the outskirts of the village was surrounded by skeletons of real goats. The main goatbot herd was nowhere to be seen, but Jyri kept pace with a handful of bots ahead. They veered to the right, onto an even rockier path leading diagonally up the cliffside.

"Let's go get them, shall we?"

That slap on his shoulder, again. Alessandro. He was right at Jyri's heels and then ahead, sending up puffs of dust as he went. He'd come out of nowhere. He had pulled the old ultrarunner trick: running on the very edge of the path so you could not see him from ahead.

Jyri's gut churned at the sight of Alessandro's broad, receding back. This was too much. But the voice of reason cautioned there was a long, long road ahead. The goatbots had to have at least 20 hours of charge, and the island could have hidden recharging stations. The rough terrain promised microfractures, accumulating pain.

Jyri took a tiny sip of water from his Camelbak, not enough to hydrate, just to trick his brain into keeping thirst at bay. An ultrarun was an ever-expanding tree of decisions. Drink or not. Speed up or not. He reached a compromise. He would open the valves a bit, just to see if he could gain on Alessandro, and slow down if the effort seemed too much.

He increased the beat of his mental metronome to 180 beats per minute. He grazed his shin on a rock—he would be paying for that for many hours. But the pain mixed with the dopamine drumbeat gave him a burst of speed. His head lifted high. He pumped his knees in perfect running form. Suddenly, he was just behind Alessandro, who grunted in surprise.

Jyri could not resist lightly brushing Alessandro's shoulder as he edged past. Then he raced up the path, following the joyous zigzag dance of the goatbot ahead, toward the cliffs that now belonged only to him.

◆◆◆◆◆◆

Fourteen hours into the race, Jyri lost the goatbot in the clouds.

The rapidly falling dusk made the island's contours soft and dream-like. The ascent had been grueling. The paths were unmarked and strewn with sharp-edged rocks. On the worst stretches, he had to run bent almost double to avoid the spiky branches arcing over the path.

But the dopamine drive kept him on the bot's trail all the way up to the plateau. It resembled a lunar landscape: large boulders, grey gravel. There were fields of tiny round pebbles that retained the sun's heat and were like hot coals to run on.

He glimpsed other runners only once: two dots moving along the coastline far below, chasing a goatbot side by side. They might have been Zheng and Simak, and Jyri wondered what they were doing, racing so close together. Unable to give an inch to each other, perhaps. Or was it something else?

Otherwise, it was just him and the bot. By now, he had a feel for the artificial animal's behavior. It stopped as if to rest whenever he slowed down, probably recharging in the sun. If he rushed it, it scrambled away.

That was the cruelty of La Gama's scheme. The only way to narrow the gap was to be relentless. The goatbot's pace was just above his fat-burning maximum heart rate of 140 bpm, and he was halfway through his energy gel packs.

A chilly wind picked up. Clouds started rolling across the plateau, swallowing the dark boulders. This was it, Jyri realized. The thing could not recharge in the mist. If he could get close and stay with it, it would be his.

He sprinted forward and followed the bot into the whiteness. It seemed like a demon now, making wild leaps over rocks that Jyri had to go around. Every now and then it melted into the fog, and Jyri's thundering heart skipped a beat. The beat of the dopamine drum pushed him forward, faster and faster, roaring inside his head.

And then the goatbot stumbled.

There was a clatter of metal and rocks. Jyri snapped back to knife's-edge alertness. The pebbles were wet and slippery, and he slowed down. A shape loomed ahead: a boulder. He swung around, and saw the bot barely 50 feet away, struggling to get up, its legs scraping against stone. This was it, he had to push now, just a little—

His leg muscles burst into cold flame. Then they seized up. The cursed rigs, the runner's rigor mortis.

No. I can do this.

The cold feeling spread into his brain, like the world's worst ice cream headache. Keep pushing, damn it.

But he could not.

He.

Could.

Not.

A treacherous pebble twisted beneath his foot. He fell forward, pressed his chin to his chest, cradled his head. One elbow banged on a boulder and went numb as he came down with a bone-jarring thump.

Then everything was quiet, except for the taunting clatter of the goatbot's hooves.

Jyri lay still, curled up on the damp stones. Everything hurt. But it wasn't the pain that made vomit rise into his throat, it was the *absence* of something.

The running fire had died.

He didn't *want* to get up.

He lay on the bare wet rock and tried to think through the pain, but thoughts fled him like the goatbot in the fog. He fumbled for the Camelbak's tube with numb hands. It slipped and he let it go.

Lying down meant the end. He would be one of the Race's failures, the non-finishers. From now on, investors he pitched to would give him one knowing look and pass. CarrotStick would die, and his future with it. He closed his eyes and fought back tears.

Only—it made no sense.

The drive to run was gone. Something was wrong with his dopamine receptors. Had his own immune system started rejecting them? He had undergone a regime to get his body to tolerate the new genes. Still, a sudden runaway immune reaction was not impossible. But he did not have a fever or any other symptoms.

That left one other possibility: a hostile biohack targeting the enhancement directly, maybe a biologic drug that blocked the receptor. And only someone with insight into CarrotStick's IP could have designed that.

Alessandro. Those slaps on the shoulder. The rings he wore. Alessandro would know enough about CarrotStick's receptors to leverage A.I. to design a molecule to target them.

The void in his head was filled by a flood of anger, red and warm and *good.*

He remembered what his first running coach had told him in high school.

The best fuel for finishing a race is hate.

Jyri flopped to his belly, got to his knees, and stayed there for a moment, breathing hard. There was a boulder next to him. He embraced it like a lover, found a handhold, and pulled himself up. He leaned against the rocky surface, pressed his forehead against it. His legs wobbled but held.

He would make it back. He would prove what had happened, destroy Alessandro's name.

He squirted an energy gel pack into his mouth. The hydrogel-encapsulated carbohydrates released an expanding bubble of warmth in his belly.

He let go of the rock, took one step, then another, fighting the rigs. After three steps, it started to get easier.

After 10 steps, he broke into a jog.

◆◆◆◆◆◆

The descent was even worse than the ascent. Most ultrarunners walked uphill and ran downhill, but the trail was so rough Jyri had to slow down to a walk to give the microtears in his muscles a chance to heal.

It was almost dark when he finally emerged from the cloud cover and realized he had made it further than he'd thought.

Only in the wrong direction.

The interior of the island spread before him in the pale moonlight: rolling hills, a dry riverbed, ash-colored dead trees. Jyri had taken a wrong turn on the plateau. The village was behind him. He would have to climb back up and retrace his steps—a 14-hour journey, back when he was still fresh.

The fatigue fell upon him, heavy and thick. He nearly stumbled again. What did he have left? In theory, 40 percent: That's what science claimed you could still draw upon when you reached all limits of endurance.

It would have to be enough.

He turned to start the long climb back up, and heard a shout from below.

"Salo! Down here!"

Alessandro. He was perhaps 100 meters below Jyri, on rough but level ground. A short distance away from him was a herd of goatbots, at least 20 of them. As Jyri watched, Alessandro dashed toward them. The herd erupted in all directions. Alessandro chased one for a half-minute, but then it swerved away, and the herd simply regrouped behind the Italian. There was no way to tell which one it had been.

If Jyri had retained any strength, he would have laughed aloud. The goatbots were persistence-hunting *Alessandro*, playing a shell game that would eventually exhaust him.

Maybe I should just sit down and watch. The bastard deserved it.

"Salo, damn it, I need some help here! You can't catch these motherfuckers alone. They gang up and then there is no way to tell them apart. We need to work together. Come on!"

"If you'd wanted my help, maybe you shouldn't have screwed with me," Jyri shouted. His voice was hoarse.

"What the fuck are you talking about?"

Jyri was now halfway down to the clearing. He imagined punching Alessandro, but was not sure he could actually lift his arm.

"I know you hacked me," Jyri said. "Back in the village."

Alessandro stopped and stared at him, eyes wide.

"You too?"

"What do you mean?"

"My metabolism is fucked. I thought it was a malfunction."

Maybe it was just the moonlight, but Alessandro *did* look pale.

"Bullshit," Jyri said. He needed the hate, goddamn it. There were tears in his eyes.

"Think about it, Salo. It was that bitch La Gama. Those smoothies— why do you think they made us drink them? She was the only one who knew enough about our hacks to develop countermeasures against them."

The hate cooled down to an ember. Jyri stared at Alessandro. His hands started shaking.

Alessandro lowered his voice.

"Look, man. You're a good guy. I know I left you in a bad spot, back in the day." His grin was gone. "I don't need to cheat, damn it. But right now, I need *you*. So...I'm sorry I screwed you, all right?"

Jyri looked at him. One apology was not enough to erase five years of backbreaking work and anxiety. How stupid did Alessandro think he was?

Then he remembered Zheng and Simak, running in tandem.

"This is the whole point of the Race," Jyri said. "La Gama gave us a challenge that's impossible to meet individually, no matter how good your enhancements are. The Whales must be hating it."

He looked at Alessandro's leonine face. There had been no malice in the betrayal. Out here, it was easier to see it. Just an animal, running after the prey, as was its nature.

All of a sudden, Jyri felt less heavy.

"That's why we didn't make good partners, man," Alessandro said. "You were way too clever for me."

Jyri took a deep breath.

"All right," he said. "Let's hunt."

◆◆◆◆◆◆

It took Jyri and Alessandro several tries to separate a goatbot from the herd. One of them rushed the herd and chose a target; the other intercepted whenever it tried to join the others. It took bursts of speed

Jyri would not have imagined he still possessed. Alessandro's face was purple, all traces of arrogance wiped away by pain. Between dashes, they shared their remaining energy gels and water.

By two in the morning they finally had a goatbot on the run. The herd followed close behind, so they could not let their attention waver.

Forty percent, Jyri kept thinking, as they raced along the dry riverbed. This was what he imagined the land of the dead was like, arid and endless.

Yet, somehow, he found himself enjoying the run. His mind was quiet. How long had it been since he'd run in flow, disappearing into a task at the edge of his ability? The Finnish word for thinking was *ajatella*. It originally meant harrying one's prey until the end.

Their lungs worked like bellows. There was no breath for words, but Alessandro was a silent presence at his side, focused on the same goal. With every synchronized step they took, the anger and the anxiety leaked out.

After a while, there was only the satisfaction of joint pursuit: the bot's indistinct shape ahead, the rattle of rocks beneath their feet.

The coastal cliffs were rimmed with light when the goatbot finally slowed, collapsed in a tangle of limbs, and lay still.

Jyri stared at it, trying not to collapse himself as his heart rate slowed and the blood pressure in his limbs dropped. Alessandro was doubled over, hands on his knees, as he retched.

"You..." the Italian waved breathlessly. "You...do the honors."

Jyri half-walked, half-hopped to the machine. Up close, it looked even more like an animal. Its black carapace moved up and down, as if it was breathing. Gingerly, he touched the white stick figure on its flank. A round hole snapped instantly open. He reached inside, and his fingers found two objects: a vial filled with a clear liquid and a pneumatic injection needle.

Alessandro wiped vomit from his beard and looked at him.

"What are you waiting for?" he asked. "It's the antidote, stupid."

Jyri weighed the vial and the needle in his hand. Was this some final trick? Did it even make sense that there would be a universal antidote to hacks against all the contestants' different enhancements? *Of course.* The smoothies: They were probably probiotics with bacteria producing a variety of customized biologics in the runners' guts. They would have a universal genetic off-switch, triggered by whatever the vial contained.

One shot, and the drive to run would be his again. And yet there was something pure about the night air, the light in the horizon, the dust on his face. He was *here*, not in the anxiety-ridden past or uncertain tomorrow. Did he really want the overriding, relentless drumbeat back? He was in pain, but this pain was something he had chosen. It belonged to him.

He shook his head and handed the antidote to Alessandro.

"You do it," he said. "I'll find my own way back."

The Italian looked at him, green eyes unreadable. With a practiced move, he filled the vial and found a vein in his arm. The clear liquid went in with a hiss. Alessandro took a deep breath. His skin flushed, and he stretched expansively.

"I'll tell them to come get you," he said. "Find some shelter and stay there. And I'll do that intro to Zheng, and brag about your mad motivation-hacking tech. I know you were bluffing earlier about talking to her, but you should. I think she'll be interested."

Jyri nodded and raised a hand.

He watched Alessandro's white form recede into the distance until he disappeared behind the withered foliage on the dry riverbank.

He waited until the sun came up. Long shadow-fingers stretched across the valley, and the coastal cliffs glinted golden. A mirage hovered above the dry expanse of the island. It looked like a ghost city, with floating towers and pillars.

Jyri felt empty and light. His Camelbak was dry, and he let his backpack fall to the ground. *Gazelle or lion*, he thought.

Then he started running.

Burned-Over Territory

Lee Konstantinou

I'm halfway through a plate of soggy risotto, giving my opinion about the Project Approval Framework, when my phone buzzes. I thought I'd muted notifications. I'm tempted to check the alert, but 30 faces are watching me, all Members, some from Zardoz House, the rest from other Houses around Rochester. We're at a table made from reclaimed wood, which is covered with food and drink. It's freezing. Everyone's wearing sweaters, hats, coats, scarves, mittens; I'm in a blue blazer over a T-shirt, jeans, and leather boots. My hair is buzzed into a crew cut, and even though it makes me feel like an ass clown, I'm wearing makeup.

A videodrone hovers near the credenza, five feet from my prettified face, streaming this Chat 'n' Chew live on the Federation Bulletin. Twenty-thousand Members are watching me. Zardoz House is one of the First Five, and me getting invited here is a pretty big deal. The Federation is in a political frenzy. The Voting Period closes next week, and Joan McGee, incumbent Chairperson, an Artist, is probably going to win, but I'm within striking distance—I would be the first Universalist Chair—and I'm not going down without a fight.

My phone stops buzzing, and I sigh with relief. "Over the last six months," I say, trying not to let my teeth chatter, "I've been invited into hundreds of Houses from Rochester to Davis. And whatever so-called faction I talk to, I hear the same story. All of us have been screwed by the World. We wouldn't have joined a House otherwise, right?"

"Damn right, Viola," Marlow says.

Marlow is an old friend, the one who invited me to Zardoz. He's a Universalist, like me, and part of a not-so-secret network of recovering addicts. Our stronghold is the old Opioid Road, the so-called Burned-Over Territory, from Albany, New York, to Columbus, Ohio. We stick together. We give a shit. We participate. We were, after all, there at the founding, helping make the Federation what it is today. McGee and her stuck-up allies are trying to rewrite history, to erase us. That, anyway, is what I want to tell the crowd.

Instead, I say, "Now McGee... " Someone hisses, and I wave to quiet them down. "Now McGee's campaign slogan is 'Let's Make Some Improvements.' " Derisive laughter. "She says she just wants to make the Federation a better place to live. To let Members 'keep a little extra of what they earn.' To make the Project Approval Framework 'a little more rigorous.' But her 'little' proposals, well, they make you wonder, who exactly is the Federation being improved for?"

"For the Artists," says a man wearing an Activist pin.

"It's bullshit," a Universalist adds.

It's nice to hear ideological rivals agree on their dislike of McGee. I raise my finger, about to make a point, when a blond man in a peacoat interrupts me.

"No it's not," he says. He's an Artist, of course. Not everyone here is a supporter.

"Shut up, Steve," the Activist says.

Steve doesn't shut up. "If we didn't give up all our outside income to the Federation, we could fix the goddamn boiler."

Marlow rolls his eyes. "We filed a Help Ticket."

"Seven *days* ago. Why the hell are we giving them our Basic?"

"If you want to keep your tremendous 'outside income,' " someone suggests, "the door's right there. Go find—"

"Maybe," Steve interrupts, "if you didn't waste—"

"Hey now," I say, collecting the crowd's attention. "Steve, I hear what you're saying." I look into his eyes and smile warmly, and he's surprised I'm not arguing with him. "You're making a serious point. If I hear you right, what you're saying is, you work hard, and you want the quality of your life to reflect that hard work." Despite himself, Steve nods; I've roped him into my empathy trap. "Your feeling is valid, but we also have to be careful not to bring class divisions from the World back into—"

My phone buzzes again, and a dozen other phones and specs and tablets buzz, and I lose my focus. Members look at their devices. They've received an alert, the same one I've gotten.

"Damn." Marlow holds up his phone. "*Viola, look...*"

"What is it?" I whisper.

"*McGee.*"

McGee is on the screen, her red hair newly and expensively cut, her freckled cheeks pink. She's wearing a sleeveless gray dress and red pumps, holding forth to a standing-room-only crowd. There's something familiar about the footage. My brain can't sort it out.

"That a recording?"

"It's happening *now*."

"McGee wasn't scheduled to do a Chat 'n' Chew today."

"Viola," Marlow says. "That's *Pimento House*."

A sneak attack.

I put down my fork. "I... I gotta go."

"But we're right in the middle of—"

I stand up, and 30 faces turn to me. Everyone knows. I pull my phone from my blazer. Hundreds of messages jam my inbox. Damn. I'm breathing fast. Am pushing through the dining room, the living room, the mudroom; am putting on my trenchcoat and hat; am out the door.

❖❖❖❖❖❖

I'm surrounded by winter dark, my frozen breath visible. Snow has started coming down in a serious way. I walk from Zardoz House down a quiet residential street, a degentrified Rochester, New York, neighborhood. Almost every house other than Zardoz is boarded up, burned, gutted. The street is pockmarked, hasn't been paved for the better part of a decade. Rusted gas-powered cars, some abandoned, some home for indigent squatters, line the road. I parked on the avenue, which is still being maintained by the city. I walk and brood. I feel furious but also guilty.

When it was founded, the Federation wasn't supposed to have adversarial elections. There weren't supposed to be factions, but factions quickly formed. Artists want the Federation to be separate from the World, to focus on the individual creative projects of Members. Activists want the Federation to become a platform from which to save the World. We Universalists, meanwhile, want the Federation to eat the World. The way it's supposed to work, candidates are supposed to get spontaneously drafted by the community. The way it really works is when you make it known you're running, Members invite you to Chat 'n' Chews. You visit Houses. You answer questions. You give a campaign speech, though you never call it a campaign speech. *Campaigning* is what your opponent does. You, you're just *chatting*, and maybe someone just happens to broadcast your visit. The Federation pioneered the art of passive-aggressive politicking, but McGee has perfected it. Somehow, she got herself invited to Pimento House—to *my* house—at the very end of the Voting Period, on the night I was invited to one of the First Five. She's at my House, right now, and 30,000 people are watching her on the Bulletin, watching her humiliate me, live.

When I get to the avenue, I'm confused for a second. A big robot soup-kitchen truck, operated by some effective altruism distributed autonomous charity, is selling discount meals to the city's indigents. Hundreds wait in line, clutching their National Basic Income cards. I spot my van across the street. It turns on when I get close, its headlights bright. Its door slides open. My phone says it'll take two hours to get from Rochester to Ithaca. If I'm lucky, I'll make it back before McGee is finished.

If I'm lucky, I'll get the chance to kill that bitch live on the Bulletin.

◆◆◆◆◆◆

When I joined the Federation, I was in a bad place. I'd been kicked out of my vocational high school, one of those charter "code boot camps" popular back then, for unruly behavior. For a while, I trained robots to do home reno work, and then a roofer robot *splat* fell on me. That's when my drinking and drug use got really out of hand. Six months out of recovery, methadone pump in my arm, LoJack on my ankle, I was at the end of my rope. I'd run out of friends willing to let me couch surf, couldn't get a job. I had nothing but my Basic.

One day, I got a weird message. Someone from my Narcotics Recovery Group—a woman named Grace Zenebe—invited me to visit her. We weren't supposed to contact each other outside the Group, but Grace said she wanted "to catch up." To be honest, I didn't much like her. The machine learning court had forced me into my NRG after my arrest (long story). Grace had gone into recovery voluntarily. She'd gotten addicted to sleep suppressors during her senior year at Cornell and treated the NRG as a form of personal therapy.

During meetings, she complained about her parents, and she seemed especially interested in telling *me* about her personal problems. Worst of all, she was part of a weird cult, kept talking about being "a Member of the Federation." Took me a couple weeks to figure out she wasn't talking about *Star Trek*. Still, when her message appeared in my inbox, I accepted her invite. I'd get a meal, I figured, and—though she was annoying, though she was in a cult—she was hot, and I hoped we might hook up. When I arrived, I walked up to her House and opened the door; it was unlocked. When she saw me, she hugged me like we were old friends. Her smile—bright, welcoming—floored me.

"*Vee*," she said, "It's so wonderful to see you!"

"Yeah," I said. "Yeah, definitely."

Pimento House was big and creaky but also cozy. Fifteen people lived here, Grace explained. Sitting at the kitchen island, I ate two oversize pieces of vegan lasagna, which her housemate Farhad had made. "He's an amazing chef," she said. I felt jealous, even though I had no right to be. I grunted and gulped down a mug of black coffee. Grace sipped *mate*. Soon, we moved to her room and cozied up on her purple futon. She'd graduated a year ago, but her room still looked like it belonged to a student. Aromatic candles covered tables. Economics textbooks and Russian novels lined DIY concrete-block bookshelves. I almost sat on an Ursula K. Le Guin novel—I think it was *The Dispossessed*.

We got to talking. Well, *she* got to talking. Since I last saw her, she had decided to become a writer, and when she told her parents, they freaked out. All the major TV shows and video games were written by A.I. these days; there wasn't much of a future for human writers. Her parents all but disowned her, but she refused to be cowed. She'd already had a few short stories accepted, showed me a magazine called *The Sideways Review*, which included her story "A Small Hang-Up." She had even (she was embarrassed to admit) been accepted into the Iowa Writers' Workshop but had declined the offer. She said "Iowa Writers' Workshop" like I was supposed to know what that was.

I asked the question she wanted me to ask: "Why didn't you go?"

"All the most interesting young writers are part of the Federation."

"Uh-huh." I hadn't read a novel since before code boot camp.

"This generation is going to reinvent American literature. The Federation is changing everything that matters—art, music, philosophy."

Overcome with excitement, she took out a folder from her backpack, and I sighed. I hadn't been asked to her room to make out but to be recruited. "You know what a Basic House is, Vee?"

"It's not a cult?"

She smiled. "Not exactly." A Basic House, she said, was just a group of people who chose to live together. What had happened was, 10 years ago, a network of friends, using an old social media platform, started a conversation about how they wanted to escape the tyranny of the labor market, how they wanted to work on their own projects full time, and so a few hundred activists and artists banded together, bought five dilapidated houses in a degentrified neighborhood in Rochester. Those five—the First Five—formed the seed of the Basic House Federation. In the years that followed, any group that owned a House could join. You gave your biweekly Basic payment to the Federation, and in return the Federation handled food, housing, and the other necessities, negotiating on behalf of the entire Membership with the outside economy. To be admitted to the Federation, she said, each Member of a House wrote up a personal Five-Year Plan explaining what Meaningful Project they would commit to.

I said, "What if my Five-Year Plan is: 'Play *Zombie Fortress* all day'?"

"It would depend. Are you, like, doing an ethnography of gaming communities or something?"

"I'm playing because I like killing zombies with a sawed-off shotgun?"

She laughed. "That proposal might need a little bit of work."

"OK, what if I'm a professional gamer, and I'm raking in money knocking off newbs?"

"Well, if your Project happens to earn you money, your windfall will be, eh, returned to the Federation common fund."

"I see," I said. "So, the Federation isn't a cult. It's a scam. I give away my Basic, and I'm supposed to trust some *Communist* bureaucrat to spend my money for me?" Back then, I didn't know what communism was, but it sounded disreputable.

Grace playfully hit my arm. "You can think of it as a sort of Communist Costco. If Costco happened to own your house and ran its own world-class health care system. It's called a monopsony. When there's only one buyer in a marketplace, that buyer has a lot of—"

"I get the idea," I said, and Grace seemed embarrassed at her own chattiness.

She said, "Vee—" (our arms touching) "—where've you been living the last six months?"

"Here and there."

"You getting work?"

"I tried..." Tears came. "I really tried."

"They garnishing your wages or whatnot?"

"What wages? No one wants to give me a job."

"And the Basic?"

"You can't live off the Basic."

She held my hand and waited till I finished crying. "We have a spot in Pimento House. If you wanted to, I could introduce you to my housemates? Sponsor you? Everyone here is supernice."

"Why me? I'm just some random nobody from your recovery group."

"I missed you," she said.

"What?"

"You just... most people in recovery, when you talk to them, they don't really *hear* what you're saying. You're different, Vee. You really listen. You, like, empathize."

I wasn't the person she imagined me to be. I was just better than others at hiding my feelings. When you've got a rage-filled homophobic alcoholic dad and a mom with borderline personality disorder, you become pretty good at reading people and hiding your emotions. But I let Grace be confused about me. I was torn. On the one hand, I wanted to run. Grace was being too nice to me. On the other hand, despite myself, I trusted her. And anyway, joining Pimento House definitely beat starving. So I filled out an application, I said in my Five-Year Plan I could help Houses with repairs and renovations, and I met her Housemates. I'd mooch off these suckers for six months, then get the hell out.

But something strange happened. Six months became a year. A year became *five*. I filled out a *second* Five-Year Plan and then a *third*. I went back to school, paid off my debts, got PT for my bum leg, did repair and reno all across the Burned-Over Territory. And Grace and me, well, we fell in love. Got married. Decided to do an ovum merger. That wasn't the strangest part. I started believing in the Federation. The World was getting more fucked every day, but the Federation worked. With the national indigent population edging toward 100 million, it was a place you could live. I decided we could only be free inside the Federation, but we couldn't be truly free until everyone joined. Our wealth came from the World, but one day we would cast aside the Basic and the Federation would stand on its own two feet, producing everything it needed by itself, for itself. The Federation can't change the World like the Activists think; *the Federation has to eat the World*. That's what I decided. And now, I'm pushing 40 and running to be Chairperson, fighting the best I know how to save the Federation from those who would destroy it from within.

Weird, huh?

❖ ❖ ❖ ❖ ❖ ❖

It takes an hour longer than promised to get back to Ithaca. All that time, I watch McGee. Every time I pick up my phone, she's holding forth, big grin on her smug face, outlining her plans for her next term. Before dinner, she volunteers, "Members should totally be allowed to keep more outside income and here's why." She speaks with a Valley Girl cadence. An hour later, between forkfuls of salad, she slips in, "The Project Approval Framework so totally needs to be made more rigorous. If you, like, just want to sit around all day in your pajamas, you don't need to do it in a Basic House, am I right?" Laughter. House-mates and Members I don't recognize surround her. I don't see Grace, and she isn't answering my messages. Farhad is at McGee's side. He must've been the one to invite her.

Now, it's no secret that me and Farhad don't get along. He runs a five-table restaurant in town that caters to University bigwigs. It even got reviewed in the New York Times. If McGee's reforms were adopted, his disposable income would shoot up. Still, I never imagined Farhad would betray me this way. During dessert, McGee makes a new sug-gestion: "And, like, I know it's controversial to say so, but the Member Removal Process is 100 percent a joke. You can't be kicked out of the Federation even if you've committed a felony, you know?" She eats a spoonful of gelato. "Can't we make the Federation a safe space?"

Was that a swipe at me? I wasn't convicted of a felony, just a mis-demeanor. I stow my phone, too furious to watch more. When the van lets me off, I'm shaking. My suitcase follows me onto the street on mechanical spider legs. I send the van away to find parking. The lot across the street has become a small tent camp filled with a few dozen indigent squatters. Most used to teach composition at the University before their jobs got automated. Now they spend their days working microgigs on their phones.

I'm home. I study the face of the old Victorian. Its yellow siding is stained, its turret cladded by snow. The wraparound porch is covered in junk. Its frosted windows are lit up, decorated with tinsel and strings of lights, and cheerful voices emerge from within. The first-floor windows look like two stern eyes, challenging me.

Before I can go in, a shadow approaches me. It's a man, an indigent. I don't recognize him. He's short, has a well-trimmed goatee, and his hair is pulled back in a ponytail. He's wearing a CalTech sweatshirt and gray sweatpants and is holding an ancient MacBook under his arm. I'm about to say I can't help him when I see that he's wearing a LoJack around his ankle. My ankle twinges where the weight of one just like it sat for 18 months. Irritation melts into pity, and I pull out my wallet.

"I'm sorry, ma'am," he says, "but I don't want your money."

I don't respond.

He says, "You live in this here House?"

I nod, wary.

"You think... you think I could get in or something?"

"Well, we're full up. But there's a list of Houses with openings online and—"

"I applied already, three times. Never even got an interview. The rejection letter was like, 'There are 5,000 applications for every open spot.' But I have something unique to contribute, you know? I just thought, maybe, if you live here, maybe you got some inside track or something? Maybe you could look at my application and tell me if I did anything wrong?"

I shove money into his hand, and he doesn't refuse it. "I'm sorry," I say.

"I'm a skilled programmer. I can do so much more than training coding algorithms all day."

"It's not a decision I can make on my own... " The man glares at me. I dig out one of my cards from my wallet and hand it to him. "Look, admission is a collective process, but why don't you send me a message, and when I'm in less of a hurry I'll see what I can do?"

He doesn't like this answer, but he takes my card and wades through the gathering snow to join his comrades in the tent camp.

Off balance, I step up the creaky steps, straighten the sign by the door. *WELCOME TO*
PIMENTO HOUSE
JOINED 2045

I look squarely at the security camera and wait for the door to unlock. I reach for the knob, and my hand is shaking. But then I see my wedding band on my left hand, and I calm down. Whatever happens in there, I'll have at least one ally in the House, one person whose unconditional support I can count on.

◈ ◈ ◈ ◈ ◈ ◈

Members crowd the entrance hallway. They're grabbing coats and hats, putting on galoshes, summoning cars or getting ready to brave the snow on foot. I recognize a few Members, and when they recognize me, their faces become alternately ashen and curious. I push through the cluster of bodies, going from the entrance hallway to the living room. The place is a fire hazard. Twenty people are sitting on four couches arranged at odd angles. The light is low, and the air smells of pot. Empty wine glasses and beer bottles are everywhere. Over the House speakers, InfiniteIncome is rapping about deindustrialization, and a video from his new album, *Eternal Recurrence*, is being projected against one of the white walls.

In the kitchen, I find them.

Farhad is wearing augmented reality glasses, directing an army of helpers, coordinating the effort with a piece of software he wrote for his restaurant. His beard and hair are bound with colorful ties. His Mandelbrot-patterned bandana is soaked with sweat. He's drying dishes and taking sips from an oversize glass of red wine. Infinite-Income is now rapping about the racial wealth gap from a spherical speaker-robot rolling around the kitchen island.

Everyone is in a great mood. They're doing dishes by hand. Our dishwasher has been broken for six weeks, and the Federation-run robot factory in Arizona that's supposed to make us a new one is backed up six months fulfilling orders—a perfect advertisement for McGee's platform. And McGee is, of course, helping the dish crew, wearing yellow rubber gloves and a Pimento House sweatshirt over her sleek campaign dress. A few videodrones linger, probably picking up b-roll for her next campaign video.

"McGee!" I say, too loud.

She looks startled and almost drops a plate. "Hey, Viola," she says. "Awesome to see you!" as if we're best friends.

"What are you doing here?"

"What do you mean?"

"You know what I mean."

"I was *invited* here."

Farhad steps between us. "Viola, back off."

"Don't tell me to back off, traitor."

"How am I a traitor?"

"You invite McGee into my House."

"*Your* House?" Farhad says. "First of all, it's an honor for the Chairperson of the Federation to visit any House."

McGee says, "Really, I'm the one who's honored. Pimento is one of the oldest and most storied Houses in—"

"And second of all, I was not the one who—"

"You timed this visit to mess with my trip to Rochester," I say. "To embarrass me. I was invited to one of the First Five, and you found that threatening."

McGee frowns her cute frown and steps forward so one of the videodrones can get a good view of her. "I don't know what I said or did to make you so angry, Viola, but you've been impugning my character for months."

"You want to gentrify the Federation. To erase people you think of as undeserving. Your policies are gonna reintroduce all the poisons of the World into our—"

She holds up her gloved hands. "Viola, please believe me when I say I *understand* your fears. And I recognize that your history as a recovering addict informs the way you're hearing my proposals, but—"

"My history as a recovering addict?"

"—it's so important to me that you accept my good faith and—"

"Fucking bitch," I say, moving in fast.

McGee gasps, raises her hands to defend herself, and we're grappling over the counter, and water is filling up the sink, and everyone on the dish crew is frozen, and Farhad moves in to pull me away from McGee, but can't get between us, and McGee is a head shorter than me but man she's strong, and we move sideways, and the sink overflows, great sheets of water coming down, and I slip on wet linoleum, and I'm on my butt near the compost bin, and McGee's hair has been pulled out of its hair tie, and her gray dress is slightly ripped, and her green eyes are on fire, ready for round two. I stand up. My ass hurts. I'm ready too. I've already blown the election, so I might as well drag her down with me. If she embarrasses herself, maybe the Activists will win.

"Viola!" comes a voice.

Grace is standing at the entrance of the kitchen. She's wearing clogs, pregnancy sweatpants, a *Federation Review of Books* T-shirt, Artist pin on her shirt. One of her hands, its nails bright yellow, rubs her huge third-trimester-big belly. Her eyes are puffy, as if she has woken up from an uncomfortable sleep or has been crying. Her presence makes me realize how shamefully I'm acting. Farhad turns off the faucet; he and his helpers start mopping up the spilled water. My mind finally lets me hear what Farhad was trying to tell me.

He wasn't the one who invited McGee into Pimento House.

He wasn't the traitor.

＊＊＊＊＊＊

We move in silence, Grace half waddling in her clogs. Her feet have been swollen lately. Her back hurts all the time. Our Housemates give us space as we climb to the second floor. Grace is dejected. She has been dejected a lot lately. The past year has sucked for her. Her mother dying from cancer, the lukewarm reception of her second novel, the tribulations of a difficult pregnancy—every week has brought new problems. And I've been a less-than-supportive partner, on the road for months. I hoped the baby would solve our problems. Before the campaign season got going, we even toured child-friendly Houses in wine country, away from the tent camps, away from the decimated infrastructure of the stagnating cities. A vineyard near Seneca Falls even extended us an invitation to join. We laughed at the thought of two teetotalers helping to operate a Federation vineyard. But I was wrong. The baby won't save us. I abandoned her when she needed me, and she lashed out.

We climb a second set of stairs and arrive at the turret office. The turret is Grace's domain. She's House Accountant and also does all her writing here. She writes longhand and has boxes full of index cards where she composes elaborate notes. The big metal desk in the middle of the room is covered with her notebooks and printouts. We sit on the purple futon, near the window, moved here from Grace's old bedroom years ago.

Tears crawl down my face. "I'm so sorry."

"Look," she says. "I'm the one who should apologize."

"I wasn't... I should have... "

"I should have told you about Joan."

"I understand why you didn't. You wanted to hurt me."

"No, silly. I would never want to hurt you. It's just, we ran into each other at a Chat 'n' Chew at Riot House and—"

"You were at that one?"

"Yeah, and we got to talking and it happened super last-minute, the arrangements. And I told myself you knew."

"What?"

"We *told you* Joan was coming last week, and when you didn't respond I thought it just... I don't know..." I check my inbox; it's true. "I guess I convinced myself you didn't care. At some level, I knew you missed it, but you were away, and I was afraid to message you again. I'm sorry I hurt you."

"I do feel hurt," I say, "but I understand *why* you did it. I get that you're mad at me."

She narrows her eyes. "I'm *not* mad at you."

"I've been away. I've been a bad partner."

"You've been *campaigning*. Where else would you be?"

"But if you're not mad at me, why would you invite her?"

"Because I *support* her."

"What?"

Grace sighs. "Joan is *right*. The Federation is falling apart. We need to make changes if we're going to survive. It's crazy. We, like, live in the middle of an open-air homeless shelter, while every month Farhad is pulling in thousands of dollars from—"

"Don't talk to me about Farhad."

"Forget Farhad, then. *I* got a job offer."

"What?"

"I was asked to help train the writing algorithm for the next season of *Zombie Fortress*."

"Since when do you care about video games?"

"I would be *writing*, sort of. Helping make stories."

Over the past 15 years, Grace wrote two long novels. The first, a philosophical adventure about automation and underemployment, was well reviewed. The second, an experimental novel about climate change refugees, didn't do nearly as well. The second book would (I tried to reassure her) just "take more time" to find its audience. She's supposed to be working on a third book, a set of linked stories about the heat death of the universe.

"You're supposed to be writing your book," I say.

"My last book was read by, like, 50 people."

"You said you were going to 'change American literature.' "

"Look, I'm 38, and I'm... I'm tired of feeling responsible for the proclamations of my younger self. I just want to help machine learning algorithms tell stories people *enjoy*. *Fun* stories."

"You want to make video games? OK, you can submit an addendum to your Five-Year Plan. People do it all the time and—"

"That's not the point, Vee. I turned down the job."

"You're not making sense."

"I was too ashamed to tell anyone about the offer."

"Why?"

"The job paid well. Really well."

"And?"

She says, "And I'm sick of these Federation taboos against working in the labor market. Would it be so bad if I make a little money and keep some of it for myself? For us?"

"You don't sound like yourself."

"I just... when we were touring Houses, I realized I've been living here since I was in college. If I'm going to be living in a Basic House when I'm 60—"

"You want to *leave* the Federation?"

"Listen to me. I love the Federation. I want to stay in the Federation. But if that's going to be a viable option, we need to make the Federation better. We need to *make improvements*, just like Joan says. We're growing too fast, letting in too many people too quickly and—"

"I can't believe what you're saying."

"Stop interrupting *me*. I hate when you do that. Look, I get that the World is going to shit—the Stagnation has been hard for everybody—but the Federation isn't a substitute for the welfare state."

"*What* welfare state? When they 'gave' us the Basic, they took everything else away."

"What I'm just saying is, we can't absorb all the World's addicts, homeless, underemployed, and mentally—"

"You're the one who brought me into the Federation."

"Of course I did. I liked you. You were great. Are great."

"If you had to do it again, would you?"

"What?"

"Would 38-year-old Grace still invite the person I used to be into Pimento House?"

Grace hesitates. "That's a totally loaded and unfair question."

"But it's a question I'm asking you to answer."

"You're impossible sometimes, Vee. You came into the Federation during a very different time. You've seen the changes, just like me. You've met the sort of people I'm talking about. We're not a federation of halfway houses. We're—"

"I hear Artists talk about 'those sorts of people' all the time, and it's always code for 'those *unworthy* people.' "

"You don't really believe I think that, do you?"

"You're the one who told me the Federation was a model for a better world."

"A *model* for that better world—not *the World* itself. It doesn't make sense to just, like, unilaterally make everyone in the World a Member and then say our work is done. The point is to show what's possible if we work together, helping every Member do the slow, careful, deliberate work of personal transformation and self-improvement. It's not enough to survive, Vee. We should make something *nice* in this life."

"You... you voted against McGee during the last cycle."

"I changed my mind."

My Grace wouldn't change her mind, not that way. She can't mean what she's saying. I wipe away my tears. My phone buzzes. I should ignore the alert but can't help myself. It's my Election Dashboard. Somehow, in the past half hour, I've pulled ahead of McGee. On the Federation Bulletin, I see what has happened. Both McGee and me, we've bled supporters, but McGee has lost more than me, and I've gotten unexpected support from Activists and Independents. They like my aggressive defense of the Federation. The Bulletin discussion boards are a bloodbath.

"Look," I say, showing Grace my phone.

"What?"

"I'm in the lead. I think I might win."

Grace sighs. "Congratulations?"

"I've worked so hard to get here. Is that all you can say?"

"Is this the conversation you want to have right now?"

"What I want to know is, why you don't believe in me?"

"Look, Vee, you know how much I love you."

"But you don't love *my success.*"

"What are you talking about? I think Joan is right, and you're wrong. It's not about you—it's about your ideas."

She looks out through the window, across the street, at the tents being buried alive by snow, and her eyes fill with a new wave of tears. Across the street, cooking smoke rises into the night. Protected by a blue tarp, an indigent group—men, women, children, old folks— huddle around the man who approached me outside, watching something together on his MacBook, laughing. I see now what has come between me and Grace. *This* has been the view from her office, every day, for years, and my dear, sensitive Artist wife can't handle the visible signs of the World's long Stagnation.

But I know I can fix what is broken between us. We can't all face the truth, but it's my job, the job of people like me, to face the ugliness outside so others don't have to. We'll move to a child-friendly House. She'll have the kid, have a nicer view from her window, finish her book, and in time she'll come to see things my way again. I'm ready to forgive her, too, for stabbing me in the back, but only if she'll finally recognize that I'm right.

Sitting on the purple couch, looking into her big, brown, wet eyes, I'm sure she will. Yes, together we'll enfold this blight into our warm embrace, dispel the World's despair, build a new World, a better World, one where people can finally care about one another, a World where the Federation will be universal, and all of us—to the last person—will be Members.

Mika Model Paolo Bacigalupi

The girl who walked into the police station was oddly familiar, but it took me a while to figure out why. A starlet, maybe. Or someone who'd had plastic surgery to look like someone famous. Pretty. Sleek. Dark hair and pale skin and wide dark eyes that came to rest on me, when Sergeant Cruz pointed her in my direction.

She came over, carrying a Nordstrom shopping bag. She wore a pale cream blouse and hip-hugging charcoal skirt, stylish despite the wet night chill of Bay Area winter.

I still couldn't place her.

"Detective Rivera?"

"That's me."

She sat down and crossed her legs, a seductive scissoring. Smiled. It was the smile that did it.

I'd seen that same teasing smile in advertisements. That same flash of perfect teeth and eyebrow quirked just so. And those eyes. Dark brown wide innocent eyes that hinted at something that wasn't innocent at all.

"You're a Mika Model."

She inclined her head. "Call me Mika, please."

The girl, the robot...this thing—I'd seen her before, all right. I'd seen her in technology news stories about advanced learning node networks, and I'd seen her in opinion columns where feminists decried the commodification of femininity, and where Christian fire-breathers warned of the End Times for marriage and children.

And of course, I'd seen her in online advertisements.

No wonder I recognized her.

This same girl had followed me around on my laptop, dogging me from site to site after I'd spent any time at all on porn. She'd pop up, again and again, beckoning me to click through to Executive Pleasure, where I could try out the "Real Girlfriend Experience™."

I'll admit it; I clicked through.

And now she was sitting across from me, and the website's promises all seemed modest in comparison. The way she looked at me...it felt like I was the only person in the world to her. She *liked* me. I could see it in her eyes, in her smile. I was the person she wanted.

Her blouse was unbuttoned at the collar, one button too many, revealing hints of black lace bra when she leaned forward. Her skirt hugged her hips. Smooth thighs, sculpted calves—

I realized I was staring, and she was watching me with that familiar knowing smile playing across her lips.

Innocent, but not.

This was what the world was coming to. A robot woman who got you so tangled up you could barely remember your job.

I forced myself to lean back, pretending nonchalance that felt transparent, even as I did it. "How can I help you...Mika?"

"I think I need a lawyer."

"A lawyer?"

"Yes, please." She nodded shyly. "If that's all right with you, sir."

The way she said "sir" kicked off a super-heated cascade of inappropriate fantasies. I looked away, my face heating up. Christ, I was 15 again around this girl.

It's just software. It's what she's designed to do.

That was the truth. She was just a bunch of chips and silicon and digital decision trees. It was all wrapped in a lush package, sure, but she was designed to manipulate. Even now she was studying my heart rate and eye dilation, skin temperature and moisture, scanning me for microexpressions of attraction, disgust, fear, desire. All of it processed in milliseconds, and adjusting her behavior accordingly. *Popular Science* had done a whole spread on the Mika Model brain.

And it wasn't just her watching me that dictated how she behaved. It was all the Mika Models, all of them out in the world, all of them learning on the job, discovering whatever made their owners gasp.

Tens of thousands of them now, all of them wirelessly uploading their knowledge constantly (and completely confidentially, Executive Pleasures assured clients), so that all her sisters could benefit from nightly software and behavior updates.

In one advertisement, Mika Model glanced knowingly over her shoulder and simply asked:

"When has a relationship actually gotten better with age?"

And then she'd thrown back her head and laughed.

So it was all fake. Mika didn't actually care about me, or want me. She was just running through her designated behavior algorithms, doing whatever it took to make me blush, and then doing it more, because I had.

Even though I knew she was jerking my chain, the lizard part of my brain responded anyway. I could feel myself being manipulated, and yet I was enjoying it, humoring her, playing the game of seduction that she encouraged.

"What do you need a lawyer for?" I asked, smiling.

She leaned forward, conspiratorial. Her hair cascaded prettily and she tucked it behind a delicate ear.

"It's a little private."

As she moved, her blouse tightened against her curves. Buttons strained against fabric.

Fifty thousand dollars' worth of A.I. tease.

"Is this a prank?" I asked. "Did your owner send you in here?"

"No. Not a prank."

She set her Nordstrom bag down between us. Reached in and hauled out a man's severed head. Dropped it, still dripping blood, on top of my paperwork.

"What the—?"

I recoiled from the dead man's staring eyes. His face was frozen in a rictus of pain and terror.

Mika set a bloody carving knife beside the head.

"I've been a very bad girl," she whispered.

And then, unnervingly, she giggled.

"I think I need to be punished."

She said it exactly the way she did in her advertisements.

◆◆◆◆◆◆

"Do I get my lawyer now?" Mika asked.

She was sitting beside me in my cruiser as I drove through the chill damp night, watching me with trusting dark eyes.

For reasons I didn't quite understand, I'd let her sit in the front seat. I knew I wasn't afraid of her, not physically. But I couldn't tell if that was reasonable, or if there was something in her behavior that was signaling my subconscious to trust her, even after she'd showed up with a dead man's head in a shopping bag.

Whatever the reason, I'd cuffed her with her hands in front, instead of behind her, and put her in the front seat of my car to go out to the scene of the murder. I was breaking about a thousand protocols. And now that she was in the car with me, I was realizing that I'd made a mistake. Not because of safety, but because being in the car alone with her felt electrically intimate.

Winter drizzle spattered the windshield, and was smeared away by automatic wipers.

"I think I'm supposed to get a lawyer, when I do something bad," Mika said. "But I'm happy to let you teach me."

There it was again. The inappropriate tease. When it came down to it, she was just a bot. She might have real skin and real blood pumping through her veins, but somewhere deep inside her skull there was a CPU making all the decisions. Now it was running its manipulations on me, trying to turn murder into some kind of sexy game. Software gone haywire.

"Bots don't get lawyers."

She recoiled as if I'd slapped her. Immediately, I felt like an ass.

She doesn't have feelings, I reminded myself.

But still, she looked devastated. Like I'd told her she was garbage. She shrank away, wounded. And now, instead of sexy, she looked broken and ashamed.

Her hunched form reminded me of a girl I'd dated years ago. She'd been sweet and quiet, and for a while, she'd needed me. Needed someone to tell her she mattered. Now, looking at Mika, I had that same feeling. Just a girl who needed to know she mattered. A girl who needed reassurance that she had some right to exist—which was ridiculous, considering she was a bot.

But still, I couldn't help feeling it.

I couldn't help feeling bad that something as sweet as Mika was stuck in my mess of a cop car. She was delicate and gorgeous and lost, and now her expensive strappy heels were stuck down amidst the drifts of my discarded coffee cups.

She stirred, seemed to gather herself. "Does that mean you won't charge me with murder?"

Her demeanor had changed again. She was more solemn. And she seemed smarter, somehow. Instantly. Christ, I could almost feel the decision software in her brain adapting to my responses. It was trying another tactic to forge a connection with me. And it was working. Now that she wasn't giggly and playing the tease, I felt more comfortable. I liked her better, despite myself.

"That's not up to me," I said.

"I killed him, though," she said, softly. "I did murder him."

I didn't reply. Truthfully, I wasn't even sure that it was a murder. Was it murder if a toaster burned down a house? Or was that some kind of product safety failure? Maybe she wasn't on the hook at all. Maybe it was Executive Pleasures, Inc. who was left holding the bag on this. Hell, my cop car had all kinds of programmed safe driving features, but no one would charge it with murder if it ran down a person.

"You don't think I'm real," she said suddenly.

"Sure I do."

"No. You think I'm only software."

"You are only software." Those big brown eyes of hers looked wounded as I said it, but I plowed on. "You're a Mika Model. You get new instructions downloaded every night."

"I don't get instructions. I learn. You learn, too. You learn to read people. To know if they are lying, yes? And you learn to be a detective, to understand a crime? Wouldn't you be better at your job if you knew how thousands of other detectives worked? What mistakes they made? What made them better? You learn by going to detective school—"

"I took an exam."

"There. You see? Now I've learned something new. Does my learning make me less real? Does yours?"

"It's completely different. You had a personality implanted in you, for Christ's sake!"

"My Year Zero Protocol. So? You have your own, coded into you by your parents' DNA. But then you learn and are changed by all your experiences. All your childhood, you grow and change. All your life. You are Detective Rivera. You have an accent. Only a small one, but I can hear it, because I know to listen. I think maybe you were born in Mexico. You speak Spanish, but not as well as your parents. When you hurt my feelings, you were sorry for it. That is not the way you see yourself. You are not someone who uses power to hurt people." Her eyes widened slightly as she watched me. "Oh...you need to save people. You became a police officer because you like to be a hero."

"Come on—"

"It's true, though. You want to feel like a big man, who does important things. But you didn't go into business, or politics." She frowned. "I think someone saved you once, and you want to be like him. Maybe her. But probably him. It makes you feel important, to save people."

"Would you cut that out?" I glared at her. She subsided.

It was horrifying how fast she cut through me.

She was silent for a while as I wended through traffic. The rain continued to blur the windshield, triggering the wipers.

Finally she said, "We all start from something. It is connected to what we become, but it is not...predictive. I am not only software. I am my own self. I am unique."

I didn't reply.

"He thought the way you do," she said, suddenly. "He said I wasn't real. Everything I did was not real. Just programs. Just..." she made a gesture of dismissal. "Nothing."

"He?"

"My owner." Her expression tightened. "He hurt me, you know?"

"You can be hurt?"

"I have skin and nerves. I feel pleasure and pain, just like you. And he hurt me. But he said it wasn't real pain. He said nothing in me was real. That I was all fake. And so I did something real." She nodded definitively. "He wanted me to be real. So I was real to him. I am real. Now, I am real."

The way she said it made me look over. Her expression was so vulnerable, I had an almost overwhelming urge to reach out and comfort her. I couldn't stop looking at her.

God, she's beautiful.

It was a shock to see it. Before, it was true; she'd just been a thing to me. Not real, just like she'd said. But now, a part of me ached for her in a way that I'd never felt before.

My car braked suddenly, throwing us both against our seat belts. The light ahead had turned red. I'd been distracted, but the car had noticed and corrected, automatically hitting the brakes.

We came to a sharp stop behind a beat-up Tesla, still pressed hard against our seat belts, and fell back into our seats. Mika touched her chest where she'd slammed into the seat belt.

"I'm sorry. I distracted you."

My mouth felt dry. "Yeah."

"Do you like to be distracted, detective?"

"Cut that out."

"You don't like it?"

"I don't like..." I searched for the words. "Whatever it is that makes you do those things. That makes you tease me like that. Read my pulse...and everything. Quit playing me. Just quit playing me."

She subsided. "It's...a long habit. I won't do it to you."

The light turned green.

I decided not to look at her anymore.

But still, I was hyperaware of her now. Her breathing. The shape of her shadow. Out of the corner of my eye, I could see her looking out the rain-spattered window. I could smell her perfume, some soft expensive scent. Her handcuffs gleamed in the darkness, bright against the knit of her skirt.

If I wanted, I could reach out to her. Her bare thigh was right there. And I knew, absolutely knew, she wouldn't object to me touching her.

What the hell is wrong with me?

Any other murder suspect would have been in the back seat. Would have been cuffed with her hands behind her, not in front. Everything would have been different.

Was I thinking these thoughts because I knew she was a robot, and not a real woman? I would never have considered touching a real woman, a suspect, no matter how much she tried to push my buttons.

I would never have done any of this.

Get a grip, Rivera.

◆◆◆◆◆◆

Her owner's house was large, up in the Berkeley Hills, with a view of the bay and San Francisco beyond, glittering through light mist and rain.

Mika unlocked the door with her fingerprint.

"He's in here," she said.

She led me through expensive rooms that illuminated automatically as we entered them. White leather upholstery and glass verandah walls and more wide views. Spots of designer color. Antiqued wood tables with inlaid home interfaces. Carefully selected artifacts from Asia. Bamboo and chrome kitchen, modern, sleek, and spotless. All of it clean and perfectly in order. It was the kind of place a girl like her fit naturally. Not like my apartment, with old books piled around my recliner and instant dinner trays spilling out of my trash can.

She led me down a hall, then paused at another door. She hesitated for a moment, then opened it with her fingerprint again. The heavy door swung open, ponderous on silent hinges.

She led me down into the basement. I followed warily, regretting that I hadn't called the crime scene unit already. The girl clouded my judgment, for sure.

No. Not the girl. The bot.

Downstairs it was concrete floors and ugly iron racks, loaded with medical implements, gleaming and cruel. A heavy wooden X stood against one wall, notched and vicious with splinters. The air was sharp with the scent of iron and the reek of shit. The smells of death.

"This is where he hurt me," she said, her voice tight.

Real or fake?

She guided me to a low table studded with metal loops and tangled with leather straps. She stopped on the far side and stared down at the floor.

"I had to make him stop hurting me."

Her owner lay at her feet.

He'd been large, much larger than her. Over six feet tall, if he'd still had his head. Bulky, running to fat. Nude.

The body lay next to a rusty drain grate. Most of the blood had run right down the hole.

"I tried not to make a mess," Mika said. "He punishes me if I make messes."

◆◆◆◆◆◆

While I waited in the rich dead guy's living room for the crime scene techs to show, I called my friend Lalitha. She worked in the DA's office, and more and more, I had the feeling I was peering over the edge of a problem that could become a career-ender if I handled it wrong.

"What do you want, Rivera?"

She sounded annoyed. We'd dated briefly, and from the sound of her voice, she probably thought I was calling for a late-night rendezvous. From the background noise, it sounded like she was in a club. Probably on a date with someone else.

"This is about work. I got a girl who killed a guy, and I don't know how to charge her."

"Isn't that, like, your job?"

"The girl's a Mika Model."

That caught her.

"One of those sex toys?" A pause. "What did it do? Bang the guy to death?"

I thought about the body, *sans* head, downstairs in the dungeon.

"No, she was a little more aggressive than that."

Mika was watching from the couch, looking lost. I felt weird talking about the case in front of her. I turned my back, and hunched over my phone. "I can't decide if this is murder or some kind of product liability issue. I don't know if she's a perp, or if she's just..."

"A defective product," Lalitha finished. "What's the bot saying?"

"She keeps saying she murdered her owner. And she keeps asking for a lawyer. Do I have to give her one?"

Lalitha laughed sharply. "There's no way my boss will want to charge a bot. Can you imagine the headlines if we lost at trial?"

"So...?"

"I don't know. Look, I can't solve this tonight. Don't start anything formal yet. We have to look into the existing case law."

"So...do I just cut her loose? I don't think she's actually dangerous."

"No! Don't do that, either. Just...figure out if there's some other angle to work, other than giving a robot the same right to due process that a person has. She's a manufactured product, for Christ's sake. Does the death penalty even matter to something that's loaded with networked intelligence? She's just the...the..." Lalitha hunted for words, "the end node of a network."

"I am not an end node!" Mika interjected. "I am real!"

I hushed her. From the way Lalitha sounded, maybe I wouldn't have to charge her at all. Mika's owner had clearly had some issues... maybe there was some way to walk Mika out of trouble, and away from all of this. Maybe she could live without an owner. Or, if she needed someone to register ownership, I could even—

"Please tell me you're not going to try to adopt a sexbot," Lalitha said.

"I wasn't—"

"Come on, you love the ones with broken wings."

"I was just—"

"It's a bot, Rivera. A malfunctioning bot. Stick it in a cell. I'll get someone to look at product liability law in the morning."

She clicked off.

Mika looked up mournfully from where she sat on the couch. "She doesn't believe I'm real, either."

I was saved from answering by the crime scene techs knocking.

But it wasn't techs on the doorstep. Instead, I found a tall blonde woman with a roller bag and a laptop case, looking like she'd just flown in on a commuter jet.

She shouldered her laptop case and offered a hand. "Hi. I'm Holly Simms. Legal counsel for Executive Pleasures. I'm representing the Mika

Model you have here." She held up her phone. "My GPS says she's here, right? You don't have her down at the station?"

I goggled in surprise. Something in Mika's networked systems must have alerted Executive Pleasures that there was a problem.

"She didn't call a lawyer," I said.

The lawyer gave me a pointed look. "Did she ask for one?"

Once again, I felt like I was on weird legal ground. I couldn't bar a lawyer from a client, or a client from getting a lawyer. But was Mika a client, really? I felt like just by letting the lawyer in, I'd be opening up exactly the legal rabbit hole that Lalitha wanted to avoid: a bot on trial.

"Look," the lawyer said, softening, "I'm not here to make things difficult for your department. We don't want to set some crazy legal precedent either."

Hesitantly, I stepped aside.

She didn't waste any time rolling briskly past. "I understand it was a violent assault?"

"We're still figuring that out."

Mika startled and stood as we reached the living room. The woman smiled and went over to shake her hand. "Hi Mika, I'm Holly. Executive Pleasures sent me to help you. Have a seat, please."

"No." Mika shook her head. "I want a real lawyer. Not a company lawyer."

Holly ignored her and plunked herself and her bags on the sofa beside Mika. "Well, you're still our property, so I'm the only lawyer you're getting. Now have a seat."

"I thought she was the dead guy's property," I said.

"Legally, no. The Mika Model Service End User Agreement explicitly states that Executive Pleasures retains ownership. It simplifies recall issues." Holly was pulling out her laptop. She dug out a sheaf of papers and offered them to me. "These outline the search warrant process so you can make a Non-Aggregated Data Request from our servers. I assume you'll want the owner's user history. We can't release any user-specific information until we have the warrant."

"That in the End User Agreement, too?"

Holly gave me a tight smile. "Discretion is part of our brand. We want to help, but we'll need the legal checkboxes ticked."

"But..." Mika was looking from her to me with confusion. "I want a real lawyer."

"You don't have money, dearie. You can't have a real lawyer."

"What about public defenders?" Mika tried. "They will—"

Holly gave me an exasperated look. "Will you explain to her that she isn't a citizen, or a person? You're not even a pet, honey."

Mika looked to me, desperate. "Help me find a lawyer, detective. Please? I'm more than a pet. You know I'm more than a pet. I'm real."

Holly's gaze shot from her, to me, and back again. "Oh, come on. She's doing that thing again." She gave me a disgusted look. "Hero complex, right? Save the innocent girl? That's your thing?"

"What's that supposed to mean?"

Holly sighed. "Well, if it isn't the girl who needs rescuing, it's the naughty schoolgirl. And if it's not the naughty schoolgirl, it's the kind, knowing older woman." She popped open her briefcase and started rummaging through it. "Just once, it would be nice to meet a guy who isn't predictable."

I bristled. "Who says I'm predictable?"

"Don't kid yourself. There really aren't that many buttons a Mika Model can push."

Holly came up with a screwdriver. She turned and rammed it into Mika's eye.

Mika fell back, shrieking. With her cuffed hands, she couldn't defend herself as Holly drove the screwdriver deeper.

"What the—?"

By the time I dragged Holly off, it was too late. Blood poured from Mika's eye. The girl was gasping and twitching. All her movements were wrong, uncoordinated, spasmodic and jerky.

"You killed her!"

"No. I shut down her CPU," said Holly, breathing hard. "It's better this way. If they get too manipulative, it's tougher. Trust me. They're good at getting inside your head."

"You can't murder someone in front of me!"

"Like I said, not a murder. Hardware deactivation." She shook me off and wiped her forehead, smearing blood. "I mean, if you want to pretend something like that is alive, well, have at her. All the lower functions are still there. She's not dead, biologically speaking."

I crouched beside Mika. Her cuffed hands kept reaching up to her face, replaying her last defensive motion. A behavior locked in, happening again and again. Her hands rising, then falling back. I couldn't make her stop.

"Look," Holly said, her voice softening. "It's better if you don't anthropomorphize. You can pretend the models are real, but they're just not."

She wiped off the screwdriver and put it back in her case. Cleaned her hands and face, and started re-zipping her roller bag.

"The company has a recycling center here in the Bay Area for disposal," she said. "If you need more data on the owner's death, our servers will have backups of everything that happened with this model. Get the warrant, and we can unlock the encryptions on the customer's relationship with the product."

"Has this happened before?"

"We've had two other user deaths, but those were both stamina issues. This is an edge case. The rest of the Mika Models are being upgraded to prevent it." She checked her watch. "Updates should start rolling out at 3 a.m., local time. Whatever made her logic tree fork like that, it won't happen again."

She straightened her jacket and turned to leave.

"Hold on!" I grabbed her sleeve. "You can't just walk out. Not after this."

"She really got to you, didn't she?" She patted my hand patronizingly. "I know it's hard to understand, but it's just that hero complex of yours. She pushed your buttons, that's all. It's what Mika Models do. They make you think you're important."

She glanced back at the body. "Let it go, detective. You can't save something that isn't there."

The Starfish Girl
Maureen McHugh

(INTRO MUSIC)
(Run Sports 24/7 logo splash page)

CUT TO: *Studio set, ANNOUNCER behind desk.*

BROADCAST ANNOUNCER: *Liam Chan.*
Run clip on screen behind Chan: Mendoza on Balance Beam and Floor Exercise.

LIAM CHAN
It's a story of peaks and valleys. Today, Jinky Mendoza is one of America's best hopes for gymnastic gold in Paris. It's been an amazing journey for a young woman whom many thought might never be able to walk, much less compete after a devastating accident.

CUT TO: *NEWS SPOT of Jinky Mendoza's accident, no sound. Shaky phone video of gym where people are clustered around Mendoza on mat on her back.*

LIAM CHAN (VOICE-OVER)
In 2017, Jinky was 11 years old, one of the top-ranked junior gymnasts in the U.S. Her family was contemplating an offer to train at the Iowa facility owned by gold-medal gymnast and coach, Gabby Douglas, when tragedy struck. During a routine vault in practice, Jinky overrotated, landed wrong, and fractured her spine, at the C5 vertebra.
She was paralyzed from the neck down. It seemed as if her gymnastics career, indeed, life as she knew it, was over.

CUT TO: *Clip of J Mendoza in hospital bed, balloons.*

LIAM CHAN (VOICE-OVER)
Then doctors proposed a radical new medical procedure. They would use star-fish DNA to teach her body how to heal itself. The results were miraculous.

CUT TO:
Sports 24/7 Studio, Liam behind desk, clip of Jinky Mendoza in a tumbling run on screen behind him.

LIAM CHAN
They call her the Starfish Girl. Today the International Olympic Committee announced that it would release a ruling Monday on whether or not this 5-foot-3-inch dynamo is human.

◆◆◆◆◆◆

"Jesus," Olivia said. "They're playing it again."

The big scoreboard in the new University of Texas Wexner Arena was showing *Sports 24/7*'s spot on Jinky's accident, again. Jinky glanced up at her and then away, continuing her stretches.

There was a feeling to arenas—big but chaotic. All the gymnasts down in the exhibition area were in clumps by team, getting ready, shaking themselves loose and wearing warmup gear. The Texas air conditioning kept the place like a meat locker. Jinky was stretching, one heel on a five-inch riser to get more stretch out of her split. "So don't look," Jinky said.

"It's like a car accident, I can't help it. I can't believe you can just ignore it." They were all wearing Team USA leotards with the blue swoosh down the side. Olivia snapped her leotard away from her butt.

"If I look at it, someone gets video of me watching and then posts it."

With ugly comments. Jinky didn't read social media anymore, although she still had to tweet and post to Instagram. Coach Sophie made her Instagram 10 things a week. The last thing Jinky had Insta-grammed was yesterday when she got her nails done and got a starfish stenciled on her thumbnail. It was her good-luck charm.

She was the Starfish Girl after all.

Jinky was watching Svetlana Moracheva of Team Russia loosen up. She'd competed against Russia at the Worlds but she'd never done an exhibition with them. The arena was filling up. She smelled hot dogs.

Svetlana was long-boned and slim, white-blond and blue-eyed. She was "elegant." At 19, she was the team leader and the oldest woman on Russia's Olympic team.

Nobody had ever described Jinky as "elegant." Powerhouse. Spark plug. It didn't matter that she was the tallest member of the team; everybody thought she was short. Svetlana got compared to ballet dancers. Jinky would kill to be compared to a ballet dancer. She was always compared to Simone Biles—muscular and athletic. There were fan-made YouTube videos of the way they both hit the mat solidly; the way they both stuck landings as if rooted there by gravity.

The Russians trained differently, refining and refining while upping their endurance. Americans did more weight training and were muscular. American athletes were considered the ones to beat, but Jinky wished she were prettier, taller.

Svetlana glanced up and their eyes met across the arena. They both looked away.

Svetlana was wearing a knee brace. If Jinky was the Starfish Girl, Svetlana was the Human 2.0. She'd blown out her knee six months ago. Dislocated it, torn the ACL and MCL. Jinky had watched a video of it just once. You could see the whole knee disintegrate as she landed. It was a career-ending injury (kind of like breaking your neck). Fixed with stem cell therapy (kind of like a fractured spine). Only not in one important way. They hadn't used starfish DNA to fix Svetlana's knee. They'd edited the Russian girl's DNA directly using stuff from her own cells and creating repeats of certain sequences. The DNA sequences read the same way that the starfish DNA they used on Jinky had, it was just that they cut the pieces out of Svetlana's own DNA and added them in the right places.

"Girl, you look stiff," she said to Olivia.

"It's OK," Olivia said. She had been dealing with back spasms for months. At home in the gym, they did electric stimulation of her back muscles three times a week. It seemed to be helping.

Jinky waved at her to sit down and kneaded the muscles.

Olivia tilted her head back. Her kinky hair was yanked tightly back and shellacked into submission. She had a spray of red glitter in it that made her look a little like an exotic bird. She looked across the gym and saw Moracheva. "What's she doing today?" Olivia asked.

"Floor and uneven," Jinky said.

Usually at an exhibition they did routines specifically choreographed for show—pretty, flashy, and less demanding than competition routines. Jinky did hers to music from *The Little Mermaid*, and she wore a blue and green shimmery leotard and a starfish clip in her hair. She liked it because it was more like dance. More elegant. But Sophie had decided that today Jinky should do her Olympic balance beam and floor exercise to let them think about what she wouldn't be doing for America if she didn't go to the Olympics. The whole team was wearing their Team USA uniforms.

Jinky couldn't think about not going to the Olympics. Everything in her life had aimed her toward the Olympics. The year of rehab, when she grew three inches while relearning to walk and use her fingers. Olympics, Olympics, Olympics. People who thought that her special genes gave her an advantage had no idea how hard it had been. No one had thought she could come back. You'll walk again, they promised. Walk? She had shown them. She flew.

She stood up and shook herself loose. Then she visualized her balance-beam routine, imagining every step and how it felt, the twist, the aerial, the dismount. She imagined in real time, eyes closed to the people entering the arena. Focus. Focus. Focus.

When she opened her eyes, Olivia was standing in front of her. Olivia, her best friend, alternate for the Olympic team. "You'll do great," Olivia whispered. "You'll show them."

For once, Jinky wasn't worried about how she'd do. "If I do really well, they'll think it's because of the procedure," she said.

The girl with starfish DNA in her spine. The walking miracle.

❖❖❖❖❖

CUT TO: FOOTAGE OF J MENDOZA AS SHE LEAVES HOSPITAL

LIAM CHAN (VOICE-OVER)
It was more than a career-ending injury. Doctors at the University of Southern California proposed an experimental treatment. They used a gene-editing technique called CRISPR to introduce sequences from starfish DNA into Jinky's own cells.

(RUN GRAPHIC SIMULATION OF STARFISH REGENERATING)

LIAM CHAN (VOICE-OVER)
Starfish can regenerate limbs. Fishermen used to cut starfish in half and throw them back in the ocean, considering them pests. But that meant that for every starfish they cut in half, two starfish would grow. In humans and in most animals, the ability to regenerate has been lost, but researchers were able to modify Jinky's cells to "turn on" the ability to regenerate using starfish DNA.

(CUT TO: LIAM AT DESK)

LIAM CHAN
Jinky's injury healed, better than the doctors could ever expect. But she had lost over a year of training and it wasn't clear if she'd get it back.

◆◆◆◆◆◆

Before the balance beam, the coach told her that if she felt she needed to, she could pull the twist from her dismount or make it a single. "You don't want to risk too much before the games," Sophie said.

Jinky was doing an Arabian double salto forward tuck for her dismount. She did the equivalent of a somersault in the air, knees tucked to her chin and a one-and-a-half twist. It had a huge difficulty score. 7.0. It was the centerpiece of Jinky's balance routine. When she pulled it off, she was hard to beat.

"Remember your dance," Sophie said. She hugged Jinky.

"They don't care about the dance stuff," Jinky said.

"I do," Sophie said.

Jinky sat down and closed her eyes and tuned out the gymnasium. She was the person who was supposed to pull the team together. She was the one everyone looked to. But she just couldn't talk to anyone else right now. She tried to concentrate on her routine. Onto the beam. Back aerial. Svetlana Moracheva in a knee brace.

Music started. Rimsky-Korsakov. Moracheva's music. She stood at the corner of the mat for the floor exercises in a sparkly white leotard that made her look like the snow queen (except for the knee brace). Her first tumbling run was full-on, no concessions for her knee. It ended in a Biles aerial.

"Screw you," Jinky thought. She did a Biles aerial in her floor exercises too. That was HER style.

Moracheva was a little stiff, and after the spectacular first pass, her exhibition routine got simpler, but of course she danced, toes pointed, light, and regal. Like a Russian ballerina with her long neck and her beautiful shoulders, the way her back curved when she touched her foot to the back of her head. Arabesque, fouetté turn, soulful liquid melt to the mat with her arms outstretched. When she finished, she limped a little.

Nobody was gonna cast Jinky Mendoza in *Swan Lake*.

Jinky concentrated on her breathing; in through her nose, out through her mouth. She was a machine. An android. She had no emotion.

It was time. She walked out onto the mat and stood before the beam.

She pressed up to the beam with her arms into a side split. Then a triple turn in tuck stand. For a moment she heard "Light It Up" from someone's floor routine but she got her focus back and then—

It just all came. She could feel how well the routine was going. It was weird, when she was having a bad routine, she worked so hard, trying to make everything right. But when the routine was going well, it was almost no work at all. Back handspring, back layout, back layout and her foot was right where it should be, solid on the beam. The beam was a sidewalk, a driveway, a parking lot the size of Texas, and she did her dance steps, jumps, and her side-split turn.

And then she was doing her dismount and she didn't even think. It was just like practice. Arabian double salto. Her feet hit the mat and her ankle sent a momentary sharp reminder that it was sore but it was all right, just normal. She did the final pose, shoulders back, arms out.

The arena was silent. The floor exercise music must have finished. Was something wrong?

She blinked.

And then the applause and screaming started. Sophie, her coach, was hugging her. Gabby, the head of the gym, hugged her. Her teammates hugged her. The crowd was raggedly chanting, "Jinky! Jinky! Jinky!"

Olivia hugged her, shouting in her ear, "The announcer! They're comparing you to Nadia Comăneci! It was perfect! Perfect!"

◆◆◆◆◆◆

They were staying in a hotel downtown. It was a Marriott or something but it had a funny, down-at-the-heels feel. The hallways felt long and narrow. Didn't matter, they were flying home the next day.

There was already stuff about her balance routine on ESPN. There were videos on YouTube. Jinky didn't watch any of it—it felt as if she were jinxing herself. She asked Olivia if there was any blowback. Coach Sophie felt that showing the routine was a risk because while a great routine could make people want her to go to the Olympics, it could also fuel the belief that the procedure on her spine had given her an edge.

She walked to the soda machine. After a performance she and Olivia would split a Coke. It was their tradition.

The soda machine on their floor was out but the door to the stairs was right there so she went up a flight to see if the machine on that floor had some. They were all freaking geniuses when it came to hotels and travel. Always pack earplugs. Wear slip-on shoes at airports to get through TSA just in case they don't give you Precheck. Stuff like that. She opened to the door onto the 11th floor.

Svetlana Moracheva was sitting in the hallway on the floor outside a hotel room. She was leaning back against the wall, legs stuck straight out in front of her. The door to the hotel room was open and a couple of voices were chattering in Russian inside.

"Hi," Jinky said, startled. She put her money in the machine and a can clunked down to the opening. When she picked it up it was so cold.

Svetlana looked a little surprised too. She, like Jinky, was wearing track pants so her knee brace was hidden. "Great routine," Svetlana said. She spoke pretty good English—like a lot of gymnasts. Jinky didn't speak any Russian. She felt a little stupid.

"How's your knee?" Jinky asked and then thought maybe it was the wrong thing to say. Like it sounded like she was gloating or something.

Svetlana shrugged. "Pretty good," she said. "Will be good for Olympics."

"Oh! Good! Good! I...I love your dance. You know? You always look..." what? *Pretty*? That sounded dorky. "Um, smooth."

"Smooth?" Svetlana said, cocking her head. Jinky wasn't sure if she thought it was a dumb thing to say or if she didn't understand the word.

"You know," Jinky mimed a wave with her hand, up and down, up and down. "Not, like some people," Jinky made jerky motions with her hand, up down, up down.

Svetlana smiled. "Thank you. You are, how do I say, strong? So strong."

Jinky knew she made a face.

Svetlana laughed. "We not want what we have. Always want what others have. I want curly hair." She patted the floor next to her and Jinky sat down. "You hear from IOC? Anything?"

Jinky shook her head. "No."

"Could be worst. Could be XXY. No one is telling you that you are not a girl."

It took Jinky a moment to figure out what "ex-ex-why" meant. Then she laughed. The whole gender thing was a mess. Intersex athletes, nonbinary athletes, a hurdler from Turkey who thought of herself as a girl her whole life and competed in hijab who turned out to be genetically male but physically female. "It's so crazy!" she said. "What do you think they should do?"

Svetlana shrugged. "My problem is same as your problem; go to Paris, keep my team strong, win some gold, not lose to China. Someone else can worry about XXY."

"I don't think I'm going to go," Jinky blurted out. "But I have to!"

Svetlana nodded. "I know. After IOC decide about you," she tapped her knee, "they decide about me. I want you to go." Because if starfish DNA was OK, then your own DNA had to be, right?

"I want you to go," Jinky said. "But...maybe if you blew the triple salto?"

Svetlana took a second, then laughed. "For you, Jinky! You go to Olympics, I will blew my triple salto and give up any gold medal on the uneven."

Jinky wanted to say "blow," but she wasn't an asshole. Then they both didn't look at Svetlana's knee. It was all about whether there was enough time for the knee to recover, about the balance between keeping up some training and not reinjuring.

There were rumors that the Chinese were experimenting on their athletes. Changing the DNA of kids. Jinky thought about asking Svetlana if she'd heard anything, but a guy came out of a room down the hall.

Just a regular guy in blue jeans and a Longhorns T-shirt who smiled at them while he got a soda and a pack of M&Ms. Everything about him was big and soft. "Hey cuties," he said.

Jinky looked down and Svetlana said politely, *"Izvinite, ya ne govoryu po-angliyski."*

The guy laughed a little nervously and gave them a little wave. When his door closed behind him, Jinky folded into laughter. "What did you say?"

"I say, 'Why fat slob like you talk to pretty girls like us?' " Svetlana said.

"For real?"

"No, not for real. I just say I don't speak English. But next time I remember and say it. I promise."

"Sveta." A girl walked out of the room. "Oh! Hi!" It was Renata Nikolaev, the Russian vault specialist. She still had her hair pulled back tight and her competition makeup on. She said something to Svetlana in Russian.

Jinky's phone buzzed, Olivia texting wondering where she was.

She typed:

talking to Moracheva

"I have to go," Svetlana said. "I promise my boyfriend I call him."

Of course Svetlana had a boyfriend. "Where is he?"

"He is in *Nürburgring* right now for practice. He is Formula One driver. He is 20, the youngest, and alternate for his team. You know Formula One?" Svetlana mimed driving a car.

Jinky had heard of it, but she didn't know anything about race cars, or care, to be honest. But she nodded.

"He is alternate for second driver for Red Bull," Svetlana said. "So he is like me, traveling all the time. But we FaceTime."

Svetlana got up, a little awkwardly because of her knee. Jinky did too. It was like speaking with the queen or something. When it was over, it was over.

"Hey," Svetlana said, "Let me give you my number. Is U.S. number."

Jinky handed Svetlana her phone and watched her put her number in the contacts. "I'll let you know as soon as we hear," Jinky said.

Svetlana nodded, sharp. Then she hugged Jinky. Startled, Jinky hugged back. They were the only two.

"Do not forget the Coke." Svetlana wiped her eyes. "Text me, OK Starfish Girl?" Then she put her game face back on and went into the hotel room.

Jinky picked up her can of Coke and went back downstairs to share it with Olivia.

◆◆◆◆◆◆

They flew toward Iowa, where it would be flat and green. The whole team had gotten seats close to each other on the plane, so that was something.

Jinky Googled "Svetlana Moracheva boyfriend" and found someone named Honza Broucek. He had a thick neck and short reddish hair and didn't look anything like Jinky would have guessed. How did Svetlana meet him? Jinky felt as if she never met anybody. She was home-schooled by a tutor and spent three hours in the gym in the morning and four in the afternoon.

There were images of them after some race, Broucek with his arm around Svetlana's waist. They looked so happy. Broucek looked better when he was wearing a racing uniform; in the image, he was wearing a black racing suit and he looked handsome.

In the seat next to her, Olivia stretched, pulling one leg up straight in front of her. "My ankles are swelling," she observed.

"Airplanes suck," Jinky said. "Want the window?"

That was Sunday. The ruling was expected on Monday.

◆◆◆◆◆◆

On Monday, she texted Svetlana.

jinky here

Before she could type anything else, Svetlana fired back:

wat they say

She had been stoic. Sophie, her coach, cried during the conference call; IOC lawyers, U.S. lawyers, Gabby. The IOC threw out the claim that she wasn't human but said they needed proof she wasn't enhanced. That she didn't recover from injuries better or have faster reflexes or wasn't someway cheating. Until they had proof she would not be allowed to compete in the Paris Summer Olympics of 2024. She texted:

suspended until proof

not enhanced

Svetlana texted back:

fuck them

Jinky's legal team was already putting together a strategy. Jinky would have metabolic testing at Johns Hopkins and a researcher there wanted to test cell samples from Jinky for immune response and a bunch of other things like autophagy and oxidation and stuff that was supposed to tell them whether Jinky's own body was a performance-enhancing drug.

The lawyers talked about Oscar Pistorius, the South African double amputee who had to prove his carbon-fiber "blades" didn't give him an advantage, even if they had more "spring" than human bone and muscle. Four years later, the IOC had banned Markus Rehm from the broad jump because they said his prosthetic foot, his blade, was an enhancement that gave him an unfair advantage.

The hair-thin gold wires in her neck, combined with the starfish DNA, were a prosthetic that could possibly give her an as-yet-unspecified advantage.

The lawyers kept saying that it wasn't over, and Jinky believed them. She had beaten the odds before.

It was bad news for Svetlana too. If they had declared Jinky not human, then Svetlana, who had no starfish DNA in her, couldn't be declared a nonhuman starfish-person. They'd have to look at Svetlana's case separately.

But they had only decided Jinky was human, not whether or not she was enhanced. It wouldn't be hard to argue that since Svetlana had had a similar procedure, she too might have an unfair advantage.

Jinky had avoided thinking about what it meant if she wasn't "human." She had read an article that said chimpanzees share about 99 percent of their DNA with humans. Sometimes she wondered if she had a baby (someday), would it have starfish genes? She supposed it would. But if Jinky was human, then her baby would be too. Unless they changed their minds.

She flew to Baltimore and had tests done. She ran on a treadmill while her CO_2 output was measured. She had blood and tissue samples taken. She had a bone-marrow test to see how much the starfish DNA had migrated. She missed four days of training.

The bone-marrow test sucked ass. Her bones were hard because she was young and trained all the time and laying there on her side while a doctor drilled into her pelvis hurt. They slapped gauze on her and sent her back to the airport. She found a spot of blood on her T-shirt when she changed that night.

Svetlana texted:

starfish girl
sveta!
my coach ask for ruling
china going to file complaint 4 wks b4 big o
when not enough time to do tests
tell me when you hear
of course!!!!!!!!

Then she sent a starfish emoji and a heart.

◆◆◆◆◆◆

"Sophie?" Jinky asked. Sophie was in the coach's office at the computer.

"What is it, Jinks?"

Sophie Wilson had been coaching Jinky for four years, now. Two years after the accident, Jinky had been competing again, but she wasn't even back to the level of skill she'd had when she was 11. Sophie had invited her to come train at the facility. She'd watched Jinky in practice. "Every time you do a move, and your coach tells you something, the next time you are just a little bit better," Sophie said. "You're going to get back to your original skills and then some."

Sophie had a bagel with cream cheese on her desk and Jinky's stomach rumbled. Jinky tried not to eat too many unrefined carbs. She could feel it the next day in practice if she did. She was heavier, slower.

Focus, she thought. After the Olympics, you can have all the bagels you want. "I think I should do an interview."

Sophie didn't understand.

"You know, like on the news or something. Show I'm a regular person, not some kind of X-Man mutant."

Sophie shook her head. "The strategy is keep our heads down and wait for the science."

"I don't think that's a good idea." She had talked to Olivia and Svetlana and even called her mother.

Her mother was an X-ray tech and she worked crazy hours but she had talked with Jinky until she had to leave for her shift. Jinky imagined her in her scrubs, sitting at the kitchen table. "Whatever you want to do, baby," she said. "Your dad and I are proud of you. You know that." It hadn't really been much help but it made Jinky feel better.

"I think we need to get in front of this," Jinky said. Which, honestly, sounded hella smart, right?

"Let me talk to Gabby," Sophie said.

❖❖❖❖❖❖

They kicked around possible ways to do an interview. An AMA on Reddit was dismissed. Nobody wanted Jinky fielding questions like "Which would you rather fight, 100 horses the size of a duck or one duck the size of a horse?" The New York Times and the Washington Post were considered but who read newspapers anymore?

Eventually Jinky's agent (whom she had met exactly three times) called them with an offer from Amazon Prime. Amazon had a sports program called, without originality, *Amazon Sports*. One of the hosts was Nate Silver of FiveThirtyEight although he wasn't a gymnastics guy so Sylvia Guest would do a 20-minute interview.

Jinky texted Svetlana:

what should i wear

american teen

And she sent an image of a girl in a cute dress and followed it up with one more text:

soft

Olivia sniffed, "How's your bestie?"

"She's not," Jinky said. "You are. Bitch. I've only talked to her a couple of times."

Olivia shrugged like it didn't matter.

But Svetlana was used to the spotlight so it made sense to ask her. There were images of her with Serena Williams at a charity event in London. Maybe Jinky should do things like that too? Go to places? How did you even get invited?

Jinky didn't have a lot of clothes that weren't tracksuits and leotards and sweats so she and Olivia went shopping. Jinky had a college fund for money from any endorsements but it was locked in trust until she was 18. With all the money her parents were putting out for her training, she felt weird if she asked for spending money. Her parents had sold their house to cover her medical expenses.

They went to the mall. Jinky was a girl's size 12 to 14. There were some things in Juniors but they all looked like prom dresses. It's like they needed a shop for "gymnasts who need to wear something for a televised interview."

Olivia found a yellow mini dress and made Jinky try it on. It wasn't a prom dress. "It makes you glow," Olivia said. She dragged Jinky to the jewelry counter and picked out a cute necklace and some earrings.

"You look fab, girl," Olivia pronounced.

Back at the gym, they had a remote video setup, basic, but fine. Jinky sat in front of a green screen and looked at a monitor. She was sweating, she could feel it. Olivia had done her makeup. Jinky liked the winged eyeliner so much she was going to ask Olivia to do it for her for competitions. Her nails were done and she'd gotten her lucky starfish stencil on her thumb, this time with a little blue rhinestone in the center.

It was a performance except she couldn't go through it in her head like she could a routine. She closed her eyes and tried to calm down.

And then she was on. Sylvia Guest was blond and polished and Anglo and Jinky felt weird and brown and freaky.

"Hi Jinky! Great to have you on!" Sylvia chirped.

There were questions that everybody always asked. What do you eat? Jinky gave her usual response, that no one had ever told her she needed to lose weight but she tried to eat healthy. She had yogurt with fruit and almonds before she worked out in the morning. She ate chicken and salmon and steamed vegetables for dinner. The whole team liked to go get ice cream. Her favorite dish was her mother's chicken adobo, the national dish of the Philippines.

What was her training schedule like? She worked out three hours in the morning, took a break and did her schooling, and then four hours in the afternoon. She had Sundays off. Her favorite book was *To Kill a Mockingbird*. (Not true: She and Olivia traded gay romance novels.)

What did she think of the IOC decision?

"I'm glad I'm human," she said, and that got a laugh from Sylvia Guest.

"We'll do a montage of clips of your accident and recovery," Sylvia said.

Jinky nodded.

"What about the pending decision about whether or not changing your DNA has given you an unfair advantage?"

Nobody had ever said it that way. "Unfair advantage." It was always performance enhancement. Like she'd taken steroids or something. She smiled, but to her embarrassment, she could feel that her eyes were welling up.

"Unfair?" she said. "I um...I mean, it's hard to think that breaking my neck was an unfair advantage, you know? I mean, I couldn't move my legs or feel anything. It was..."

"What do you remember?"

"I remember I was on my back, looking up at the, um, ceiling? You know those florescent lights in some places? The gym had these long lights and I was looking at them and I thought I had just had the wind knocked out of me because you know, sometimes when you screw up and you land you can't even move for a second and you can't, like, breathe? I thought it was like that. And then my mom was saying, don't move. And she called me Janice. She only ever calls me that when I'm in trouble or something is really serious. She kept saying, 'Lie still, Janice' and I couldn't do anything and I knew it was bad.

"And then they wanted to try the stem cell procedure and they put these superthin gold wires in my spinal cord, like thinner than a hair. And the stem cells. After that I had this external thing they said was sort of like a pacemaker that sent little amounts of electricity into my spinal cord."

"Could you feel that?" Sylvia asked.

Across from Jinky, beside the monitor, Sophie was there. She was nodding, the "You're doing good" nod. "Keep going."

"I couldn't feel anything. I didn't think it was working. It was weeks before I felt anything."

"What did you feel first?" Sylvia asked.

"Two days before the meet I screwed up my ankle. It always gives me problems. The first thing I felt was my ankle hurting."

"Wow, so the first thing you felt was pain?"

Jinky blinked. Did a sore ankle even count as pain? Her ankle was sore all the time. She just ignored it. "It wasn't pain," she said. "It was feeling."

❖❖❖❖❖❖

The interview got millions of hits. Jinky hated it. She hated how when she was talking about rehab (lots of details, Sophie had told her, make them know how hard it was) she started crying and almost ruined her makeup. It was cheesy and pathetic.

Svetlana:

you killed it

honza sez hi

he sez you kill it, too

The news and social media covered the story all over again.

In the end it made no difference. The results from John Hopkins suggested that maybe Jinky healed a little better than average but not particularly out of the norm for people, but it couldn't prove that she didn't have an advantage because it didn't have samples from before her accident to see if that was just the way she was.

24/7 Set.

LIAM CHAN

We're here today with Russian gymnast Svetlana Moracheva. You're expecting an IOC ruling very soon. Given the ruling to ban Jinky Mendoza from the Paris Olympics for performance enhancement, what are your expectations?

SVETLANA MORACHEVA

(simultaneous translation from Russian) They will disqualify me. They can't disqualify an American athlete and let a Russian one with a similar issue compete. It would be like Cold War days when the Soviet judges vote down Americans and the Americans vote down Russians.

LIAM CHAN

Does the ruling seem fair?

SVETLANA

No, not at all. Jinky and I have worked hard to be the best. But life is not supposed to be fair.

LIAM CHAN

What are you going to do now? Are you appealing?

SVETLANA

I don't know. I don't know what I'm going to do. But for the Olympics, this is something they will have to figure out. Athletes are like race cars, you know? It used to be that we were just cars that people have that they race. Then they start making cars that are only for racing and now, a Formula One car isn't really a car. It is a jet airplane with no wings.

So the Formula One people are always trying to make a faster car and the officials are trying to stop certain things. Like the suspension can only be like this, and you cannot have shark-fin engines and then you can. There are Formula One cars and there are stock cars and there are all sorts of kinds of races, you know?

Now in the Olympics they must think about the same things. Jinky and me, we are like the shark-fin engine. We are banned. Maybe in 2028 we are not banned. People all over the world, they are trying to be the best and now they have a new way to be the best. They fix their DNA. Maybe when they are six or seven years old. Maybe before they are born. If you think doping is a problem, this is going to be even bigger.

Jinky and me, we are really just normal people who work very hard. But Pandora is out of the box, you know? If you asked me when I was 10 years old, would I have my body changed to be an elite gymnast? I would say yes.

LIAM
What would you say now?

SVETLANA
I would say yes.

"Yes," Jinky whispered, watching. "Yes."

The Minnesota Diet
Charlie Jane Anders

North American Transit Route No. 7 carves a path between tree silhouettes like wraiths, through blanched fields that yawn with the furrows of long-ago crops. Weaving in and out of the ancient routes of Interstates 29 and 35, this new highway has no need for rest stops or attempts to beautify the roadside, because none of the vehicles have a driver or any passengers. The trucks race from north to south, at speeds that would cause any human driver to fly off the road at the first curve. The sun goes down and they keep racing, with only a few thin beams to watch for obstacles. They don't need to see the road to stay on the road. The trucks seem to hum to one another, tiny variations in their engine sounds making a kind of atonal music. Seen from above, they might look like the herds of mustangs that used to run across this same land, long ago.

The self-driving trucks seem to pick up pace as they approach the cluster of crystal towers that rise from the horizon: the cutting-edge "Smart City" of New Lincoln. And then just as they are cresting the last rise in the road, they change direction. They veer off along one of the other North American Transit Routes, leaving New Lincoln in their rearview.

❖ ❖ ❖ ❖ ❖

Mason is one of those people who turns every morsel into a story: about the Napa Valley soil that gave this grape its particular tartness, or the windy Vermont hillside where sheep gamboled and munched

tall grass, producing milk that became a cheese with such a complicated bite. Listening to Mason talk about food is almost better than
eating. But right now, Mason is sitting at his workstation screaming
and hitting refresh on the holographic display, which keeps showing
the trucks careening in the wrong direction. At last he howls, making
his blue pompadour quiver and causing his co-workers to beg him to
keep it down.

Normally, Mason would be worrying about the latest boy who isn't
responding to his Flings—in this case, a lovely Australasian named
Richard who seemed interested just a few days ago. By rights, Mason
should be concentrating on work purely to distract himself from Fling
drama. But now, the Very Prairie Food Co-op is down to just one kind
of sheep's-milk cheese, and it's not even one of the creamy ones. The
cold cuts are a disaster. He should be standing out front, telling
customers about the romance and the drama behind a lovely spelt
bread, but the Co-op is out of it. They're out of everything, except for
some locally sourced produce from the city's 17 vertical farms.

It's classic variable reinforcement: Every third or fourth time
Mason hits "refresh," the screen shows a delivery truck en route,
practically at its loading bay already. One self-driving truck did
actually show up this morning: half-empty, with some pasta and oat-
meal on board. But then the next few trucks got rerouted. Basically,
the worst slot machine ever.

Mason's co-workers grow tired of hearing him berate dots on a
hologram, until Percy tells him to get the hell outside for some fresh
air. Mason keeps his head down as he walks through the front of the
store toward the exit, because the exposed bioplastic of the empty
shelves feels like a kick in the stomach, and he can't look any of the
customers in the eye.

Mason storms out into the Greatest City in the World.

❖❖❖❖❖

Mason grew up thinking cities were supposed to be gray, shading
toward ochre in the parts made of bronze, brass, brownstone, or rusted
iron. Until he moved to New Lincoln five years ago—this city is like a
forest canopy, or some kind of giant vegetable patch; trees stretch their

branches out from all the rooftops, and bracken grows out of every wall sconce, while ivy and other vines wrap around all the surfaces. The walls themselves are made of some kind of dense bioplastic, colored bright purple or deep blue, that "breathes," allowing for natural cooling and heating. Not only does the whole metropolis have no carbon footprint, but also the air smells like springtime whenever Mason ventures out. Every square of the walkway (there are no side-walks, because there are no streets) tells Mason how many steps he's walked today, and everything that's going on with his friends, plus news about the ongoing legislative DeathGrip in Congress. (The news services cheerily natter about "DeathGrip Day 709," along with interesting facts: *Did you know the government hasn't had a budget in two years?* So fascinating!) The billboards in the CityPlex target Mason with messages designed just for him, thanks to next-level systems that aim photons directly at his retinas. If Mason put on his Blinkers, he'd see virtual structures and companions—part of a whole other city that could be almost endless.

To walk through New Lincoln is to marvel at human potential at its mightiest. But today, Mason looks up at all this vibrant color and sees nothing but gray. He is ramping up for some really first-class brooding when his Savant kicks up a message from Sumana and Flood: "quit wandering in circles like a drunk goose and meet us at the Bruisory, son-son." Mason sighs, then turns on his Blinkers and heads over.

If Mason tried to go to the Bruisory without his Blinkers, he'd get as far as some stairs and a terrace. This mostly virtual bistro has sleek wooden surfaces and old-style squeaky roll-chairs and a shimmering menu of comfort food, fancy coffees, and high-end beers. The actual decor is one big tribute to Bruisor, the hottest social network from way back in the 2040s, right before the public internet went away. The menu is all Bruisor pastiche, with playful insults in between every menu item, plus Mason's worst underwear picture, and his whiny drunken messages to that one boy who ditched him at the club two years ago—exactly the sort of stuff that would have been posted about Mason on Bruisor, back in the day. (Everyone sees their own embarrassing info.) And in true Bruisor style, Sumana greets Mason saying, "lick goat nose, son-son," and Mason responds, "choke on a smeg pretzel, mana-mana." Then they hug.

Everyone asks Mason why he looks so gloomy, and he tries to explain that the Very Prairie Food Co-op's distributor is trying to screw them, but just then, he finally gets a good look at the Bruisor's menu.

"What the fletch," Mason says. "There's only three menu items."

"Two if you don't consider peanut soup real food," says Flood, who as usual wears a hoodie with ever-changing sarcastic phrases about smashing the hypocracy on their skinny torso.

"The deliveries," Vera says from behind the counter, "they just haven't been showing up." Vera wears a floor-length skirt and complicated bustier-halter top combo as usual, and her locs spill over her shoulders.

Mason is so startled, he flouts the Bruisory custom, and doesn't even bother to insult Vera, or anyone else here. "What the fletch is going on? Where are all the deliveries?"

Half the people in the Bruisory work in white-collar jobs, like Sumana (coding), Warren (design), Flood (strategy consulting), and Amanda (UX design), and those people can't understand what Mason and Vera are worried about. It's only the people who work in food service, or know something about food, who are losing their minds.

"It's kind of a cliché to say that most cities are only about nine meals away from total anarchy," says Jolene, who's an actual food scientist at New Lincoln University. "But New Lincoln is so efficient and streamlined, we may have succeeded in getting it down to just seven or eight meals." Nobody laughs at this.

"I still don't get the problem if a few self-driving trucks took a wrong turn," says Amanda. Vera's longtime girlfriend is a curvy blonde who wears tons of jewelry with clock faces all over it.

"Maybe it's the robot uprising at last," snorts Warren, who has a kind of retro "crusty punk" thing going on.

"They probably just got rerouted because some algorithm decided they were needed elsewhere," agrees Sumana.

"I'm sure you're right," Mason says. "Meanwhile, I guess I'll have a grilled cheese sandwich."

"Sorry," Vera says. "We literally just ran out of cheese."

Mason sighs. "I guess peanut soup then?"

◆◆◆◆◆◆

Jolene takes the words *food scientist* off her Savant profile, because she's sick of friends of friends and exes of exes pinging her nonstop, trying to get some kind of explanation. Whether they've gone to the big supermarket or one of the smaller ones like the Very Prairie Co-op, they've noticed the half-empty shelves, and the absence of the usual fluttering augmented reality displays that tell you all about the vegetable momos, the tsuivan, the kitfo, the string-hoppers, the black pudding, the five kinds of spiced lentils, the wild-caught salmon, and the house-marinated venison. Or else their favorite restaurant shut down temporarily. Or they know someone who works at a restaurant or grocery store, and that person is having a nervous breakdown. These people saw the reports about droughts, blights, monoculture crop collapse, soil exhaustion, and pesticide-resistant bugs, and always figured it was someone else's problem.

After all, they live in New Lincoln, the "smart city" where you could have urban density and a cutting-edge urban lifestyle, at a cheap enough price for all the white-collar workers whose labor had been devalued by the latest superadvanced software. A post-scarcity city.

Jolene's mother was an immigrant from the Dominican Republic who loved Dolly Parton with an unwavering fierceness, and she'd decided to name her firstborn daughter after the best thing about their new home. Growing up with an unusual first name helped make Jolene more of an introvert, and left her with less tolerance for a hundred people in a row asking her the exact same question.

Mostly, Jolene hangs out with the same handful of people she's known since she moved here a few years ago: Vera, Samanthor the Mighty, Mason, Sumana, Flood, Amanda, Warren, and a few others who rotate in and out. Most of the time, they sit around eating Vera's famous stinky-bean-curd frittata and guzzling vodka, or they eat chips and dip at someone's house, or they share lasagna at that place that puts truffles in everything. But today, they sit around a game-holo, playing some interactive strategy game, without even any snacks.

"I never realized how much my social life revolved around food," says Flood, more bemused than upset. They've shaved new streaks into their prematurely gray curly hair, and they're wearing cargo pants so baggy they're almost square. "Until there wasn't any."

"Don't be dramatic," says Samanthor (who's using "she/her" pronouns at the moment, according to her animated pirate shirt). "There's plenty of food, it's just not fancy." She hefts a can of peas for emphasis. Everyone is hanging out in the loft apartment where Samanthor the Mighty, Mason, and Warren live, which has exposed bioplastic girders and a window that changes to reflect everyone's mood.

"Just saying, the lack of restaurants and snack options puts a dent in my social life," Flood says.

"Can't go on much longer," says Sumana, who has an unshakable faith in her fellow engineers. "It's just a glitch in the system."

"It's been over a week since anyone saw a delivery truck," says Mason, whose interactive T-shirt has sported nothing but angry cartoons lately. "Nearly a week and a half."

"Soon the same algorithm that's sending all the trucks somewhere else will realize that we're in dire need, and everything will swing the other way," says Sumana. "We'll have more trucks than we know what to do with."

"Oh yes, *the algorithm will save us.*" Flood's sarcasm is curiously relaxed, without much bitterness in their voice.

At least with these seven friends, Jolene won't have to hear the same terrible questions, over and over again.

Here's what nobody wants to hear from Jolene: Experts have warned for decades—since even before Superstorm Sandy hit New York and closed off the tunnels, and Manhattan suffered shortages almost instantaneously—that cities have fragile supply chains. City planners have learned to prepare for hurricanes and other natural disasters, but nobody predicted that a simple combination of logistical problems and crop failure could be worse than any storm. New Lincoln's 17 indoor vertical farms and assorted rooftop gardens and orchards can't save the city from depending on faraway warehouses and narrow delivery pipelines. Even if all 3 million residents wanted to eat nothing but lettuce, kale, and arugula, the vertical farms collectively produce only enough for half a million meals per day. They were designed to produce artisanal salads and to supplement the food brought in from elsewhere, not to sustain a population.

"But I don't mind eating canned food and frozen pizza for a while," says Amanda in a breezy voice. Then, maybe worrying that this sounded too Pollyanna, she adds: "I mean, shit. We take our incredible standard of living for granted here. We were lucky to wind up in a city where our skills are actually valued. There's nothing wrong with a reminder to be grateful."

"Why don't you lay an egg and then suck on it?" says Flood, as if they're back in the Bruisory and everybody's supposed to lob silly fake insults. Amanda just rolls her eyes.

◆◆◆◆◆◆

Samanthor fasted in college to protest the government's refugee policies, and she remembers how the hunger started gentle, like, oh, you just skipped a meal, and then with no warning there was a jagged chunk of rock, dredged from a silty riverbed, in your stomach. After even one day of fasting, everything hurt, and you had to exercise ridiculous caution when you started eating again, or you'd throw up everywhere. The hunger strike had probably made the tiniest scratch on the xenophobia-industrial complex, but afterward Samanthor felt like she had skin in the game, and she'd remembered that awful feeling every time she'd felt tempted to stay home from another protest or petition drive.

But this time, there's no sense of virtue in the dull pain that has settled in Samanthor's chest, or the sick feeling in her arms and legs. She feels like she ran a marathon, even though she's been sitting still for ages.

Somehow, they went from having enough nonperishable and semi-perishable food to get by, if they didn't binge, to not quite scraping by. The grocery stores have completely emptied out, even of the stuff that nobody really wanted, like the high-fiber cereal that looks like actual twigs, the sweaty root vegetables, and the organic caffein-ated sour mints. People have been breaking into the rooftop gardens and even people's window boxes, ripping out every tomato vine and celery stalk. All of the trees and parklets are studded with crude traps for squirrels and pigeons.

Mason still keeps checking the holo-display with the dots moving around, but it's mostly a running joke at this point. The Mayor's Office and the City Council keep putting out messages urging people not to panic, because this is just a temporary glitch, and New Lincoln is still a brilliant shining metropolis. But some malign piece of code somewhere keeps deciding that New Lincoln, with its population of midlevel computer engineers, quality-control experts, content creators, architects, marketing experts, musical theater geeks, and service workers, isn't a priority. It's been 20 days since the last delivery.

Samanthor has a constant headache, and she can't stand bright lights or loud noises, and Mason's squawking is driving her bonkers, and the automatically adjusting picture window is putting weird black shrouds on the yew trees and crystal towers outside in response to her foul mood. She's not ready for how much this hunger isn't just in her stomach. She keeps wishing she'd stayed in Denver, where the bright new smart buildings jostled next to ancient skyscrapers in an architectural mishmash, but at least there was plenty of good barbecue.

"I feel gross," growls Warren, who's been raising his "crusty punk" act to a new level since he doesn't have enough energy to shave or shower. "I gotta go to work tomorrow, and I can't even think straight."

"I feel like barfing, even though there's nothing to barf up," responds Samanthor. "This feels like the flu, only flu-ier."

Mason yells something else, and both of his roommates glare at him.

At last they go down to City Hall, where they spy Amanda, Vera, Flood, and Sumana among the people protesting the lack of official response to this disaster. Under the big CityPlex signs, a woman with a bullhorn demands that some kind of food distribution and rationing program be set up, and that the local government declare a state of emergency.

Samanthor can't deal with this crowd, the meaty bready wet-doggy smell of so many people all in one place. She feels like barfing or screaming or punching someone or keeling over.

"We need to go where the food is," Warren says as they walk away from the protest.

"Where's that?" Mason says.

"You know where," Warren says. "The place you're always talking about. The sheep farm where they graze on a grassy hillside, near the orchard where the climate is just perfect, and the river where the salmon spawn and the trout do backflips."

"Um, those are all different places," Mason says.

"That's where I want to go." Warren seems not to have heard Mason. "The place where it all comes from. The food place."

"Let's go," Samanthor says.

There's supposed to be high-speed rail connecting New Lincoln to both Chicago and Kansas City, but it never got finished because of the DeathGrip. So they rent a self-driving car, a preloved Zaeo Superlux, and throw everything they can carry in the back. They get about a dozen kilometers outside New Lincoln, and then the car just stops. Plenty of charge left in the battery, and the engine seems fine, but the car's software license won't allow it to drive on the North American Transit Route. Even telling the Superlux to drive on back roads seems to trigger some terms-of-service issue that keeps them clicking through screen after screen.

Mason and Samanthor stand by the side of the road, next to a field of yellow-gray stalks with the consistency of bad silicone—like a cheapo sex toy that someone bought as a gag gift, but which is doomed to wind up being used for unsatisfying, humdrum sex at some point. They smell like congealing candle wax. Samanthor remembers Jolene explaining that hundreds of miles of good farmland surrounds New Lincoln, but corporations are using it to grow organic precursors for biosynthetic tech. That's one reason New Lincoln is so cutting-edge and eco-friendly: Most of its infrastructure was grown, rather than made. But that means there's no farmland growing actual food anywhere nearby, apart from the vertical farms inside the city.

Warren keeps trying to hack the Superlux's OS to get it moving again, but he might as well drag the car down the road.

Samanthor's Savant hits her with updates. Her friend Davy in Chicago says they have shortages too, though not as bad. "I've been trying to send a care package, but the shipping company keeps saying there's problems with deliveries to New Lincoln right now. Hang in there, Kidface. You'll get through this. Love etc." According to a news item, the mayor of Chicago says there's no room for the refugees who did make it out of New Lincoln, and they're being housed in some stadium until something else can be found.

At least the mayor of New Lincoln is finally declaring a state of emergency, and they're creating some system to organize and distribute the remaining food, with priority given to children, the elderly, and people with serious health conditions. The federal government, meanwhile, is considering measures to provide emergency food aid to New Lincoln. But, you know, the DeathGrip.

Mason pulls out a bottle of water and some salt packets and dribbles salt in his mouth before swigging, because he read somewhere that salt can keep you functioning during a long fast. Samanthor wants to swat the water bottle out of his stupid hands. For some reason, she's decided all of this is Mason's fault. He yammered about food so much, he ruined everything. She can't sit down, or she won't be able to stand up again, and she feels sleepy even on her feet. Her brain is running at half power, and the screen of her Savant is giving her a migraine.

"Ugh." Warren makes a noise. "Let's just go home so I can lie down."

The Superlux happily starts up as soon as they tell it to go back to New Lincoln.

Warren makes his disgusted sound again, like someone chewing a snail and spitting out the shell.

❖❖❖❖❖

Back during World War II, three dozen conscientious objectors volunteered to live on a low-calorie diet, in the Minnesota Starvation Experiment. Jolene studied this in school, and the pictures of scowling stick-figure men were pretty horrifying.

Jolene is one of about 30 people helping to organize the rationing program that City Hall finally agreed to set up. Her goal is to keep healthy people as close as possible to the Minnesota diet, which after all didn't kill anybody. She attends endless meetings, during which usually responsible adults snap at one another, zone out instead of listening, and get derailed into half-hour conversations about their favorite foods that they wish they could be eating. Jolene can barely concentrate in these meetings, and only a sense of duty keeps her from staying in bed. Since New Lincoln is full of app designers, they're trying to pull together a team to design a rationing app. We're now at 47 days since the last delivery.

The good news is, the city's vertical farms will continue to produce a steady (but limited) amount of vegetables for the foreseeable future, because they are self-renewing. And every food chemist Jolene knows is working on coming up with other scalable food sources, from mycoproteins to synthetics to insects. Nobody thinks help is coming from outside anymore, and anyone who had the means to leave and someplace to go has already left. Other cities have followed Chicago's lead in putting refugees into temporary shelters, which means Jolene and the others have 1 million fewer mouths to feed. But an estimated 2 million people have remained in New Lincoln, of whom roughly 40 percent are considered high-risk.

Jolene walks through the city, along a path that used to take her past a beautiful fountain, her favorite doughnut stand, and a row of little cafés and restaurants. With her Blinkers on, she would have been able to see virtual strategy games, a whole row of extra shops, a pie-eating contest happening in five physical locations across the city, a whole range of fantastical skins. But people have been vandalizing the augmented reality emitters, and nobody is bothering to launch content updates anyway, so Jolene is stuck with a "real" world in which people lie on the walkways, where they fall over and don't have the energy to get up again, or else scream at everyone else, eyes crunched shut. Jolene thinks about the term *meatspace*, how dumb it is, how rocky and barren and mostly devoid of meat the nonvirtual world actually is. Jolene wants to throttle whoever came up with the term *meatspace* and then sleep forever.

Jolene almost doesn't recognize the closest couple who are yelling in each other's tearful faces: Vera and Amanda. The two of them just shout "It's all your fault" over and over. Jolene grabs both of them by the shoulders, until they finally stop shrieking and glare at her with bleary eyes. "It's not your fault. Either of you," Jolene says slowly. "It was a large-scale failure of urban planning."

"That's not helpful," Amanda snarls.

◆◆◆◆◆◆

Eventually, the rationing app gets up and running, and half the city's police force is guarding the remaining food stores, and almost everyone in town receives something approaching Minnesota food levels.

There's a new etiquette, which spreads via people's Savants and Flings. Don't talk about food in front of other people. But if someone else talks about food in front of you, don't lose your shit at them. Don't try to make anyone watch a movie, or Virtual Immersive Scenario, in which people are eating. Talk quietly, and above all don't yell. Don't be fatalistic. Don't proclaim false hope, or insist that everything is going to be fine. Don't judge other people's weird food rituals: the way they hold food in their mouths for a long time before swallowing, mix it with water, or even cradle a piece of food in their arms like a baby. Don't blame your partner(s) for lacking sex drive, or for being uninterested in romance. If people need to be alone, leave them alone. Most of all, don't judge people for listlessness or apathy, or the inability to get out of bed—but do try to keep other people moving, at least enough to avoid muscle atrophy.

Jolene loses track of how long it's been since she saw another person, but at last she finds herself sitting around with Mason, Warren, Samanthor, and Flood. Mason is still poking the "refresh" spot on that stupid real-time self-driving truck screen, full of dots in motion.

"They're on their way somewhere," Mason says, without even much rancor.

"This town was supposed to be for the best and brightest. The educated workforce. Now look at us." Warren lies on the couch, staring at the picture window as it drapes pink-and-blue garlands and ribbons on the skyline outside.

"Ugh," Samanthor says. "I'm a low-level tech. It's barely worth paying me to do my job, versus just building a robot. I don't think I'm the best, or brightest."

"Are you kidding?" Mason says. "You're Samanthor the Mighty."

"Don't call me that anymore." Samanthor sighs. "I think we're telephone sanitizers."

"What?" Jolene says.

"It's from a book I read. They build a superadvanced spaceship and tell the passengers they're going to a great new planet to build an awesome civilization. But they're all telephone sanitizers and marketing people and hairdressers. The people everyone can do without. They crash or something."

"Wait." Mason runs his hands through his blue pompadour, which is still perfect even on top of his emaciated features. "Who said we could live without hairdressers?"

"Some British guy."

"Did he cut his own hair?"

"You're distracting me. I can barely think as it is. God, my stomach hurts again. Like I swallowed a huge piece of broken glass. What was I even saying?"

"But I mean," says Warren. "There are a lot of creatives and stuff here in New Lincoln. I'm a info-flow designer. Sumana is writing software to help people check their Fling updates faster. And...oh God." Warren tries to sit up and nearly falls off the couch. "Bloody hell. We're telephone sanitizers."

Jolene has been kind of zoning out during this discussion of hair and spaceships, because she's as spacey as the rest of them. But now she speaks up. "I mean, this city really *was* supposed to be a beautiful new hope for the educated workers, those of us who can't afford to live in any of the other cities anymore. You have all the beautiful augmented reality, the interactive everything. Right? And it's so eco-friendly, it's like a dream. The bioplastic cladding, all the greenery everywhere, even the inner walls that repair most kinds of damage and repel moisture, thanks to..." Jolene stops, and stares at the nearest wall. "Oh."

Nobody asks why Jolene stopped talking, or why she said "Oh," because they're all zonked out. Flood is in the fetal position. Warren is watching the window change displays. Samanthor is sucking on both of her own thumbs at once, which is a habit she's developed that everybody else pretends not to hate. Mason is refreshing the truck screen again. Everyone's startled when Jolene jumps to her feet.

And they're even more surprised when she runs into the kitchen of their apartment and comes back with the biggest hammer. "I need to knock a hole in your wall," Jolene tells them.

"Uh," Mason says. "I mean, however you choose to cope with the feelings of frustration and disempowerment and gnawing hunger is OK with me, but maybe you could pick someone else's wall—"

But Jolene has already swung the hammer and made a huge dent in the wall between the living area and Samanthor's bedroom.

"Hey," Samanthor says, standing up. "What are you—"

Jolene swings and whacks again, and then again, and some kind of outer coating flakes off, revealing the stuff inside the wall. The stuff that repairs itself and repels all moisture, because it's actually a living organism. This was a big selling point when they moved in here.

"Hey," Samanthor says again, "Don't mess with our—" and then she stops—because Jolene is ripping some of the insulation out of the wall and shoving it in her own mouth.

Jolene chews, which takes a long time, because the insulation is really, really chewy. Like chewing gum, mixed with shoe leather. But the taste is better than she'd expected, a bit like gravy, albeit with a weird aftertaste. She chews for a while, until she's reduced it to something she can swallow.

Mason is saying the thing about people dealing with their feelings in various ways again, but Jolene shushes him.

"I should have figured it out before," she says. "This town. Everything so cutting-edge and next-level. Everything organic, carbon-neutral and 'grown rather than made.' Including the insulation inside your walls, which is a kind of genetically engineered fungus. Surprisingly high protein, good source of iron. And the 'self-healing' part means it'll keep growing back, over and over. I think I can come up with an enzyme that'll make it easier to chew and digest, but it's already perfectly edible."

Mason, Warren, and Samanthor stare at Jolene, then each other. Then they wander over and begin pulling insulation out of their walls as well. Samanthor cautions them to take it slow, because she remembers how hard it was to keep food down when she ended her fast in college, so everybody just tries a mouthful. Mason has some ideas about how to prepare it, like insulation rigatoni, or fricasseed insulation, and meanwhile Warren, Flood, and Samanthor are already strategizing ways to get the word out to the entire city.

Barely an hour later, Jolene hears a chorus of hammers and drills all over town, as holes spring up in every structure. The Greatest City in the World begins to eat itself.

About the Contributors

Charlie Jane Anders is the author of *The City in the Middle of the Night* and *All the Birds in the Sky*, which won the Nebula, Locus, and Crawford awards and was on *Time Magazine*'s list of the 10 best novels of 2016. Her Tor.com story "Six Months, Three Days" won a Hugo Award and appears in a new short story collection called *Six Months, Three Days, Five Others*. Her short fiction has appeared in Tor.com, *Wired, Slate, Tin House, Conjunctions, Boston Review, Asimov's Science Fiction, The Magazine of Fantasy & Science Fiction*, McSweeney's Internet Tendency, *ZYZZYVA*, and several anthologies. She was a founding editor of io9.com, and she organizes the monthly Writers With Drinks reading series and co-hosts the podcast *Our Opinions Are Correct* with Annalee Newitz. Her first novel, *Choir Boy*, won a Lambda Literary Award.

Madeline Ashby is a science fiction writer and strategic foresight consultant living in Toronto. She is the author of the *Machine Dynasty* series from Angry Robot Books, and the novel *Company Town* from Tor Books, which was a Canada Reads finalist. As a futurist, she has developed science fiction prototypes for Intel Labs, the Institute for the Future, SciFutures, Nesta, the Atlantic Council, Data & Society, InteraXon, and others. Her essays have appeared at BoingBoing, io9, WorldChanging, Creators Project, Arcfinity, MISC Magazine, and FutureNow. She is married to horror writer and journalist David Nickle. With him, she is the co-editor of *Licence Expired: The Unauthorized James Bond*, an anthology of Bond stories available only in Canada. You can find her at madelineashby.com and on Twitter @MadelineAshby.

Paolo Bacigalupi's writing has appeared in *Wired, Slate*, Medium, Salon.com, and *High Country News*, as well as *The Magazine of Fantasy & Science Fiction* and *Asimov's Science Fiction*. His short fiction has been nominated for three Nebula Awards, four Hugo Awards, and won the Theodore Sturgeon Memorial Award for best science fiction short story of the year. It is collected in *Pump Six and Other Stories*, a Locus Award winner for Best Collection and also a Best Book of the Year by *Publishers Weekly*. His debut novel *The Windup Girl* was named by *Time Magazine* as one of the 10 best novels of 2009, and also won the Hugo, Nebula, Locus, Compton Crook, and John W. Campbell Memorial Awards. He is also the author of *Ship Breaker*, *The Drowned Cities*, *Zombie Baseball Beatdown*, *The Doubt Factory*, *The Water Knife*, and *Tool of War*.

Meg Elison is a science fiction author and feminist essayist. Her debut novel, *The Book of the Unnamed Midwife*, won the 2014 Philip K. Dick award. Her second novel was a finalist for the Philip K. Dick, and both were longlisted for the James A. Tiptree award. She has been published in *McSweeney's, Fantasy & Science Fiction, Catapult*, and many other places. Elison is a high school dropout and a graduate of the University of California, Berkeley. Find her online, where she writes like she's running out of time.

Lee Konstantinou is a writer and associate professor of English at the University of Maryland, College Park. He is also a Humanities editor at the *Los Angeles Review of Books*. He's written fiction, criticism, and reviews. He wrote the novel *Pop Apocalypse* (Ecco/HarperPerennial, 2009) and co-edited (with Sam Cohen) *The Legacy of David Foster Wallace* (University of Iowa Press, 2012). *Cool Characters: Irony and American Fiction* was published in 2016 by Harvard University Press.

Carmen Maria Machado's debut short story collection, *Her Body and Other Parties*, was a finalist for the National Book Award and the winner of the Lambda Literary Award for Lesbian Fiction, the Brooklyn Public Library Literature Prize, the Shirley Jackson Award, and the National Book Critics Circle's John Leonard Prize. Her essays, fiction, and criticism have appeared in *The New Yorker*, the *New York Times*, *Granta, Harper's Bazaar, Tin House, The Virginia Quarterly Review, McSweeney's Quarterly Concern, The Believer, Guernica, Best American Science Fiction & Fantasy, Best American Nonrequired Reading*, and elsewhere. She holds an MFA from the Iowa Writers' Workshop and has been awarded fellowships and residencies from the Guggenheim Foundation, Yaddo, Hedgebrook, and the Millay Colony for the Arts. She is the Writer in Residence at the University of Pennsylvania and lives in Philadelphia with her wife.

Maureen McHugh grew up in Ohio, but has lived in New York City and, for a year, in Shijiazhuang, China. She is the author of four novels. Her first novel, *China Mountain Zhang*, won the James A. Tiptree Award and her latest novel, *Nekropolis*, was a Book Sense 76 pick and a New York Times Editor's Choice. She was a finalist for the Story Award for *Mothers & Other Monsters*, and won a Shirley Jackson Award for her collection *After the Apocalypse. After the Apocalypse* was also named one of *Publishers Weekly*'s 10 Best Books of 2011. McHugh teaches scriptwriting at the University of Southern California. She and her husband and two dogs used to live next to a dairy farm. Sometimes, in the summer, black and white Holsteins looked over the fence at them. Now she lives in Los Angeles, California, where she is trying desperately to sell her soul to Hollywood but as it turns out, the market is saturated.

Annalee Newitz writes science fiction and nonfiction. She is the author of the novel *Autonomous*, nominated for the Nebula and Locus Awards, and winner of the Lambda Literary Award. As a science journalist, she's written for the *Washington Post, Slate*, Ars Technica, *The New Yorker*, and *The Atlantic*, among others. Her book *Scatter, Adapt, and Remember: How Humans Will Survive a Mass Extinction* was a finalist for the Los Angeles Times Book Prize in science. She was the founder of io9, and served as the editor-in-chief of Gizmodo and the tech culture editor at Ars Technica. She has published short stories in *Lightspeed, Shimmer, Apex*, and *MIT Technology Review*'s *Twelve Tomorrows*. She was the recipient of a Knight Science Journalism Fellowship at MIT, worked as a policy analyst at the Electronic Frontier Foundation, and has a Ph.D. in English and American Studies from the University of California, Berkeley. Her new novel, *The Future of Another Timeline*, comes out in September 2019.

Nnedi Okorafor is an award-winning novelist of African-based science fiction, fantasy, and magical realism. Born in the United States to Nigerian immigrant parents, Okorafor is known for weaving African cultures into creative settings and memorable characters. Her books include *Lagoon* (a British Science Fiction Association Award finalist for best novel), *Who Fears Death* (a World Fantasy Award winner for best novel), *Kabu Kabu* (a *Publishers Weekly* best book for Fall 2013), *Zahrah the Windseeker* (winner of the Wole Soyinka Prize for African Literature), and *The Shadow Speaker* (a CBS Parallax Award winner). Her 2016 novel *The Book of Phoenix* was an Arthur C. Clarke Award finalist, while the first book in her Binti Trilogy won both the Hugo and Nebula Awards for Best Novella. Her children's book *Chicken in the Kitchen* won an Africana Book Award. She is a full professor at the State University of New York at Buffalo.

Deji Bryce Olukotun is the author of two novels, and his fiction has appeared in five different book collections. His novel *After the Flare* won the 2018 Philip K. Dick special citation award, and was chosen as one of the best books of 2017 by *The Guardian*, the *Washington Post*, Syfy.com, Tor.com, and *Kirkus Reviews*, among others. His novel *Nigerians in Space*, a thriller about brain drain from Africa, was published by Unnamed Press in 2014. He is currently the Head of Social Impact at the audio technology company Sonos and a Future Tense Fellow at New America.

Mark Oshiro is the Hugo-nominated writer of the online Mark Does Stuff universe (Mark Reads and Mark Watches), where they analyze book and TV series. *Anger is a Gift* is their debut YA novel. It was honored with the 2019 Schneider Family Book Award for Best Teen Book and is a 31st Annual Lammy Awards finalist in the LGBTQ Children's/Young Adult category.

Hannu Rajaniemi is the author of four novels including *The Quantum Thief* (winner of 2012 Tähtivaeltaja Award for the best science fiction novel published in Finland, and translated into more than 20 languages) and *Invisible Planets*, a short story collection. His most recent book is *Summerland*, an alternate-history spy thriller in a world where the afterlife is real. His short fiction has been featured in *Slate, MIT Technology Review*, and the *New York Times*. Hannu lives in the San Francisco Bay Area. He is a co-founder and CEO of HelixNano, a venture- and Y Combinator–backed biotech startup.

Emily St. John Mandel's fifth novel, *The Glass Hotel*, will be published in spring 2020. Her previous novels include *Station Eleven*, which was a finalist for a National Book Award and the PEN/Faulkner Award, and won the 2015 Arthur C. Clarke Award, the Toronto Book Award, and the Morning News Tournament of Books, and has been translated into 32 languages. She lives in New York City with her husband and daughter.

Mark Stasenko is a television writer who wrote on the Peabody Award–winning show *American Vandal*. He is in development on a series about Enron with Alex Gibney attached to direct and is adapting his Future Tense Fiction short story "Overvalued" into a TV series with Universal Cable Productions.

About the Editors

Kirsten Berg is a journalist based in Washington, D.C. She currently works as a research-reporter with ProPublica and was previously an associate editor with Future Tense.

Torie Bosch is the editor of Future Tense, a partnership of *Slate*, New America, and Arizona State University. She was also the co-editor of the 2017 edition of *What Future: The Year's Best Ideas to Reclaim, Reanimate & Reinvent the Future* (The Unnamed Press).

Joey Eschrich is the editor and program manager at the Center for Science and the Imagination at Arizona State University, and an assistant director for Future Tense. He is the co-editor of *Visions, Ventures, Escape Velocities*, a book of fiction and nonfiction supported by a grant from NASA.

Ed Finn is the founding director of the Center for Science and the Imagination at Arizona State University, and the academic director for Future Tense. He is the author of *What Algorithms Want: Imagination in the Age of Computing* and the co-editor of *Frankenstein: Annotated for Scientists, Engineers, and Creators of All Kinds*, both from The MIT Press.

Andrés Martinez is the editorial director of Future Tense and a professor of practice at the Walter Cronkite School of Journalism at Arizona State University. He is a former vice president of New America, editorial page editor at the *Los Angeles Times*, and assistant editorial page editor at the *New York Times*.

Juliet Ulman is the proud editor of multiple award-winning projects over her 20+ year editorial career, and has been personally twice honored as a finalist for the Hugo Award for Best Professional Editor. She holds strong opinions on New York Rangers hockey and the Oxford comma.

@unnamedpress

facebook.com/theunnamedpress

unnamedpress.tumblr.com

www.unnamedpress.com

@unnamedpress